Fernán Caballero

La Gaviota

A Spanish Novel

Fernán Caballero

La Gaviota
A Spanish Novel

ISBN/EAN: 9783337033248

Printed in Europe, USA, Canada, Australia, Japan

Cover: Foto ©Andreas Hilbeck / pixelio.de

More available books at **www.hansebooks.com**

A SPANISH NOVEL.

BY

FERNAN CABALLERO.

TRANSLATED BY

J. LEANDER STARR.

NEW YORK:
PUBLISHED BY JOHN BRADBURN,
(SUCCESSOR TO M. DOOLADY,)
49 WALKER-STREET.
1864.

THE HON. GEORGE OPDYKE,

EX-MAYOR OF THE CITY OF NEW YORK.

SIR:

 I am honored with your permission to dedicate to you this translation of the best novel in the Spanish language. This honor I can well appreciate. The urbanity of your character, and your firm integrity as a gentleman, a merchant, and while so ably filling the civic chair of this great city, have rendered you both distinguished and respected.

Glowing hopes and confident expectations were formed of your success in the performance of the arduous duties of Mayor, when, two years ago, you were inaugurated. Yesterday was a yet prouder day to yourself and to your friends, when the mantle of office fell gracefully from your shoulders, amid the applause and homage of citizens of all classes and shades of political opinion, the only strife among whom was, who should show to the courteous, impartial, and zealous retiring mayor the greatest respect.

Well may the king of Israel have exclaimed: "Let not him that girdeth on his harness boast himself as he that putteth it off."

Your career has been marked by the most devoted patriotism, and you have stood forth at the period of the nation's trials as an unflinching supporter of constitutional government, and throughout every loyal State in the Union will your name be revered as such.

May, sir, at some far distant day, that tribute be paid to you which honored the memory of the immortal Pitt

"Non sibi, sed pro patria vixit."

With great respect,
I have the honor to be, sir,
Your obedient servant,
J. LEANDER STARR.

17 Lafayette Place,
New York, *Jan. 5th*, 1864.

PREFACE,

BY THE TRANSLATOR.

GAVIOTA (sea-gull) is the *sobriquet* which Andalusians give to harsh-tongued, flighty women of unsympathetic mien and manners; and such was applied to the heroine of this tale by a youthful, malicious tormentor—Momo.

Fernan Caballero is, indeed, but a pseudonym : the author of this novel, passing under that name, is understood to be a lady, partly of German descent. Her father was Don Juan Nicholas Böhl de Faber, to whose erudition Spain is indebted for a collection of ancient poetry. Cecelia, the daughter of Böhl de Faber, was born at Morges, in Switzerland, in 1797, and subsequently married to a Spanish gentleman. Indeed, since the death of her first husband, she has successively contracted two other marriages, and is now a widow.

We have it on the authority of the Edinburgh Review, that the novels of this gifted authoress were " published at the expense of the Queen." The same authority remarks, " Hence it might have been foretold, that of the various kinds of novels, the romantic and descriptive was the least repugnant to the old Spanish spirit ; and that in order for a writer

successfully to undertake such a novel, it would be necessary for him to have a passionate attachment to the national
manners and characteristics, and a corresponding dislike to
the foreign and new—such are the qualities we find united
in Fernan Caballero: *La Gaviota is perhaps the finest story
in the volumes."* Its advent is a real literary event: the
most severe critics have dissected this new work, and have
unhesitatingly proclaimed the authoress to be the Spanish
Walter Scott. Among the painters of manners, the best,
without doubt, are the Spanish writers. We are certain to
find there truth, joined to a richness and piquancy of details; and, above all, a spirited tone, which singularly
heightens and sets off their recitals. They have, however,
what in us is a defect, but with them a natural gift—*the
being a little prolix.*

In translating it is easy to avoid this prolixity. This has
been attended to in the present translation. I have preserved all the character of truth and originality of this
novel; curtailing only such passages as seemed, in my judgment, too long and tedious for those who are not initiated
into those *agreeable familiarities* of Spanish intimate conversation, and others, which are without attraction to those
who were not born under the bright sun of Iberia. In regard to the translation, I would again quote from the
review of it by the " Edinburgh Review :" " One quality
which distinguishes their talk it is impossible to give any
notion of in translation, and that is the enormous quantity
of proverbs, in rhyme or in assonance, with which they in-
tersperse their speech ; and even when they are not actually

quoting a proverb, their expressions have all the terseness of proverbial language."

In rendering into English the ballads and other poetry, so profusely interspersed throughout this novel, I had to decide between the preservation of the original thoughts and ideas, in all their quaintness and integrity, and wrest from my translation that poetic elegance which, as English poetry, I could have wished to have clothed it in; or to abandon all the original, save the mere text, and write independent stanzas in English, as though I had composed original poetry, borrowing only the *thought* from the Spanish text. My habitual desire, in *all* my translations, being to preserve the *original* sense in its *fullest force*, I adopted the former of these two views; and thus, while the reader will find no poetic beauty, he will have before him the entire original thoughts. The translation of any foreign poetry into chaste and elegant English verse is acknowledged to be a very difficult task. At the end of this volume are four specimens, to satisfy the curious, of a *strictly literal* verbal translation of short poetic sprinklings towards the conclusion of the tale.

A writer remarks, on the Andalusian character: "Seeing nothing about them but a smiling fertility, the hierarchy of the Catholic Heaven are to them beneficent beings, to be approached with trust and confidence, and the familiarity with which they speak of God, the Saviour, the Virgin, and the saints, *must not be mistaken for irreverence;* on the contrary, it springs from the belief that they are really the favored sons of the faith, and from the vividness with which they realize the existence and beneficent watchfulness of their Divine protectors."

And again. "There is hardly a bird, or a shrub, or an odor, about which the Andalusians have not some pious and simple legend. The white poplar was the first tree the Creator made, and therefore it is hoary, as being the oldest. San Joseph told the serpent to go on its belly, because it attempted to bite the infant Saviour in their flight into Egypt. Rosemary has its sweetest perfume and its brightest blossoms on Fridays, the day of the Passion, because the Virgin hung on a rosemary-bush the clothes of the infant Christ. Everybody loves the swallows, because they plucked out the thorns of our Saviour's crown on the cross; while the owl, who dared to look impassively on the Crucifixion, has been. sick and afflicted ever since, and can utter nothing but *Cruz! Cruz!* The rose of Jericho was once white, but a drop of the blood of the wounded Saviour fell on it, and it has been red ever since. Children smile in their sleep because angels visit them. When there is a buzzing noise in the ears, it is because a leaf of the tree of life has fallen."

LA GAVIOTA.*

CHAPTER I.

In November, in the year 1836, the steamer "Royal Sovereign" took her departure from the foggy coast of Falmouth, lashing the waves with her paddle-wheels, and spreading her sails, gray and wet, in the mist still grayer and more wet than they.

The interior of the hull presented the uncheerful spectacle of the commencement of a sea voyage. The passengers, crowded together, were struggling with the fatigue of sea-sickness. Women were seen in extraordinary attitudes, with hair disordered, crinolines disarranged, hats crushed: the men pale, and in bad-humor; the children neglected and crying; the servants traversing the cabin with unsteady steps, carrying to their patients tea, coffee, and other imaginary remedies; while the ship, queen and mistress of the waters, without heeding the ills she occasioned, wrestled powerfully with the waves, triumphing over resistance, and pursuing the retreating billows.

The men who had escaped the common scourge were

---

* Gaviota is the name of a sea-gull. It applies familiarly to the female scold, imprudent, stupid, and of harsh manners, indicated by the well-known proverb: "The sea-gull—the older she is, the louder she screams."

enabled to walk the deck, either by being so constituted as to withstand the ship's motion, or by being accustomed to travel.

Among them was the governor of an English colony, a tall, fine-looking fellow, accompanied by two of his staff officers. There were several who wore their mackintoshes, thrusting their hands into their pockets; some' had flushed countenances, others blue, or very pale, and, generally, all were discontented. In fine, that beautiful vessel seemed to be converted into a palace of discontent.

Among all the passengers was distinguished a youth, who appeared to be about twenty-four years of age; gallant, noble, and of ingenuous countenance, and whose handsome and affable face gave no signs of the slightest caprice. He was tall, and of gentlemanly manners; and in his deportment there was grace, and an admirable dignity. A head of black, curly hair adorned his fair and majestic forehead; the glances of his large, black eyes were placid and penetrating by turns. His lips were shaded by a light, black mustache; his bland smile indicated talent and vivacity; and in his noble person, in his actions, and in his gestures, there were evidences of the elevated class to which he belonged, with a soul freed from the least symptom of that disdainful air which many unjustly attribute to all kinds of superiority. He travelled for pleasure, and was essentially good; nevertheless, a virtuous sentiment of anger impelled him to launch out against the vices and extravagances of society. He often affirmed that he did not feel it to be his vocation to battle with windmills, like Don Quixote. He would much more agreeably consort with those who seek the good, with the same satisfaction and purity that the artless young damsel feels in gathering violets. His physiognomy, his grace, the freedom

with which he muffled himself in his Spanish cloak, his
insensibility to cold and to the general disquietude
around him, established decidedly that he was Spanish.

He was walking backwards and forwards, observing
at a glance the assemblage which, mosaic-like, chance
had thrown together on those boards which constitute a
large ship, and which, in smaller dimensions, would constitute a coffin. But there is not much to be observed
in men who thus presented the appearance of those who
are intoxicated, or in women whose appearance resembles that of a corpse.

Notwithstanding, he was much interested in the family of an English official, whose wife had been brought
on board greatly indisposed, and who was immediately
carried to her berth; the same was done with the nurse,
and the father followed, with the infant boy in his arms;
afterwards he led in three other little creatures, of two,
three, and four years of age, enjoining upon them to
remain silent, and not to move from thence. The poor
children, although they felt inclined to cry, remained
motionless and silent, like the angels which are represented in paintings at the feet of the Virgin. Little by
little the beautiful bloom of their cheeks disappeared;
their large eyes opened wide, and they remained molli-
fied and stupid; and while no movement or expression
of anger announced that they suffered, such was clearly
denoted by the expression of their frightened and pallid
countenances. No one noticed this silent torment, this
amiable and sad resignation.

The Spaniard went to summon the steward, while
that official was answering a young man, who, in German, and with expressive gestures, appeared to be im-
ploring assistance in favor of some wretched victim of
sea-sickness.

As the person of this young man did not indicate either elegance or distinction, as he spoke nothing but German, the steward turned his back, saying he did not understand him.

Then the German descended to his berth in the fore-castle, and returned immediately, bringing a pillow, a quilt, and a heavy overcoat. With these auxiliaries he made up a kind of bed. He laid the children in it, and covered them with great care, and stretched himself on the deck beside them. But the sea-sick man had scarcely reclined, when a violent vomiting commenced, despite his efforts, and, in an instant, pillow, quilt, and great-coat were bespattered and ruined. The Spaniard then noticed the German, in whose physiognomy he saw a smile of benevolent satisfaction, which seemed to say, "Thank God, these little ones are cared for!"

He attempted a conversation with him in English, in French, and in Spanish, and received no other answer than a silent inclination of the head, and with but little grace, repeating this phrase: "Ich verstehe nicht" (I do not understand).

When, after dinner, the Spaniard again ascended to the deck, the cold had increased. He enfolded himself in his cloak, and commenced promenading. Then he noticed the German seated on a bench, and looking at the sea; which, as if to exhibit its sparkling, displayed on the sides of the ship its pearls of foam, and their brilliant phosphoric light. This young observer was dressed very insufficiently, because his frock-coat had become worn and unserviceable, and the cold must have pierced him.

The Spaniard advanced several paces to approach him; but he hesitated, he knew not how to institute a conversation. Immediately he smiled, as if a happy thought had occurred to him, and that he was going the right way towards it, and said to the German, in *Latin:* "You must feel very cold."

That voice and short phrase produced on the stranger the most lively satisfaction, and harmonized, also, with his questioner, they were in accord in the same dialect; he replied:

"The night is, indeed, somewhat severe; but I was not thinking of that."

"Then what were you thinking of?" demanded the Spaniard.

"I was thinking of my father and mother, and of my brothers and sisters."

"Why do you travel, then, if you so much feel the separation?"

"Ah! señor; necessity—that implacable despot."

"Why not travel for pleasure?"

"Pleasure is for the rich, and I am poor. For my pleasure! If I avow the motive of my voyage, then truly pleasure would be very far off."

"Where then do you go?"

"To the war. To the civil war, the most terrible of all, at Navarre."

"To the war!" exclaimed the Spaniard, examining the kind and docile, almost humble, and very little belligerent, countenance of the German. "Then you would become a military man?"

"No, sir; that is not my vocation. Neither my affections nor my principles induce me to take up arms, if it were not to defend the holy cause of the independence of Germany, if the foreigner will become the invader. I go to the army of Navarre to procure employment as a surgeon."

"You do not know the language?"

"No, sir; but I can learn it."

"Nor the country?"

"Neither. I have never left my native town, except for the university."

"But you are provided with recommendations?"

"None whatever."

"Do you count upon any patron?"

"I know nobody in Spain."

"What then do you rely upon?"

"My conscience, my good-will, my youth, and my confidence in God."

This conversation rendered the Spaniard thoughtful. He gazed on that face, in which candor and docility were impressed; those blue eyes, pure as those of a girl; those smiles, sad, but at the same time confident, earnestly interested him, and moved his pity.

"Will you descend with me," he said, after a brief pause, "and accept some hot punch to keep out the cold? In the interim let us converse."

The German inclined his head in token of his gratitude, and following the Spaniard, they descended to the dining-room.

At the head of the table were seated the governor, with his two officers; on one side were two Frenchmen. The Spaniard and the German seated themselves at the foot of the table.

"But how," exclaimed the first, "have you ever conceived the idea of going to this distracted country?"

The German hesitated, and then related to him faithfully his life: "I am the sixth son of a professor in a small city of Saxonia, and who had spent much in the education of his sons. Finding ourselves without occupation or employment, like so many young paupers you find in Germany, after having devoted their youth to

excellent and profound studies, and who had studied
their art under the best masters, our maintenance was a
burden on our family; for which reason, without feeling discouraged, with all my German calmness, I took
the resolution to depart for Spain, where the disgraceful
and sanguinary wars of the North opened up hopes that
my services there might be useful.

"Beneath the linden-trees which cast their shadows on
the door of my homestead, I decided to carry out this
resolution. I embraced for the last time my good father,
my beloved mother, my sister Lotte, and my little
brothers, who clamored to accompany me in my pere-
grinations. Profoundly moved, and bathed in tears, I
entered on life's highway, which others find covered
with flowers. But—courage; man is born to labor, and
I felt that Heaven would crown my efforts. I like the
profession which I had chosen, because it is grand and
noble; its object is the alleviation of our fellows, and the
results are beautiful, although the drudgery seems painful."

"And you made progress?"

Fritz Stein replied in German, inflicting an excited
blow on his seat, and making a slight reverence.

A short time afterwards, the two new friends separated. One of the Frenchmen, who was placed in front
of the door, saw that he was about to ascend the stair-
case, and offered to place on the shoulders of the German his Spanish cloak, lined with fur, to which the
other showed some resistance, and the Frenchman, with
a look of scorn, replaced it in his berth.

"Have you understood what they were talking about?"
demanded he of his countryman.

"Truly," rejoined the first (who was a commission
merchant), "Latin is not my forte; but the red and

pale youth seems to me a species of pale *Werther*, and I
have heard there is in his history something of Charlotte.
So is it with those little children described in a German
novel. By good luck, instead of recurring to the pistol
to console him, he prefers punch; it is less sentimental,
but much more philosophical, and more German. As to
the Spaniard, I believe he is a species of Don Quixote,
protector of the destitute, who shares his cloak with the
poor; that joined to these high allurements, his look,
firm and ardent like a flame, his countenance, dull and
wan like the light of the moon, form an altogether perfect Spaniard."

"You know," said the first, "that in my quality of
painter of history, I go to Tarifa with the object of painting the siege of that city at the moment when the son of
Guzman made a sign to his father to sacrifice him before
surrendering the place, and this young man will serve
me for a model, and I am thus sure to succeed with my
tableau. I have never in my life seen nature approach
so near the ideal."

"There, then, ye gentlemen-artists! Always poets!"
replied the commercial traveller. "For my part, if I am
not deceived by the natural grace of this man, his lady
foot well cast, the elegance of his profile, and his form, I
would characterize him as a taureador (bull-fighter).
Who knows? perhaps it is Montés himself, possessing
the joint attractions of riches and generosity."

"A taureador!" cried the artist; "a man of the people! You jest."

"Not at all," said the other; "I am very far, indeed,
from jesting. You have not lived, like me, in Spain,
and you do not know the aristocratic type of the nation.
You will see, you will see. This is my opinion. Thanks
to the progress of equality and fraternity, the insulting

manners of the aristocracy disappear daily, and in a short time hence they will be found only among the men of the people."

"Believe that this man is a taureador!" repeated the artist, with a smile so disdainful that the commercial traveller, wounded by the reply, rose and said:

"We will know very soon who he is; come with me, we will get information of him from his servant."

The two friends mounted to the deck, where they were not long in meeting the man they searched for.

The commercial traveller, who volunteered to converse with the Spanish servant, led the conversation, and, after some trivial remarks, asked: "Your master," he said to him, "has he retired to his chamber?"

"Yes, sir," replied the servant, casting on the questioner a look full of penetration and malice.

"Is he rich?"

"I am not his intendant, I am only his valet-de-chambre."

"Is he travelling on business?"

"I do not believe he has any."

"Is he travelling for his health?"

"His health is excellent."

"Is he travelling incognito?"

"No, sir; he travels with his name and Christian names."

"And he is called—"

"Don Carlos de la Cerda."

"An illustrious name, very certainly," cried the painter.

"My name is Pedro de Guzman," added the servant, "and I am humble servant to you both." He then made a very humble reverence, and went away.

"Gil Blas is right," said the Frenchman· "in Spain

nothing is more common than glorious names. It is true that in Paris my boot-maker was named Martel, my tailor called himself Roland, and my laundress, Madame Bayard. In Scotland, there are more Stuarts than paving-stones."

"We are humbugged! That insolent servant is mocking us. But, every thing considered, I have a suspicion that he is an agent of the factions, an obscure emissary of Don Carlos."

"Certainly not," replied the artist; "it is my Alonzo Perez de Guzman the Good—the hero of my dreams." The other Frenchman shrugged his shoulders.

When the ship arrived at Cadiz, the Spaniard took leave of Stein. "I am obliged to remain some short time in Andalusia," he said to him. "Pedro, my servant, will accompany you as far as Seville, and take a place for you in the diligence for Madrid. Here are some letters of recommendation for the Minister of War and the general-in-chief of the army. If it happens that you have any friendly service to ask of me, write to me at Madrid, to this address."

Stein, stifled with emotion, could not speak. With one hand he took the letters, and with the other he pushed back the card which the Spaniard presented to him. "Your name is engraven here," he said in placing his hand on his heart. "Oh! I will not forget it while I live; it is that of a soul the most noble, the most elevated, the most generous; it is the name of the best of men."

"With this address," replied Don Carlos, smiling, "your letters would never reach me. You must have another, more clear and more brief," and he handed him his card, and departed.

Stein read: "The Duke of Almansa."

And Pedro de Guzman, who was close by, added: "Marquis de Guadalmonte, de Val-de-Flores, and de Loca-Fiel; Comte de Santa-Clara, de Encinasala, et de Laza; Chevalier of the Golden Fleece, and Grand Cross of Charles III.; Gentleman of the Chamber of his Majesty; Grandee of Spain, of First Class; &c., &c., &c."

CHAPTER II.

ONE morning in October, in the year 1838, a man on foot descended a little hill in the county of Niebla, and advanced towards the coast. His impatience to arrive at a little port which had been indicated to him was such that, thinking to shorten his route, he found himself in one of those vast solitudes so common in the south of Spain, real deserts, reserved to raise cattle, and in which the flocks never go beyond the limits. This man, although not more than twenty-six years of age, appeared already old. He wore a military tunic, buttoned up to the chin. On his head he wore a common cloth cap. He carried on his shoulder a large stick, at the end of which was suspended a little casket of mahogany, covered with green flannel, a package of books, fastened together with pack-thread, a handkerchief covering a little white linen, and a great cloak rolled up. This light baggage appeared to be beyond the strength of the traveller, who, from time to time, paused, supporting one hand on his oppressed chest, or passing it over his burning forehead. At times he fixed his looks on a poor dog which followed him, and which, whenever he halted, stretched himself at full length at his feet. "Poor Fidele!" said the master; "the only being who makes me believe there is yet in the world a little of affection and of gratitude. No! I will never forget the day when I saw you for the first time. Thou wast, with a poor herdsman, condemned to be shot, because he would not be a traitor. He was on his knees, he awaited his death,

and it was in vain he supplicated a respite. He asked
that thou shouldst be spared, and no one listened to
him. The shots were fired, and thou, faithful friend of
the unfortunate, thou didst fall cruelly wounded beside
the inanimate corpse of thy master. I rescued thee, I
cured thy wounds, and since then thou hast not abandoned me. When the wits of the regiment called me a
dog-curer, you came and licked the hand that had saved
you, as if you would say to me, 'Dogs have gratitude.'
Oh! my God, I have a loving heart! It is two years
since, full of life, of hope, and good-will, I arrived in this
country, and offered to my brethren my will, my care,
my knowledge, and my heart. I have cured many
wounds; for my recompense they have made me feel
sorrow the most profound, and it is my soul they have
lacerated. Great God! great God! discouragement has
seized me. I see myself ingloriously driven from the
army, after two years of incessant labor—labor without
repose. I see myself accused and pursued, for nothing
but for having given my care to a man of an opposite
party; to an unhappy man, who, driven like a beast, fell
dying into my arms. Is it possible that the rules of war
convert into a crime what morality recognizes as a virtue, and which religion proclaims to be a duty!

"What can I do at present? Go and repose my
head, prematurely bald, and cure my lacerated heart in
the shade of the linden-trees which surround my father's
house. There, at least, they will not charge me with
crime for having showed pity for a dying man."

After the pause of a few minutes, the unhappy man
made an effort. "Let us go, Fidele," said he; "move
on! move on!" and the traveller and his faithful animal
pursued their painful route.

But soon the man lost the right path, which he had

until now followed, and which had been beaten by the
steps of the shepherds. The ground was covered more
and more with briers and with high and thick bushes; it
was impossible to follow a straight line; he must turn
aside alternately to the right and left.

The sun had finished his course, and no part of the
horizon discovered the least appearance of any human
habitation. There was nothing to be seen but limitless
solitude; nothing but the desert tinged with green, and
uniform as the ocean.

Fritz Stein, whom our reader no doubt already recognizes, perceived too late that he had placed too much
confidence in his strength. With pain and difficulty his
swollen and aching feet could barely sustain him. His
arteries throbbed with violence, a sharp pain racked his
temples, an ardent thirst devoured him, and to heighten
the horror of his situation, the deafening and prolonged
bellowings announced the approach of some droves of
wild bulls, so dangerous in Spain.

"God has saved me from many perils," said the poor
traveller; "he will yet protect me. If not, his will be
done."

He redoubled his speed; but what was his terror,
when, after having passed a little plantation of mastic-
trees, he found himself face to face with a bull!

Stein remained immovable, and, to say truly, petrified.

The animal, surprised at this encounter and at so much
audacity, remained also without motion; his eyes were
inflamed like two burning coals. The man immediately
understood that at the least movement he was lost. The
bull, who was, by instinct, conscious of his strength and his
courage, waited to be provoked to fight; lowering and
raising his head three or four times impatiently, he began to paw the earth and to fill the air with dust, in token

of his defiance. Stein preserved his immobility. The
animal then stepped one pace backward, lowered his
head and prepared for the attack—when he felt himself
bitten in the ham. At the same time the furious barking of his brave companion informed Stein who was his
rescuer. The bull, full of rage, turned to repel this
unlooked-for attack; Stein profited by this movement
and took to flight. The horrible situation from which
he had with so great difficulty escaped, gave him new
strength to fly past the green oaks and through the briers,
the thickness of which sheltered him from his formidable adversary.

He had already passed a little dale, and climbed a hillock, and then he stopped nearly out of breath. He turned
round to observe the place of his perilous adventure.
He saw through the clearing his poor companion, which
the ferocious animal tossed in the air as if diverting himself.

Stein extended his arms towards his dog, so coura-
geous, so devoted, and, sobbing, he exclaimed:

"Poor Fidele! poor Fidele! my only friend! you well
merit your name! You pay dear for the affection you
have shown for your masters."

Then, to distract his thoughts from this frightful spectacle, Stein hurried on, shedding profuse tears. He thus
arrived at the summit of another hill, where was spread
open to his view a magnificent landscape. The ground
sloped almost insensibly to the borders of the sea, which,
calmly and tranquilly, reflected the last rays of the sun,
and presented the appearance of a vast field spangled
with rubies and sapphires.

The white sail of a vessel, which appeared as if held
stationary by the waves, seemed detached like a pearl
in the midst of these splendid riches.

The line formed by the coast was marvellously un
even; the shore seemed covered with golden sands,
where the sea rolled its long silver fringes.

Bordering the coast, rose rocks whose gigantic boul-
ders seemed to pierce the azure sky. In the distance, at
the left, Stein discovered the ruins of a fort—human labor
which could resist nothing; and whose base was the rock
—divine work which resisted every thing: at the right
he perceived a cluster of houses, without being able to
perceive whether it was a village, a palace, or a convent.

Nearly exhausted by his last hurried walk, and by his
saddened emotions, it was towards this point he would
direct his steps. He could not reach it until night had
set in. What he saw was, in fact, one of those convents
constructed in the times of Christian faith and enthusiasm.
The monastery had been in the olden time brilliant, sump-
tuous, and hospitable; now it was abandoned, poor,
empty, dismantled, offered for sale—as was indicated by
some strips of paper pasted on its ruined walls. Nobody, however, desired to purchase it, however low was
the price asked.

The wide folding-doors which formerly offered an easy
access to all comers, were now closed as if they would
never again be opened.

Stein's strength abandoned him, and he fell almost
without consciousness upon a stone bench: the delirium
of fever attacked his brain, and he was only aroused by
the crowing of a cock.

Rising suddenly, Stein with pain walked to the door,
took up a stone and knocked. A loud barking replied to
his summons. He made another effort, knocked again;
but his strength was exhausted—he sank on the ground.

The door was opened, and two persons appeared.

One of them was a young woman, holding a light in

her hand, which she directed towards the object lying at
her feet.

"Jesus!" she cried, "it is not Manuel—a stranger!
God aid us!"

"Help him," replied the other, a good and simple old
woman. "Brother Gabriel! brother Gabriel!" she called
out in entering the court, "come quickly, there is here
an unfortunate man who is dying."

Hurried steps were heard: they were those of an old
man of ordinary height, with a placid and high complex-
ioned face. His dress consisted of pantaloons and a large
vest with gray sleeves, and the remnant of an old frock-
coat; he had sandals on his feet; a cap of black wool
covered his shiny forehead.

"Brother Gabriel," said the elder female, "we must
succor this man."

"He must be cared for," replied brother Gabriel.

"For God's sake," cried the woman who carried the
light, "where can we place here a dying man?"

"We will do the best we can, my daughter, without
being uneasy about the rest. Help me."

"Would to God," said Dolores, "that we may have
no disagreement when Manuel returns."

"It cannot be otherwise," replied the good old woman, "than that the son will concur in what his mother
has done."

The three conveyed Stein to the chamber of brother
Gabriel. They made up for him a bed with fresh straw,
and a good large mattress filled with wool. Grandma
Maria took out of a large chest a pair of sheets, if not
very fine, at least very white. She then added a warm
woollen counterpane.

Brother Gabriel wished to give up his pillow; the
Grandma opposed it, saying she had two, and that one

2

would suffice for her. During these preparations some one knocked loud at the door, and continued to knock.

"Here is Manuel," said the young woman. "Come with me, mother; I do not wish to be alone with him, when he learns that we have admitted a stranger."

The mother-in-law followed the steps of her daughter.

"God be praised! Good evening, mother; good evening, wife," said, on entering, a strong and powerfully constructed man. He seemed to be thirty-eight to forty years old, and was followed by a child of about thirteen years.

"Come, Momo!* unlade the ass and lead him to the stable; the poor beast is tired."

Momo carried to the kitchen, where the family was accustomed to assemble, a supply of large loaves of white bread, some very plump woodcock, and his father's cloak.

Dolores went and closed the door and then rejoined her husband and her mother in the kitchen.

"Have you brought my ham and my starch?" she asked.

"Here there are."

"And my flax?"

"I had almost a desire to forget it," answered Manuel, smiling, and handing some skeins to his mother.

"Why, my son?"

"Because I recollected that villager who went to the fair, and whom all the neighbors loaded with commissions: Bring me a hat, said one; Bring me a pair of gaiters, said another; a cousin asked for a comb; an aunt wished for some chocolate; and for all these commissions no one gave him a *cuarto*. He had already bestrode his mule, when a pretty little child came to him

---

* Brief name for Geronimo, in Andalusia.

and said : 'Here are two *cuartos* for a flageolet, will you bring me one ?' The child presented his money, the villager stooped, took it, and replied, 'You shall be flageoleted.' And in fact when he returned from the fair, of all the commissions they had given him he brought only the flageolet."

"Be it so! it is well," said the mother : "why do I pass every day in sewing ? Is it not for thee and thy children ? Do you wish that I imitate the tailor who worked for nothing, and furnished the thread below the cost ?"

At this moment Momo reappeared on the threshold of the kitchen ; he was small and fat, high shouldered ; he had, besides, the bad habit to raise them without any cause, with an air of scorn and carelessness, almost to touch his large ears which hung out like fans. His head was enormous, his hair short, lips thick. Again—he squinted horribly.

"Father," said he, with a malicious air, "there is a man asleep in the chamber of brother Gabriel."

"A man in my house !" cried Manuel, throwing away his chair. "Dolores, what does this mean ?"

"Manuel, it is a poor invalid. Your mother would that we receive him : it was not my opinion : she insisted, what could I do ?"

"It is well; but however she may be my mother, ought she for that to lodge here the first man that comes along ?"

"No—he should be left to die at the door like a dog, is it not so ?"

"But, my mother," replied Manuel, "is my house a hospital ?"

"No. It is the house of a Christian ; and if you had been here you would have done as I did."

" Oh! certainly not," continued Manuel; "I would have put him on our ass and conducted him to the village, now there are no more convents."

" We had not our ass here, and there was no one to take charge of this unfortunate man."

" And if he is a robber ?"

" Dying men do not rob."

" And if his illness is long, who will take care of him ?"

" They have just killed a fowl to make broth," said Momo, "I saw the feathers in the court."

" Have you lost your mind, mother!" cried Manuel furiously.

" Enough, enough," said his mother, in a severe tone. " You ought to blush for shame to dare to quarrel with me because I, have obeyed the law of God. If your father were still living, he would not believe that his son could refuse to open his door to the unfortunate, ill, without succor, and dying."

Manuel bowed his head: there was a moment of silence.

" It is well, my mother," he said, at last. "Forget that I have said any thing, and act according to your own judgment. We know that women are always right."

Dolores breathed more freely.

"How good he is !" she said joyously to her mother-in-law.

"Could you doubt it ?" she replied, smiling, to her daughter, whom she tenderly loved ; and in rising to go and take her place at the couch of the invalid, she added :

" I have never doubted it, I who brought him into the world."

And in passing near to Momo, she said to him :

"I already knew that you had a bad heart; but

you have never proved it as you have to-day. I complain of you: you are wicked, and the wicked carry their own chastisement."

"Old people are only good for sermonizing," growled Momo, in casting a side look at his grandmother.

But he had scarcely pronounced this last word, when his mother, who had heard him, approached and applied a smart blow.

"That will teach you," she said, "to be insolent to the mother of your father; towards a woman who is twice your mother."

Momo began to cry,.and took refuge at the bottom of the court, and vented his anger in bastinadoing the poor dog who had not offended him.

CHAPTER III.

THE grandma and the brother Gabriel took the best care of the invalid; but they could not agree upon the method which should be adopted to cure him.

Maria, without having read Brown, recommended substantial soups, comforts, and tonics, because she conceived that Stein was debilitated and worn out.

Brother Gabriel, without ever having heard the name of Broussais pronounced, pleaded for refreshments and emollients, because, in his opinion, Stein had a brain fever, the blood heated and the skin hot.

Both were right, and with this double system, which blended the soups of the grandma with the lemonade of brother Gabriel, it happened that Stein recovered his life and his health the same day that the good woman killed the last fowl, and the brother divested the lemon-trees of their last fruit.

"Brother Gabriel," said the grandma, "to which State corps do you think our invalid belongs? Is he military?"

"He must be military," replied brother Gabriel, who, except in medical or horticultural discussions, had the habit of regarding the good woman as an oracle, and to be guided wholly by her opinion.

"If he were military," continued the old woman, shaking her head, "he would be armed, and he is not armed. I found only a flute in his pocket. Then he is not military."

"He cannot be military," replied brother Gabriel.

" If he were a contrabandist ?"

" It is possible he is a contrabandist," said the good brother Gabriel.

" But no," replied the old woman, " for to be a contrabandist, he should wear stuffs or jewelry, and he has nothing of these."

" That is true, he cannot be a contrabandist," affirmed brother Gabriel.

" See what are the titles of his books. Perhaps by that means we can discover what he is."

The brother rose, took his horn spectacles, placed them on his nose, and the package of books in his hands, and approached the window which looked out on the grand court. His inspection of the books lasted a long time.

" Brother Gabriel," asked the old woman, " have you forgotten to know how to read ?"

" No—but I do not know these characters; I believe it is Hebrew."

" Hebrew! Holy Virgin of Heaven, can he be a Jew ?"

At that moment, Stein, awaking from a long lethargy, addressed him, and said in German :

" Mein Gott, wo bin ich ? My God, where am I ?"

The old woman sprang with one bound to the middle of the chamber; brother Gabriel let fall the books, and remained petrified after opening his eyes as large as his spectacles.

" In what language have you spoken ?" she demanded.

" It must be Hebrew, like these books," answered brother Gabriel. " Perhaps he is a Jew, as you said, good Maria."

" God help us !" she cried. " But no, if he were a Jew, would we not have seen it on his back when we undressed him ?"

"Good Maria," replied the brother, "the holy father said that this belief which attributes to a Jew a tail at his back is nonsense, a piece of bad wit, and that the Jews laugh at it."

"Brother Gabriel," replied the good Mama Maria, "since this holy constitution, all is changed, all is meta-morphosed. This clique, who govern to-day in place of the king, wish that nothing should remain of what for-merly existed; it is for that they no longer permit the Jews to wear tails on their backs, although they always before carried them, as does the devil. If the holy father said to the contrary it is because it is obligatory, as they are obliged to say at Mass, 'Constitutional king.'"

"That may be so," said the monk.

"He is not a Jew," pursued the old woman; "rather is he a Turk or a Moor, who has been shipwrecked on our coast."

"A pirate of Morocco," replied the good brother, "it may be."

"But then he would wear a turban and yellow slip-pers, like the Moor I have seen thirty years ago, when I was in Cadiz. They called him the Moor Seylan. How handsome he was! But for me his beauty was nothing: he was not a Christian. After all, be he Jew or Moor let us relieve him."

"Assist him, Jew or Christian," repeated the brother. And they both approached the bed.

Stein had raised himself up in a sitting position, and regarded with astonishment all the objects by which he was surrounded.

"He does not understand what we say to him," said the good Maria. "Let us try, nevertheless."

"Let us try," added Gabriel.

In Spain, the common people believe that the best way

to make themselves understood is to speak very loud.
Maria and Gabriel, with this conviction, cried out both
together: "Will you have some soup?" said Maria.
"Will you have some lemonade?" said the brother.

Stein, whose ideas became clearer little by little, asked
in Spanish:

"Where am I? who are you?"

"He," replied the old woman, "is brother Gabriel; I
am grandma Maria, and we are both at your orders."

"Ah!" said Stein, "from whom do you take your
names? The holy archangel and the holy Virgin, guar-
dians of the sick and consolers of the afflicted, will
recompense you for your good action."

"He speaks Spanish!" cried Maria with emotion;
"and he is a Christian! and he knows the litanies!"

In her access of joy, she approached Stein, pressed
him in her arms and bravely kissed his forehead.

"Decidedly, who are you?" she said, after having
made him take a bowl of soup. "How, ill and dying,
have you reached this depopulated village?"

"I am called Stein, and I am a surgeon. I was in the
war at Navarre. I came by Estremadura to seek a port
whence I could embark for Cadiz, and then regain Germany, my country. I lost myself in my route: I made
a thousand detours and finished by arriving here, worn
out by fatigue and ready to give up the ghost."

"You see," said Maria to brother Gabriel, "that his
books are not in the Hebrew language, but in the language of surgeons."

"That's true," repeated brother Gabriel.

"And which party do you belong to?" asked the old
woman. "Don Carlos, or the other?"

"I serve in the troops of the Queen," replied
Stein.

Maria turned towards her companion, and with an expressive gesture, said in a low voice:

"He is not with the good."

"He was not with the good," repeated brother Gabriel, in bowing his head.

"But where am I?" again demanded Stein.

"You are," replied the old woman, "in a convent; which is no longer a convent. It is a body without a soul. There remain but the walls, the white cross, and brother Gabriel. The *others* have taken away all the rest. When there was nothing more to take, some *gentlemen* whom they call the public credit searched for a good man to guard the convent—that is to say, its carcass. They heard my son spoken of, and we came and established ourselves here, where I live with my son, the only one who would remain. When we entered into the convent, the fathers went away. Some retired to America or rejoined the missions in China; some returned to their families; some demanded their subsistence or work, or had recourse to alms. We have with us a monk, borne down by age and grief, who, seated on the steps of the white cross, weeps sometimes for the absent brethren, sometimes for the convent which they have abandoned. 'Will not your Reverence come here,' a child but lately attached to the services of the chapel said to him. 'Where would you that I go?' he replied. 'I will never go away from these walls, where I was, poor and an orphan, received by the good fathers. I know nobody in the world, and know nothing but how to take care of the garden of the convent. Where shall I go? What shall I do? I can live only here.' 'Then remain with us.' 'Well said, mother,' replied my son; 'we are seven seated at the same table; we will be eight, and, as the proverb says, We will eat more, and we will eat less.' "

"Thanks to this act of charity," said Gabriel, "I remain here, I take charge of the garden; but since they have sold the large pump, I do not know how to water a foot of ground; the orange.and lemon trees dry up under my feet."

"Brother Gabriel," continued the grandma, "will not quit these walls to which he is attached like the ivy; he also says, 'Very well, there remain but the walls. The barbarians! They have proved this maxim: Destroy the nest, the birds will never come back again.'"

"Notwithstanding," hazarded Stein, "I have heard said there are too many convents in Spain."

Maria fixed her black sparkling eyes on the German, and said to herself in an undertone:

"Were our first suspicions well founded?"

CHAPTER IV.

THE end of October had been rainy, and November sheltered herself under her thick green mantle.

Stein took a walk one day in front of the convent. A magnificent panorama presented itself to his sight: at the right, the limitless sea; at the left, solitude without end. Between them, on the horizon, was painted the black profile of the fort San Cristobal. The sea undulated softly, in raising without effort the waves gilded by the sun's rays, like a queen who spreads out her gorgeous mantle.

Not far from thence was situated the village of Villamar, near a river as impetuous during winter, as calm and muddy during summer. The grounds around, well cultivated, presented the aspect of a chess-board, where each square revealed the thousand shades of green. Here shone the warm tints of the vine, then covered with leaves; there, the ash-colored green of the olive-tree; the emerald green of the fig-trees, which the rains of autumn had imparted growth to; further off still, the bluish-green hedges of aloes. At the mouth of the river were collected several fishermen's boats.

Near the convent, upon a light hillock, stood a chapel; in front, a cross based on a block of masonry whitened with lime; behind this cross, a retreat of verdure: it was the cemetery. Stein went there to meditate upon the powerful magic of the works of nature, when he saw Momo leaving the farm and going towards the village.

In perceiving Stein, Momo proposed to him to accompany him, and they both commenced their route. They arrived soon at the top of the hillock, near the cross and the chapel. This ascension, however short and easy, had taken away Stein's strength, who was yet scarcely convalescent. He rested an instant; then he entered the chapel, whose walls were covered with "*exvotos.*" Among these *exvotos* there was one which singularly attracted by its strangeness. The front of the altar contracted itself towards the base in describing a curved line. Stein perceived there in the obscurity an object supported against the wall, and the form of which he could not distinguish. Fixing his earnest scrutiny on this object, he became assured it was a carbine. The size was such, and the weight must have been so great that it was incomprehensible how one single man could have the strength to place it in that position: it is but the reflection which is always inspired by the sight of the armor of the middle ages. The mouth of the carbine was so large that an orange could easily be introduced. The arm was broken, and the pieces were artistically put together by means of little cords.

"Momo," said Stein, "what does this signify? Is it really a carbine?"

"In looking at it," replied Momo, "it seems to me to be one."

"But why do they place a murderous weapon in this holy and peaceful place? In truth, it is not sense to arm Christ with a pair of pistols."

"But see, then," replied Momo, "the carbine is not placed in the hands of our Lord; it is at his feet, as an offering. The day on which this carbine was brought here, they called this Christ, the Christ of *Good Help*."

"And from what motive?" demanded Stein.

"For what motive!" said Momo in opening his eyes,
"everybody knows that, and you know it not!"

"Have you forgotten that I am a stranger?" replied
Stein.

"That is true; I will tell you then: there was formerly
in this country a highway robber who did not content
himself with robbing, he murdered the people as if they
were insects, whether from hatred, whether from fear of
being denounced, or whether from caprice. One day
two men of this village, two brothers, would undertake a
journey. All their friends assembled to conduct them
part of the way. There were abundance of good wishes
that they might not encounter the bandit who gave
quarter to no one, and who terrified everybody. But
they, good children, commended themselves to Christ,
and departed full of confidence in his protection. At the
entrance of a wood of olives, they found themselves face
to face with the robber, who came before them, with
carbine in hand, rested his gun and aimed. In this
extreme peril the two brothers fell on their knees,
addressing themselves to Christ: 'Help us, Lord!' The
bandit pulled the trigger, but whose soul was launched
into another world? It was that of the robber: God
caused the carbine to burst in the hands of the bandit.
And you see now that, in memory of this miraculous
assistance, they repaired the carbine with cords, and
deposited it here, and it is the Christ who, since then,
we implore help from. You knew nothing about it,
Don Frederico?"

"Nothing, Momo," he replied, in adding as if his own
reflections: "If you know all that others are ignorant
of, they who pretend know every thing."

"Let us go! will you come?" said Momo after a
moment's silence. "You know I cannot wait."

"I am fatigued," replied Stein; "go along, I will wait for you here."

"God protect you!" and Momo resumed his route, singing:

> " God's sweet protection be your lot,
>   Is the usual affiance.
>   Poor be ye rich ! for science,
>   The rich can buy it not."

Stein contemplated this little village, so tranquil, at once fishing, commercial, and laborious.

It was not like the villages of Germany, an assemblage of houses scattered without order, with their roofs of straw, and their gardens; they resembled in no way those of England, sheltered by the shades of their large trees; nor those of Flanders, which retired to the borders of the roads. It was composed of large streets, although badly made, where the houses, without separate stories, were of various heights, and covered with old tiles; windows were rare, and still more rare, glass and every species of ornament.

But the village contained a grand square, which, in spring, was green as a prairie; on this square was situated a beautiful church: the general aspect was one of charming neatness.

Fourteen crosses, of dimensions equal to that which was near to Stein, were placed equidistant from each other; the last, which was raised in the middle of the square, was opposite to the church: it was the *Road of the Cross.*

Momo came back, but with a companion, who was old, tall, dry, thin, and stiff as a wax taper. This man was dressed in a coat and pantaloons made of coarse gray cloth; a waistcoat enamelled in faded colors, and embellished with some repairs, real *chef-d'œuvres* of their

kind; a red belt, such as is worn by the peasants; a
slouched hat with large rim, ornamented with a cockade
which had been red, and which time, the rain, and the
sun had colored with the brilliant shades of a water-
melon. On each shoulder was a narrow strip of lace,
probably destined to secure two much-used epaulets;
and then an old sword, suspended from a belt of the same
age, completed this *ensemble*, half military and half rural.
Long years had exercised great ravages upon the front
part of the long and narrow skull of this being. To
supply the natural ornament, he had coaxed towards the
forehead the sad remnant of his head of hair, and fixing
them there by means of a cord of black silk on the top
of his skull, he formed a tuft as gracious as that of a
Chinese coxcomb.

"Momo, who is this man?" asked Stein in a low voice.

"The commandant," the other replied, very simply.

"The commandant of what?" anew asked Stein.

"Of the Fort de San Cristobal."

"The Fort de San Cristobal!" cried Stein in ecstasy.

"Your servant," said the newly arrived, saluting him
with courtesy; "my name is Modesto Guerrero, and I
place at your entire command my useless services."

The compliment of usage had an application so exact
to him who made it, that Stein could not resist a smile
in returning his military salute.

"I know who you are," pursued Don Modesto; "I
have taken a prominent part in your *contretemps* and
your misfortunes; I congratulate you on your re-establishment, and on your rencounter with the Alerzas, who
are, by my faith, very good kind of people. My person
and my house are entirely at your orders; I reside at
the *Plaza de la Iglesia*, that is to say, Place of the Constitution, for that is the name at present. If sometime

you would favor it with a visit, the inscription will indicate to you the place."

"As if he possessed all the village!" said Momo with a sneer.

"Then there is an inscription?" again demanded Stein, who, in the busy life of a camp, had never had time to learn the language of studied compliments, and could not therefore reply to those of the courteous Spaniard.

"Yes, sir," replied Don Modesto, "the subordinate should obey the orders of his superiors. You should comprehend that in this little village it is not easy to procure a slab of marble with letters of gold, like those you can purchase in Cadiz or Seville. We must have recourse to the schoolmaster, who writes a good hand, and who, to paint the inscription on the walls of common houses, is obliged to place himself at a certain height. The schoolmaster prepared a black color with soot and vinegar mixed, mounted the ladder, and commenced the work by tracing the letters about a foot long. Unfortunately, in wishing to make an elegant flourish, he gave such a violent shake to the ladder that it fell to the earth, carrying with it in its fall the schoolmaster with his pot of black, and all rolled together into the stream. Rosita, my hostess, who from the window had been a witness of this catastrophe, and having seen the unfortunate man come out black as coal, was frightened to that degree that she went into spasms, and continued thus for three days; and in truth I was myself not without some uneasiness. The Alcalde, notwithstanding, gave orders to the poor bruised schoolmaster to complete his work, and saw that the inscription gave only the letters CONSTI. The unfortunate man was ill at ease, but this time he would not use the ladder; he would bring a cart, and place a table on it, and secure it with strong cords. Hoisted upon this improvised scaffolding, the poor devil was so astounded that, reflecting on his accident, he had but one thought, which was, to complete his work as speedily as possible. This is the reason why the last letters, in lieu of being a foot long like the first, are not longer than your thumb; and that is not the worst of it —in his eagerness he forgot one letter at the bottom of his pot of black; and the inscription thus appears:

PLAZA DE LA CONSTItucin.

" The Alcalde was thrown into a pious fury; but the schoolmaster stoutly declared that neither for God nor for all the Saints would he recommence it, and that he preferred to mount a bull of eight years old rather than to work upon that mountebank plank. Thus has the inscription remained as it was: happily no one reads it. He is sorry that the schoolmaster had not completed it, for it would have been very handsome and done great honor to Villamar."

Momo, who carried on his shoulder some saddlebags, well filled, and who was in a hurry, asked the commandant if he was going to Fort San Cristobal.

" I go there, and on my way I will first go to see the daughter of Pedro Santalo; she is ill."

" Who! The Gaviota?" asked Momo; " don't believe it: I saw her yesterday on the top of a rock, screaming like the sea-gull."

" Gaviota!" said Stein, with surprise.

" It is," said the commandant, " a wicked nickname, which Momo has given this young girl."

" Because she has long legs," replied Momo, " because she lives equally on the sea and on the earth, because she sings, cries, and leaps from rock to rock like the sea-gulls."

"Your grandmother," replied Don Modesto, "loves her much, and never calls her any thing but Marisalada (witty Maria), on account of her piquant frolics, the grace of her song and her dance, and her beautiful imitation of the singing of birds."

"It is not that," replied Momo. "It is because that her father is a fisherman, and brings us salt and fish."

"And does she live near the port?" asked Stein, whose curiosity was much excited by all these details.

"Very near," replied the commandant. "Pedro Santalo possessed a bark: having made sail for Cadiz he encountered a tempest, and was shipwrecked on our coast. All perished, crew and cargo, with the exception of Pedro and his daughter, whom he had with him; the desire to save her doubled his strength: he gained the shore, but his ruin was complete. His sadness and discouragement were so profound that he would not return to his country. With the debris of his bark he constructed a little skiff among the rocks, and commenced as a fisherman. It was he who furnished the convent with fish: the brothers in exchange gave him bread, oil, and vinegar. It is now twelve years that he has lived here in peace with all the world."

This recital finished when they had arrived at a point where the paths divide into two roads.

"I will return soon," said the old commandant; "in an instant I will be at your disposal, and salute your hosts."

"Say to Gaviota," cried Momo, "that her illness does not alarm me, bad weeds never die."

"Has the commandant been long at Villamar?" asked Stein of Momo.

"Let me count—a hundred and one years before the birth of my father."

"And who is this Rosita, his hostess?'

"Who? Señorita Rosa Mistica!" replied Momo, with grotesque gesture. "It is a first love: she is uglier than hunger; she has one eye which looks to the east, and the other to the west; and her face, which the small-pox has not spared, is filled with cavities, each sufficient to hold an echo. But, Don Frederico, the heavens scorch, the clouds rush as if they would pursue us—let us hasten our steps."

CHAPTER V.

BEFORE we continue our recital, it is well, we believe, to make the acquaintance of this new personage. Don Modesto Guerrero was the son of an honorable farmer, who, like many others, was possessed of excellent parchments of nobility. During the war of independence, the French burned these parchments in burning his house, under the pretext that the children of a laborer are brigands,—that is to say, that they have committed the unpardonable crime of defending their country. The brave man could reconstruct his house; but as to the parchments, they were not of the class of phœnix. Modesto was called to the military service, and, in default of a substitute, he entered a regiment of infantry as a cadet. Sufficiently good-natured, he was not long in becoming a butt, the object of coarse jokes from his companions. These, encouraged by his forbearance, pushed their mockeries so far that Don Modesto put an end to them, as we will directly see. On a grand parade day he took his station at the end of a file. Near by was a cart. His comrades, with as much address as promptitude, passed a noose round his leg, and attached it to the wheels of the cart. The colonel gave the orders to "March!" The trumpets sounded, and all the men were in motion, with the exception of Modesto, who was brought up with his feet in the air, in the position which the sculptors give to the Zephyrs ready to fly.

The review ended. Modesto returned to quarters calm and tranquil as he had set out, and, without changing his step, he demanded satisfaction of his companions. Neither of them would assume the responsibility of the trick played. He then declared he would fight with them all, one after the other. Then he who had planned and executed the trick came forward, and they went out to fight. In the combat, Modesto's adversary lost an eye. "If you desire to lose the other," the vanquisher said to him, with his habitual phlegm, "I am at your service when you please."

Without relations or patrons at court, without ambitious views, and no fondness for intrigue, Modesto continued his career at a tortoise pace, until the siege of Gaëte, in 1805, a period at which his regiment received an order to join the troops of Napoleon. Modesto distinguished himself so well by his bravery and coolness, that he merited a cross, and the praises of his chiefs. His name was blazoned at Gaëte like a meteor, to disappear immediately in eternal obscurity.

These laurels were the first and the last which he had an opportunity of gathering during his military career: severely wounded in the arm, he was obliged to quit active service, and received as compensation the post of commandant of the ruined fort of San Cristobal. It was then forty years that he had under his orders the skeleton of a fort, and a garrison of lizards of all varieties. In the commencement, our Guerrero could not content himself with this abandonment. No one year passed without his pressing a request to the government to obtain the necessary repairs; also the guns and troops which this point of defence demanded. All these requests remained unnoticed, although, according to circumstances, he did not fail to represent the possibility of an invasion, whether by the English or the American insurgents, whether by the French, or the revolutionists, or the Carlists. A similar reception was accorded to his continual solicitations to obtain part: the government took no account whatever of these two ruins—the fort, and its commander. Don Modesto was patient; he finished by submitting to his destiny. When he arrived at Villamar, he lodged with the widow of the sacristan, who, in company with her then young daughter, lived a life of devotion. It was the abode of excellent women, a little meagre, and tainted with excessive intolerance, and scolds; but good, charitable, and of exquisite neatness.

The inhabitants of the village, who had great affection for the commandant, and who, at the same time, knew how irksome his position was, did all they possibly could to render his situation less irksome. They never killed a pig without sending him a supply of lard and pudding. At harvest-times they brought him some wheat, pease,- oil, and honey. The women made him presents of the fruits of their orchards; and his happy hostess had always an abundance of provisions, thanks to the generous kindness which inspired the good Modesto, who, of a nature corresponding with his name, far from feeling pride from so many favors, was accustomed to say that Providence was everywhere, but that his headquarters were at Villamar. He knew, in truth, how to show his gratitude for all these bounties by being serviceable to every one, and complaisant in the extreme. He arose with the sun, and his first duty was to assist the *cura* in the services of the mass. One villager charged him with a commission; another besought him to write to his son, who was a soldier; a mother confided to his care her little children, while she attended out doors to some little household affairs: he watched at the bedsides of the sick, and mingled his prayers with those

of his hostesses; indeed, he sought to be useful to everybody in all that was in his power, consistent with deco-
rum or honor. The widow of the sacristan died, leaving
her daughter Rosa, now full forty-five years of age, and
of an ugliness which you would travel far to see the like
of. The mournful consequences of the varioloid did not
contribute a little to augment this last misfortune. The
evil was concentrated on one of her eyes, and chiefly on
the pupil, which she could but half open; and it resulted
that the pupil half effaced gave to all her physiognomy
an aspect devoid of intelligence and mind, forming a singular contrast with the other eye, from which shot out
flames like the fire of a brier-bush at the slightest cause
of scandal; and certainly the occasions which presented
themselves were frequent enough.

After the funeral, the nine days of mourning passed,
the Señorita Rosita said one morning to Don Modesto:
"I regret much, señor, the duty of announcing to you
that we must separate."

"We part!" cried the brave man, opening his large
eyes, and placing his cup of chocolate on the table-cloth,
instead of placing it on the tray. "And why, Rosita?"

Don Modesto was accustomed, during thirty years, to
employ this pet name when he spoke to the daughter of
his old hostess.

"It seems to me," she replied, elevating her eyelids,
"it seems to me you need not ask me why. You know
it is not proper that two honest persons live together
under the same roof. It gives rise to scandal."

"And who could bring scandal against you?" replied
Don Modesto; "you, the village model!"

"Are you sure there will not be something? What
will you say when you learn that you yourself, despite
your great age, your uniform, and your cross, and I, a

poor girl who thinks only of serving God, that we afford amusement to these scandal-mongers?"

"What say you?" demanded Don Modesto, saddened.

"What you have just heard. And no one knows us but under nicknames which they apply to us, these cursed!"

"I am stunned, Rosita. I cannot believe—"

"So much the better for you if you do not believe it," said the devout girl; "but I avow to you that these impious ones,—God pardon them!—when they see us arrive together at the church, at the early morning mass, they say, one to the other: 'Sound the mass, here come the *Mystic Rose* and the *Tower of David,* in armor and in company, as in the litanies.' They have thus dubbed you, because your figure is so erect, so tall, and so solid."

Don Modesto remained, his mouth open, and his eyes fixed on the ground.

"Yes, señor," continued the Mystic Rose; "the neighbor who told me this was scandalized, and advised me to go and complain to the cura. I replied to her it were better that I restrained myself, and suffered. Our Lord suffered more than I, without complaining."

"Well!" said Modesto; "I will not permit that they mock me, and still less you."

"The best will be," continued Rosa, "to prove by our patience that we are good Christians, and by our indifference that we care little for the world's opinion. Beyond this, if these wicked persons are punished, they will be worse, believe me, Don Modesto."

"You are, as always, right, Rosita. I know these babblers; if you cut out their tongue, they will speak with their nose. But if, in by-gone days, any of my

comrades had dared to call me *Tower of David*, he
would have had to add, 'Pray for us!' How is it that
you, a saint, have any fear of these slanders?"

"You know, Don Modesto, what say the vulgar, who
think evil of all the world: 'Between saint and saint
there should be a strong wall.' "

"But between you and I there is no need of a wall.
I am old, and never in all my life was I ever, except
once, in love; and then it was with a very pretty young
girl, whom I would have married, if I had not surprised
her in a counter-flirtation with the drum-major, who—"

"Don Modesto!" cried Rosita, choked with this dis-
course. "Honor your name and your position, and
abandon your souvenirs of love."

"My intention was not to offend you," replied Don
Modesto, in a contrite tone. "Know that well; and I
swear to you that I never had, and never will have, an
evil thought."

"Don Modesto," replied Rosa, with impatience (she
looked on him with her eye of fire, while the other eye
made vain efforts in the hope of being inflamed in uni-
son), "do you judge me so simple as to think that two
persons, like you and I, having both the fear of God,
could conduct ourselves like those hair-brained people
who have neither shame nor horror of sin? But in the
world it is not sufficient to do well. We must even not
give cause for scandal, and guard on all sides even
against appearances."

"That is another thing," replied the commandant.
"What appearances can there be between us? Do you
not know that they who excuse, accuse themselves?"

"I tell you," replied the devotee, "there will not be
wanting persons to blame us."

"And what can I do without you?" demanded Don

Modesto, afflicted. "Alone in the world, what can you do without me?"

"He who gives food to the little birds," said Rosita, in a solemn tone, "will take care of those who trust in Him."

Don Modesto, disconcerted, and knowing not what further to say, went to consult with the cura, who was at the same time his friend and Rosita's.

The cura persuaded the good girl that her scruples were exaggerated, and her fears without reason; that the projected separation would much more give rise to ridiculous comments.

They continued then to live together, as formerly, in peace, and in the fear of God;—the commandant always good and useful; Rosa always careful, attentive, and disinterested: because, on the one hand, Don Modesto was not the man to take any recompense for his services; and, on the other, if the handle of his gala-sword had not been silver, she could well have forgotten the color of that metal.

CHAPTER VI.

WHEN Stein returned to the convent, all the family were assembled in the court. Momo and Manuel arrived at the same time, each from his direction. The last had been going his rounds of the farm in the exercise of his functions as gamekeeper; he held his gun in one hand, and in the other three partridges and two hares.

The children ran to Momo, who at once emptied his wallet, from which escaped, as from a horn of abundance, a multitude of winter fruits, which, according to Spanish custom, served to celebrate All Saints' Eve; viz., nuts, chestnuts, and pomegranates.

"If Marisalada brings us the fish," said the eldest of the little girls, "to-morrow we will have a famous feast."

"To-morrow," said Maria, "is All Saints; father Pedro will certainly not go out to fish."

"Then," said the little one, "it will be for the next day."

"They no longer fish on the 'Dia de los Difuntos.'"

"And why?" demanded the child.

"Because it would be to profane a day which the church consecrates to sanctified souls. The proof is, that the fishermen having once cast their lines on such a day, and delighted with the weight they were drawing in, were doomed to find only snakes instead of fish. Is it not true, brother Gabriel?"

"I did not see it, but I am sure of it," replied the brother.

"And is it for that you make us pray so much on the 'day of the dead?'" asked the little girl.

"For that same," said the grandma; "it is a holy custom, and God is not willing that we should ever neglect it."

"Certainly," added Manuel, "nothing is more just than to pray to the Lord for the dead; and I remember a fellow of the Congregation of Souls who begged for them in these terms, at the door of the chapel: 'He who places a small piece of money in this place, withdraws a soul from purgatory.' There came along a wag who, after having deposited his piece: 'Tell me, brother,' asked he, 'do you believe the soul is yet clear of purgatory?' 'Do you doubt it?' replied the brother. 'In that case,' replied the other, 'I take back my piece; I know this soul; she is not such a fool as to go back when she is once out.'"

"You may be assured, Don Frederico," said Maria, "that with every thing, good or bad, my son finds always something appropriate to a story, a witticism, or a *bon-mot*."

At this moment Don Modesto entered by the court; he was as stiff and grave as when he was presented to Stein at the end of the village. The only change was, that he carried suspended to his stick a large stock of fish covered over with cabbage leaves.

"The commandant! The commandant!" was the general cry.

"Do you come from your citadel, San Cristobal?" asked Manuel of Don Modesto, after exchanging the preliminary compliments, and an invitation to be seated on the same stone bench where Stein was seated.

"You might join my mother, who is so good a Christian, to pray to the saints to build again the walls of the

fort, contrary to that which, by report, Joshua did at
the walls of Jericho."

"I have to ask of the Lord things more important
than that," replied the grandma.

"Certainly," said brother Gabriel, "Maria has more
important things than the reconstruction of the walls
of a fort to ask of the Lord. It would be better of her
to implore Him to reconstruct the convent."

Don Modesto, on hearing these words, turned with a
severe gesture towards the monk, who, at this moment,
went and placed himself behind the old mother, and
dissimulated so well, that he disappeared almost entirely
to the eyes of the others present.

"After what I see," continued the old commandant,
"brother Gabriel does not belong to the church mili-
tant. Do you not remember that the Jews, before
building their Temple, had conquered the promised land,
sword in hand? Would there have been churches and
priests in the Holy Land if the crosses had not conquered
it, lance in hand?"

"But," then said Stein, with the laudable intention to
divert from this discussion the commandant, whose bile
commenced to be stirred, " why does Maria ask for what
is impossible?"

"That signifies little," replied Manuel; " all old women
act the same, except she who asked God to tell her a
good number in the drawing of a lottery."

"Was it sent her?" they asked.

"It had been well kept, if I had gained the prize. He
who could do all things, where the miracle?"

"That which is certain," declared Don Modesto, "is,
that I will be very grateful to the Lord, if he will inspire
the government with the happy idea of re-establishing
the fort of San Cristobal."

"To rebuild, would you say?" observed Manuel; "take care and repent at once, as it happened to a woman consecrated to the Lord, and who had a daughter so ugly, so stupid, and so awkward, that she could not find even a despairing man to espouse her. The poor woman, much embarrassed, passed all her days on her knees at prayer, asking a husband for her daughter. At last one presented himself: the joy of the mother was extreme, but of short duration. The son-in-law was so bad, he so maltreated his wife and his mother-in-law, that the latter went to the church, and there posted before the saint this inscription:

'Saint Christopher! with hands and feet,
Whose measure could a giant's meet!
(And with a head of bony horns),
Is't thou among the saints I saw?
Thou—Jewish as my son-in-law.'"

While the conversation was going on, Morrongo, the house cat, awoke from a long sleep, bent his croup like the back of a camel, uttered a sharp mew, opened out his mustaches, and approached, little by little, towards Don Modesto, just so as to place himself behind the perfumed pocket suspended to the baton. He immediately received on his velvet paws a little stone thrown by Momo, with that singular address which children of his age so well know how to cast. The cat skipped off in a gallop, but lost no time in returning to his post of observation, and made believe to sleep. Don Modesto saw him, and lost his tranquillity of mind.

"You have not said, Señor Commandant, how Marisalada is?"

"Ill, very ill, she grows weaker every day. I am much afflicted to see her poor father, who has had so much to

suffer. This morning his daughter had a high fever; her
cough did not quit her for an instant."

"What do you say, Señor Commandant?" cried
Maria.

"Don Frederico, you who have made such wonderful
cures, you who have extracted a stone from brother Gabriel and restored the sight of Momo, can you not do
something for this poor creature?"

"With great pleasure," replied Stein; "I will do all
in my power to relieve her."

"And God will repay you. To-morrow morning we
will go and see her. To-day you are too much fatigued
from your walk."

"I am not jealous of his kind," said Momo, grumbling.
"The proudest girl—"

"That is not so," exclaimed the old woman; "she is a
little wild, a little ferocious; one can see she has been
educated alone, and allowed to have her own way by a
father more gentle than a dove, although a little rough
in manner, like all good sailors. But Momo cannot bear
Marisalada, since one day when she called him Romo
(flat-nosed), as indeed he is."

At this moment a noise was heard; it was the commandant pursuing at a quick pace the thief Morrongo,
who had deceived the vigilance of his master and ran off
with the stock fish.

"My commandant," cried out Manuel to him, laughing, "the sardine which the cat carries will not come
to the dish except late or never, but I have here a partridge in exchange."

Don Modesto seized the partridge, thanked him, took
leave of the company, and went away, inveighing
against cats.

During all this scene, Dolores had given the breast to

her nursing infant; she tried to hush him to sleep, cradling him in her arms and singing to him:

> "There high on Calvary, in their fresh retreats,
> Woods of olives, wood of perfume meets;
> A nightingale—four larks—whose breath,
> Would warble forth a Saviour's death."

For those who suppress the circulation of poetry of the people, as the child crushes with its hand the feeblest butterfly, it would be difficult to say why larks and nightingales warble the death of Christ; why the swallow plucked out the thorns of his crown; why the rosemary is an object of veneration, in the belief that the Virgin dried the swaddling-clothes of the infant Jesus on a bush of this plant? Why, or rather how do they know that the willow is a tree of bad augury, since Judas hung himself on a branch of this tree? Why does no misfortune ever happen in a house if it has been perfumed with rosemary during Christmas eve? Why in the flower which is called the *passion-flower* are found all the instruments of the passion of Christ? In truth, there are no answers to these questions. The people do not possess them, nor demand them. These beliefs have accumulated like the vague sounds of distant music, without research into their origin, without analyzing their authenticity.

· "But, Don Frederico," said Maria, while Stein was occupied with reflections on the proceedings, "you have not told us how you find our village."

"I have seen nothing," replied Stein, "save only the chapel of our Lord of Good-Help."

"Miraculous chapel, Don Frederico. Hold," pursued the old woman, after some instants of silence, "the only motive why I am not as much pleased here as in

3*

the village is, that I cannot follow out my devotions.
Yes, Manuel, thy father, who had not been a soldier,
thought like me.   My poor husband!—he is in heaven—
my poor husband was brother of Rosaire of the dawn;
Rosaire who went out after midnight to pray for souls.
Fatigued with a long day's work he slept profoundly;
and precisely at midnight a brother rang a bell, came to
the door, and chanted:

> ' Here is then the faithful bell!
> It is not she the warnings tell;
> Of thy parents 'tis the voice!
> The cross's foot then make thy choice;
> Raise thee, my son, so full of zeal,
> And prayerful in the chapel kneel.
> On thy knees in the holy place,
> For parents supplicate God's grace.'

When thy father heard this chant, he felt no longer
fatigue nor need of sleep.   In the twinkling of an eye he
got up and followed the other brother.   It seems to me
I yet hear him singing in the distance:

> ' The Virgin raised the Sovereign crown,
> And meekly laid the sceptre down;
> Presenting them to Christ was seen,
> Exclaiming—I no more am Queen.
> If not held back thy wrath from o'er the human race,
> Then is thy crown divine with too just rigor placed.'

Jesus answered her:

> ' My mother!
> Without thy grace so pure, and thy sweet hallowed prayer,
> The thunderbolt had hurled the sinner to despair.' "

The children, who love so much to imitate what they
see as at all great or remarkable, undertook to sing in
a beautiful tone the couplets of the aurora:

> " Hark! how the trumpet's shrill-blast clarion sounds!
> The voice of the Angel through Heaven resounds:

Jerusalem ! within thy walls,
An infant's foot triumphant falls ;
What was the people's homage in that hour ?
What grand equipments decked the kingly bower ?
The all-powerful whom Heaven had sent,
Rode on an ass which men had lent."

"Don Frederico," said Maria, after a moment's silence, "in the world which God has made, is it true that there have been men without faith?"

Stein was mute.

"Can you not cure the blindness of their intelligence, as you have cured the eyes of Momo?" replied, with sadness, the good old woman, who remained altogether pensive.

CHAPTER VII.

THE following day Maria set off for the house of the invalid, in company with Stein and Momo, foot-equerry to his grandmother, who travelled mounted on the philosophic Golondrina. The animal, always good, gentle, and docile, trotted on the road, the head lowered, ears depressed, without making a single, rough movement, except when he encountered a thistle in proximity with his nostrils.

When they were arrived, Stein was astonished to find, in the middle of this arid country, of a nature so dry and so sterile, a village so leafy and so coquettish.

The sea had formed, between two great rocks, a little circular creek, and surrounded by a coast of the finest sand, which appeared like a plateau of crystal placed on a table of gold. Several rocks showed themselves timidly, as if they wished to repose themselves, and be seated on the tranquil shore. At one of them was made fast a fisherman's bark; balancing herself at the will of the waves, she seemed as impatient as a horse reined in.

On one side of the rocks was elevated the fort of San Cristobal, crowned by the peaks of wild figs, like the head of an old Druid adorned with green oak-leaves.

The fisherman had constructed his cabin with the wrecked remains of his vessel, which the sea had thrown on the coast; he had based all against the rocks, which formed, in some sort, three stories of the habitation. The roof was horizontal, and covered with *aquatica*, the first layer of which, rotted by the rains, had given growth to a great quantity of herbs and of flowers; so that in the autumn, when the dryness disappeared with the heat of summer, the cabin appeared covered as with a delicious garden.

When the persons just arrived entered the cabin, they found the fisherman sad and cast down, seated near the fire, opposite to his daughter ; who, her hair in disorder, and falling down on both sides of her pale face, bent up and shivering, her emaciated limbs enveloped in a rag of brown flannel. She seemed to be not more than thirteen years of age. The invalid turned, with an expression of but little kindliness, her large, black, and sullen eyes upon the persons who entered, and instantly sank down anew in the corner of the chimney.

"Pedro," said Mariá, "you forget your friends, but they do not forget you. Will you tell me why the good God has given you a mouth ? Could you not have let me known of the illness of the little girl? If you had let me known of it sooner, I had sooner come with this gentleman, who is such a doctor as is seldom seen, and who in no time will cure your daughter."

Pedro Santalo rose brusquely, and advanced to Stein ; he would speak to him, but he was so overcome with emotion that he could not articulate a single word, and he covered his face with his hands. He was a man already advanced in life, his aspect sufficiently rude, and his form colossal. His countenance, bronzed by the sun, was crowned by a gray head of hair, thick and un-combed ; his breast, red as that of an Ohio Indian, was also covered with hair.

"Come, Pedro!" said Maria, from whose eyes the tears began to flow at the sight of the poor father's despair; "a man like you, big as a church, a man they believe ready to devour infants uncooked, to be discouraged thus without reason! Come! I see here nothing but what appears solid."

"Good mother Maria," replied the fisherman, in a feeble voice, "I count, with this one, five children in their tombs."

"My God! and why thus lose courage? Remember the saint whose name you bear, and who threw himself into the sea when he had lost the faith which sustained him. I tell you that, with the grace of God, Don Frederico will cure the child in as little time as you could call on Jesus."

Pedro sadly shook his head.

"How obstinate are these Catalans!" said Maria, with a little anger; and passing before the fisherman, she approached the invalid: "Come, Marisalada, come; rise up, daughter, that this gentleman may examine you."

Marisalada did not stir.

"Come, my daughter," repeated the good woman; "you will see that he will cure you as by enchantment." At these words, she took the girl by the arm, and wished to raise her up.

"I have no desire," said the invalid, rudely disengaging herself from the hand which held her.

"The daughter is as sweet as the father; 'he who inherits steals not,' " murmured Momo, who appeared at the door.

"It is her illness that renders her impatient," added the father, to exculpate his child.

Marisalada had an access of coughing. The fisherman wrung his hands with grief.

"A fresh cold," said Maria; "come, come, it is not a very extraordinary thing. But then he will consent to what this child does; the cold she takes, running, with naked feet and legs, on the rocks and on the ice."

"She would do it," replied Pedro.

"And why not give her healthy food—good soups, milk, eggs? But no, she eats only fish."

"She does not wish them," replied the father, with dejection.

"She dies from negligence," suggested Momo, who, with arms crossed, was posted against the door-post.

"Will you put your tongue in your pocket!" said his grandma to him. She returned towards Stein:

"Don Frederico, try and examine our invalid, as she will not move, for she will let herself die rather than make a movement."

Stein commenced by asking of the father some details of the illness of his daughter. He then approached the young girl who was drowsy, he remarked that the lungs were too compressed in their right cavity, and were irritated by the oppression. The case was grave, the invalid was feeble, from want of proper food; the cough was hard and dry, the fever constant; the consumption indeed would not allow it to pause.

"Has she always had a taste for singing?" demanded the old woman during the examination.

"She would sing crucified, like the bald mice," said Momo, turning away his head, that the wind would carry his hard speech, and that his grandma could not hear him.

"The first thing to do," said Stein, "is to forbid this girl to expose herself to the rigors of the season."

"Do you hear, my child?" said the father with anxiety.

"She must," continued Stein, "wear shoes and dress warm."

"If she will not?" cried the fisherman, rising suddenly, and opening a box of cedar, from whence he took numerous objects of toilet.

"Nothing is wanting: all that I have and all that I can amass are hers. Maria! my daughter! you will put on this clothing! Do this for the love of heaven!—Mariquita, you see it is what the doctor orders."

Marisalada, who was aroused by the noise made by her father, cast an irritated look on Stein, and said to him in a sharp voice:

"Who governs me?"

"And say that they do not give this government to me, by means of a good branch of wild olive!" murmured Momo.

"She must have," continued Stein, "good nourishment, and substantial soups."

Maria made an expressive gesture of approbation at the same time.

"She should be nourished with milk diet, and chickens, and fresh eggs."

"Did I not tell you so!" interrupted the old woman, exchanging a look with Pedro: "Don Frederico is the best doctor in the world."

"Take care that she does not sing," remarked Stein.

"Am I never to listen to her again?" cried poor Pedro with grief.

"See, then, what a misfortune!" replied Maria. "Let her be cured, and then she can sing night and day, like the ticking of a watch. But I think it will be best to have her taken to me, for there is no one to nurse her, nor any one who knows like me how to make good soup for her."

"I can prove that," said Stein, smiling, "and I assure

you one might set before a king a soup prepared by my good nurse."

Maria never felt more happy.

"Thus, Pedro, it is useless talking of it; I will take her home."

"Remain without her! no, no, it is impossible."

"Pedro, Pedro, it is not thus we should love our children," replied Maria. "To love them is to do above all that which will benefit them."

"So let it be!" replied the fisherman, rising with resolution; "I place her in your hands, I confide her to this doctor's care, and commend her to the divine goodness."

With difficulty could he pronounce these last words, which flowed rapidly, as if he feared to recall his determination; and he went to harness his ass.

"Don Frederico," asked Maria, when they were alone with the invalid, who remained drowsy, "is it not true, that, with God's help, we will cure her?"

"I hope so," replied Stein; "I cannot tell you how much this poor father interests me."

Maria made a package of the linen which the fisherman had taken out of the box, and Pedro came back leading the ass by the bridle. They placed the invalid on the saddle: the young girl, enfeebled by the fever, opposed no resistance. Before Maria had mounted Golondrina, who appeared quite content to return in company with Urca (name given to a great sea-fish, and which was that of Pedro's ass), the fisherman took Maria aside, and said to her, in trying to slip some pieces of gold in her hand:

"This is all I could save from my shipwreck, take it, and give it to the doctor, for all I have is for him who can give me back my daughter."

"Keep your gold," replied Maria, "and know, in the first place, it is God who has conducted the doctor hither; in the second place—it is I."

Maria pronounced these last words with a light tinge of vanity.

They commenced their journey.

"Do not stop, grandma," said Momo, who walked behind; "however large may be the convent, it must be filled with people. Eh! what? the cabin was not good enough for the Princess Gaviota?"

"Momo," replied the grandma, "mind your own affairs."

"But what do you see in her? And what touches you in this wild Gaviota, to take her thus under your care?"

"Momo, a proverb says, 'Who is thy sister? thy nearest neighbor;' another adds, 'Wipe the nose of thy neighbor's child, and take her to thee.' And here is the moral: 'Treat thy neighbor as thyself.'"

"There is yet another proverb," added Momo, "which says, 'He is mad who occupies himself about others.' But it is of no use. You were obstinate about raising the palm to *San Juan de Dios.*"

"You will not be the angel to aid me," said Maria with sadness.

Dolores received the invalid with open arms, as approving the resolution of her mother-in-law.

Pedro Santalo, who had accompanied his daughter, called the charitable nurse before he returned, and, putting the pieces of gold in her hand, said—

"This is to defray the expenses, and that she may want for nothing. As to your care, God will recompense you."

The good old woman hesitated an instant, took the gold, and said—

" It is well, she shall want for nothing. Depart without uneasiness, Pedro, your daughter is in good hands."

The poor father went away hurriedly, and did not stop till he reached the coast. Then he returned to the side of the convent, and wept with bitterness.

Maria said to Momo: "Bestir yourself. Go to the village, and bring me a ham from Serrano's, who will please send me a good one, when he knows it is for a poor sick girl. Bring me at the same time a pound of sugar and a quart of almonds."

" Just so, always sent about! Throw away every thing you possess," cried Momo. " Think you they will give me all this on credit, and for my handsome face ?"

" Here is to pay for them," replied the grandma, and she placed in his hand a piece of gold of four *duros* (about 4 dollars).

" Gold !" cried Momo, stupefied : for the first time in his life he saw this metal in the form of money. " From what demons have you snatched this ?"

" What is it to you ?" replied Maria; " don't worry yourself."

" It needs no more than this," replied Momo, " that I serve as domestic to this magpie, this accursed Gaviota ! I will not go."

" Go, boy, at once, and nimbly too."

" Ha! Well—no, I will not go; I will not annoy myself," repeated Momo.

" José," said Maria, on seeing the shepherd go out, " do you go to the village ?"

" Yes, Señora; what orders have you for me ?"

The good woman gave him the· commission, and added—

" This Momo has a bad heart, and will not go. And I have not the strength to complain to his father, who

would make him march quickly, and caress him in a
manner to break his bones."

"Yes, yes, do every thing to take care of this crow
who will tear out your eyes," said Momo. "You will
receive payment in the trouble she will give you; if it is
not so now, it will be in time."

CHAPTER VIII.

A MONTH after the scenes we have described, Mari-salada was more sensible, and did not show the least desire to return to her father's. Stein was completely re-established; his good-natured character, his modest inclinations, his natural sympathies, attached him every day more to the peaceful habits of the simple and generous persons among whom he dwelt. He felt relieved from his former discouragements, and his mind was invigorated; he was cordially resigned to his present existence, and to the men with whom he associated.

One afternoon, Stein, leaning against an angle of the convent which faced the sea, admired the grand spectacle which the opening of the winter season presented to his view. Above his head floated a triple bed of sombre clouds, forced along by the impetuous wind. Those lower down, black and heavy, seemed like the cupola of an ancient cathedral in ruins, threatening at each instant to sink down. When reduced to water, they fell to the ground. There was visible the second bed, less sombre and lighter, defying the wind which chased them, and separating at intervals sought other clouds, more coquettish and more vaporous, which they hurried into space, as if they feared to soil their white robes by coming in contact with their companions.

"Are you a sponge, Don Frederico, so to like to receive all the water which falls from heaven?" demanded José, the shepherd, of Stein. "Let us enter, the roofs are made expressly for such nights as these. My sheep would give much to shelter themselves under some tiles."

Stein and the shepherd entered, and found the family assembled around the hearth.

At the left of the chimney, Dolores, seated on a low chair, held her infant, who, turning his back to his mother, supported himself on the arm which encircled him, like the balustrade of a balcony; he moved about incessantly his little legs and his small bare arms, laughing, and uttering joyous cries addressed to his brother Anis. This brother, gravely seated opposite the fire, on the edge of an empty earthen pan, remained stiff and motionless, fearing that, losing his equilibrium, he would be tossed into the said earthen pan, an accident which his mother had predicted.

Maria was sewing at the right side of the chimney; her grand-daughters had for seats dry aloe-leaves, excellent seats, light, solid, and sure. Nearly under the drapery of the chimney-piece slept the hairy Palomo, and a cat, the grave Morrongo, tolerated from necessity, but remaining, by common consent, at a respectful distance from each other.

In the middle of this group there was a little low table, on which burned a lamp of four jets; close to the table the brother Gabriel was seated, making baskets of the palm-tree; Momo was engaged in repairing the harness of the good "Swallow" (the ass); and Manuel, cutting up tobacco. On the fire was conspicuous a stew-pan full of Malaga potatoes, white wine, honey, cinnamon, and cloves. The humble family waited with impatience till the perfumed stew should be sufficiently cooked.

"Come on! Come on!" cried Maria, when she saw her guest and the shepherd enter. "What are you doing outside in weather like this? 'Tis said a hurricane has come to destroy the world. Don Frederico, here, here! come near the fire. Do you know that the invalid has supped like a princess, and that at present she sleeps like a queen! Her cure progresses well—is it not so, Don Frederico?"

" Her recovery surpasses my hopes."

" My soups!" added Maria with pride.

" And the ass's milk," said brother Gabriel quietly.

" There is no doubt," replied Stein, " and she ought to continue to take it."

" I oppose it not," said Maria, " because ass's milk is like the turnip—if it does no good it does no harm."

" Ah! how pleasant it is here!" said Stein, caressing the children. " If one could only live in the enjoyment of the present, without thought of the future!"

" Yes, yes, Don Frederico," joyfully cried Manuel, '*Media vida es la candela; pan y vino, la otra media.*' " (Half of life is the candle ; bread and wine are the other half.)

" And what necessity have you to dream of the future?" asked Maria. " Will the morrow make us the more love to-day ? Let us occupy ourselves with to-day, so as not to render painful the day to come."

" Man is a traveller," replied Stein, " he must follow his route."

" Certainly," replied Maria, " man is a traveller ; but if he arrives in a quarter where he finds himself well off, he would say, ' We are well here, put up our tents.' "

" If you wish us to lose our evening by talking of travelling," said Dolores, " we will believe that we have offended you, or that you are not pleased here."

" Who speaks of travelling in the middle of December?" demanded Manuel. " Goodness of heaven ! Do you not see what disasters there are every day on the sea ?

hear the singing of the wind! Will you embark in this weather, as you were embarked in the war of Navarre, for, as then, you would come out mortified and ruined."

"Besides," added Maria, "the invalid is not yet entirely cured."

"Ah! there," said Dolores, besieged by the children, "if you will not call off these creatures, the potatoes will not be cooked until the last judgment."

The grandmother rolled the spinning-wheel to the corner, and called the little infants to her.

"We will not go," they replied with one voice, "if you will not tell us a story."

"Come, I will tell you one," said the good old woman.

The children approached. Anis took up his position on the empty earthen pot; and the grandma commenced a story to amuse the little children.

She had hardly finished the relation of this story, when a great noise was heard.

The dog rose up, pointed his ears, and put himself on the defensive. The cat bristled her hair, and prepared to fly. But the succeeding laugh very soon was frightful: it was Anis, who fell asleep during the recital of his grandmother. It happened that the prophecy of his mother was fulfilled as to his falling into the earthen pan, where all his little person disappeared, except his legs which stuck out like plants of a new species. His mother, rendered impatient, seized with one hand the collar of his vest, raised him out of this depth, and, despite his resistance, held him suspended in the air for some time—in the style represented in those card dancing-jacks, which move arms and legs when you pull the thread which holds them.

As his mother scolded him, and everybody laughed at him, Anis, who had a brave spirit, a thing natural in an infant, burst out into a groan which had nothing of timidity in it.

"Don't weep, Anis," said Paca, "and I will give you two chestnuts that I have in my pocket."

"True?" demanded Anis.

Paca took out the two chestnuts, and gave them to him. Instead of tears, they saw promptly shine with joy the two rows of white teeth of the young boy.

"Brother Gabriel," said Maria, "did you not speak to me of a pain in your eyes? Why do you work this evening?"

"I said truly," answered brother Gabriel; "but Don Frederico gave me a remedy which cured me."

"Don Frederico must know many remedies, but he does not know that one which never misses its effect," said the shepherd.

"If you know it, have the extreme kindness to inform me of it," replied Stein.

"I am unable to tell you," replied the shepherd. "I know that it exists, and that is all."

"Who knows it then?" demanded Stein.

"The swallows," said José.

"The swallows?"

"Yes, sir. It is an herb which is called *pito-real*, which nobody sees or knows except the swallows: when their little ones lose their sight they rub their eyes with the *pito-real*, and cure them. This herb has also the virtue to cut iron—every thing it touches."

"What absurdities this José swallows without chewing, like a real shark!" interrupted Manuel laughing. "Don Frederico, do you comprehend what he said' and believes as an article of faith? He believes and says that snakes never die."

"No, they never die," replied the shepherd. "When

4

they see death coming they escape from their skin, and run away. With age they become serpents; little by little they are covered with scales and wings: they become dragons, and return to the desert. But you, Manuel, you do not wish to believe any thing. Do you deny also that the lizard is the enemy of the woman, and the friend of man? If you do not believe it. ask then of Miguel."

"He knows it?"

"Without doubt, by experience."

"Whence did he learn it?" demanded Stein.

"He was sleeping in the field," replied José. "A snake glided near him. A lizard, which was in the furrow, saw it coming, and presented himself to defend Miguel. The lizard, which was of large form, fought with the snake. But Miguel not awaking, the lizard pressed his tail against the nose of the sleeper, and ran off as if his paws were on fire. The lizard is a good little beast, who has good desires; he never sleeps in the sun without descending the wall to kiss the earth."

When the conversation commenced on the subject of swallows, Paca said to Anis, who was seated among his sisters, with his legs crossed like a Grand Turk in miniature, "Anis, do you know what the swallows say?"

"I? No. They have never spoken to me."

"Attend then: they say (the little girl imitated the chirping of swallows, and began to sing with volubility),

'To eat and to drink!
And to loan when you may;
But 'tis madness to think
This loan to repay.
Flee, flee, pretty swallow, the season demands,
Fly swift on the wing, and reach other lands.'"

"Is it for that they are sold?"

"For that," affirmed his sister.

During this time, Dolores, carrying her infant in one hand, with the other spread the table, served the potatoes, and distributed to each one his part. The children ate from her plate, and Stein remarked that she did not even touch the dish she had prepared with so much care.

"You do not eat, Dolores?" he said to her.

"Do you not know the saying", she replied laughing, "'He who has children at his side will never die of indigestion,' Don Frederico? What *they* eat nourishes *me.*"

Momo, who found himself beside this group, drew away his plate, so that his brothers would not have the temptation to ask him for its contents. His father, who remarked it, said to him—

"Don't be avaricious; it is a shameful vice: be not avaricious; avarice is an abject vice. Know that one day an avaricious man fell into the river. A peasant who saw it, ran to pull him out; he stretched out his arm, and cried to him, ' *Give me your hand!*' What had he to give? A miser—give! Before giving him any thing he allowed himself to be swept down by the current. By chance he floated near to a fisherman; ' *Take my hand!*' he said to him. As it was a question of taking, our man was willing, and he escaped danger."

"It is not such wit you should relate to your son, Manuel," said Maria. "You ought to set before him, for example, the bad rich man, who would give to the unfortunate neither a morsel of bread, nor a glass of water. 'God grant,' answered the beggar to him, 'that all that you touch changes to this silver which you so hold to.' The wish of the beggar was realized. All that the miser had in his house was changed into metals as hard as his heart. Tormented by hunger and thirst, he went into the country, and having perceived a fountain of pure water, clear as crystal, he approached with longing to taste it; but the moment his lips touched it, the water was turned to silver. He would take an orange, and the orange was changed to gold. He thus died in a frenzy of rage and fury, cursing what he had desired."

Manuel, the strongest-minded man in the assembly, bowed down his head.

"Manuel," his mother said to him, "you imagine that we ought not to believe but what is a fundamental article, and that credulity is common only to the imbecile. You are mistaken: men of good sense are credulous."

"But, my mother, between belief and doubt there is a medium."

"And why," replied the good old woman, "laugh at faith, which is the first of all virtues? How will it appear to you, if I say to you: 'I have given birth to you, I have educated you, I have guided your earliest steps—I have fulfilled my obligations!' Is the love of a mother nothing but an obligation! What say you?"

"I would reply that you are not a good mother."

"Well, my son, apply that to what we were speaking of: he who does not believe except from obligation, and only for that, cannot cease to believe without being a renegade, a bad Christian; as I would be a bad mother, if I loved you only from obligation."

"Brother Gabriel," interrupted Dolores, "why will you not taste my potatoes?"

"It is a fast day," replied brother Gabriel.

"Nonsense! There is no longer convent, nor rules, nor fasts," cavalierly said Manuel, to induce the poor old man to participate in the general repast. "Besides, you have accomplished sixty years: put away these scruples, and you will not be damned for having eaten our potatoes."

"Pardon me," replied brother Gabriel, "but I ought to fast as formerly, inasmuch as the Father Prior has not given me a dispensation."

"Well done, brother Gabriel!" added Maria; "Manuel shall not be the demon tempter with his rebellious spirit, to incite you to gormandize."

Upon this, the good old woman rose up, and locked up in a closet the plate which Dolores had served to the monk—

"I will keep it here for you until to-morrow morning, brother Gabriel."

Supper finished, the men, whose habit was always to keep their hats on in the house, uncovered, and Maria said grace.

CHAPTER IX.

MARISALADA was already convalescent, as if nature had desired to recompense the excellent treatment of Stein, and the charitable care of the good Maria. She was decently dressed; and her hair, well combed and gathered behind her neck, bore evidence of the attention which Dolores had shown in putting her *coiffure* in order.

One day when Stein was reading in his chamber, whose window overlooked the grand court where the children amused themselves in company with Marisalada, he heard her imitate the songs of various birds with such rare perfection, that he closed his book to admire this really extraordinary talent.

Soon after commenced one of those recitations so common in Spain, and which consist of playing and singing at the same time. Marisalada took the part of the mother; Pepe that of a young cavalier who came to demand of her the hand of her daughter; the mother refused him; the young man would take possession of her by force of his love; and all this dialogue, composed of couplets, was sung with exquisite melody.

The book fell from the hands of Stein, who, like all good Germans, passionately loved music.

Never had so beautiful a voice struck his ear. It was a metal pure and ringing like crystal, smooth and flexible as silk. Stein hardly dared to breathe, so much did he fear to lose a single note.

"You are there, all ears," said Maria, who entered the chamber unknown to Stein. "Have I not warned you that she is a canary set free?"

And upon this she descended to the court and asked Marisalada to sing her a song.

She refused, with her accustomed tartness.

At this moment Momo entered, singularly dressed and driving before him the ass laden with charcoal. He had his hands and face bedaubed and black as ink.

"*El Rey Melchor! El Rey Melchor!*" cried Marisalada on seeing him. "*El Rey Melchor! El Rey Melchor!*" repeated the children.

"If I had nothing else to do," replied Momo furiously, "but to sing like you, great mountebank, I would not be daubed from head to foot. Fortunately, Don Frederico has forbidden you to sing, and you will not stun my ears."

Marisalada, as a response, struck out in a song in her loudest tones. The Andalusian people have at their command an infinite quantity of songs. There are the *boleros*, now joyous, now sad; the *ole*, the *fandango*, the *cano*, so pretty and so difficult to execute; and many others, among which is distinguished the *romance*. The tone of the romance is monotonous, and we dare not affirm that this song, receiving the honors of written notation, could satisfy the dilettante and the melodrama. But its charm, or, if you will, its enchanting grace, consists in the modulations of the voice in singing, as it were to cast out certain notes, to blend them, to *balance* them, so to say, very softly, in' raising or lowering the tone, in swelling it or allowing it to die. It is thus that the *romance*, composed of a number of notes strongly bound, presents the great difficulties of expression, and the purity of execution.

The song belongs so essentially to the peasantry;
that the common class of the people alone, and very
few among them, attain perfection. Those who sing
well appear to sing by intuition. When towards evening, in the country, one hears at a distance a fine voice
singing the *romance* with a melancholy full of originality, he feels an extraordinary emotion, which can only
be compared to that produced in Germany by the
sounds of the postilion's cornet, so deliciously repeated
by the echoes in the magnificent forests, and on the
splendid lakes. The words of the *romance* refer generally to some history of the Moors, or recount either pious
legends or the sad exploits of brigands. That ancient
and celebrated romance which we have received from
our fathers like a melodious tradition, has been more
lasting as to some of its notes than all the grandeur of
Spain achieved by her cannon, and sustained by the
mines of Peru. There are still many other popular
songs, very pretty, very expressive, of which the music is
specially adapted to words. Witness that which was
sung by Marisalada, and which we transcribe here in all
its simplicity.

> "A cursed cavalier
>   Loved a noble dame ;
> Who to his love gave ear,
>   Echoing his flame.

> "Her manor, happy once,
>   Silent entered he ;
> And in her lord's absence,
>   Found security.

> "And now the wrapt embrace
>   Seemed from danger free ;
> When knelled the master's voice,
>   'Open quick to me.'

" He gayly cried, ' Sweet dove !
　　Let me thee embrace ;
　Fever is it, or love,
　　Palors now thy face ?'

" ' Scold me thou would'st again,
　　Fear then pales me thus ;
　The key ?　Let me explain ?
　　Thy treasure key is lost.'

" ' Gold is preferred to steel,
　　Then still be calm, my dear ;
　But say why, if you will,
　　Is this proud courser here ?'

" ' Yours is yon race horse, lord,
　　Presented by papa ;
　Who asks, with knightly word,
　　Your presence shortly there.'

" ' Your father is most kind,
　　Such noble gift to make ;
　This pistol, too, I find !
　　Is there not some mistake ?'

" ' 'Tis yours, please comprehend,
　　From him : he bade me say,
　He hopes you will attend
　　My sister's wedding day.'

" ' Contemptuous of law,
　　Thus in my wedded bed ;
　Who is the wretch to dare,
　　My fatal ire to goad ?'

" ' My youngest sister 'tis,
　　Whom father to me sent ;
　To share with me my bliss,
　　And see how sweet life went.'

" But suddenly the truth,
　　Flashed on the husband's mind ;
　' Father ! take back thy Ruth,
　　I but a traitress find !

4*

"' No longer is she mine,
   Betwixt us is a gulf;
   But vain 'tis to repine,
   Be man! avenge thyself.'

" The wife paid for her wrong,
   At the sharp poignard's point;
   And the false knight was hung,
   The only death he'd grant."

Marisalada had scarcely finished singing this ballad, when Stein, who had an excellent ear for music, took his flute and repeated, note by note, the song he had just heard. At this the young girl nearly fainted with astonishment; she looked around on all sides to discover whence came this echo so pure and faithful.

"It was not an echo," cried the little girls, "it was Don Frederico, who whistled in a reed pierced with holes."

Marisalada then quietly entered the chamber of Stein, and began to listen with the greatest attention, her body bent forward, a smile on her lips, and her soul in her eyes.

Within this instant the rude ferocity of the fisherman's daughter was changed, and her regard for Stein induced a certain confidence and docility which caused the greatest surprise to all the family.

Maria advised Stein to profit by the ascendency he obtained day by day over the mind of Marisalada, to engage her to be instructed and employ her time in learning the law of God, and to try and become a good Christian; a woman of sense and reason; a good manager.

The grandmother added, that to obtain the end proposed, to bend the entire character of Marisalada, and to make her abandon her bad habits, the best thing would

be to pray the Señora Rosita, the mistress of the
school, to be so good as to take charge of her, because
she was a very honest woman, fearing God, and very expert in all her handy-work.

Stein much approved of this idea, and obtained the
consent of Marisalada. He promised, in return, to go
and see her every day, and play airs on the flute to divert her.

The disposition of the young girl awakened in her an
extraordinary taste for the study of music, and the first
impulse was given her by the ability of Stein.

When Momo found that Marisalada had put herself
under the tuition of Rosa Mistica, to learn there to sew,
to sweep, to cook, and above all, as he said, to have
judgment; when he knew that it was the doctor who
had decided this, he declared he believed what Don
Frederico had recounted respecting his country, where
there were certain men whom all the mice followed when
they heard a whistle.

Since the death of her mother, Señorita Rosa had established a school for little girls. School is the name
which they give in villages; but the school in cities
bears a more pompous title, and it is called an academy.
The little village children attend school from the morning until midday; all the information is composed of
Christian doctrine and of sewing. In cities they learn
to read, to write, to embroider, and to sketch. It is
true that these schools cannot create the wells of science,
nor become the nurseries of artists, or produce models
of an education equal to that of a *mujer emancipada*;
but in return they produce ordinarily good workers and
excellent mothers of families, which is still better.

The invalid perfectly cured, Stein urged upon her
father that he would confide his daughter for some time,

to the honest woman who would replace the mother she
had been deprived of, and who would instruct her in the
duties of her sex.

When it was proposed to the Señorita Rosa to admit
to her house the *indomitable* daughter of the fisherman,
her first reply was decidedly negative, as she was accustomed to make, in such circumstances, to persons of her
character.

Notwithstanding, she finished by consenting, when she
was made to understand the good effects expected to
result from this work of charity. It is impossible to recount all that the unfortunate schoolmistress suffered
during the time she had Marisalada in charge. On one
side were mockeries and rebellion; on the other, ser-
mons without profit, and exhortations without result.
Two causes exhausted the patience of Rosa; with her
patience was not an inborn virtue, but laboriously ac-
quired.

Marisalada had succeeded in organizing a kind of
conspiracy in the little battalion commanded by Rosa.
This conspiracy burst forth one fine morning, timid and
undecided at first, then audacious and walking with a
lofty head. Thus was the event:

"The rose mallow does not please me," suddenly said
Marisalada.

"Silence!" cried the mistress, whose severe discipline
forbade conversation during school-hours.

Silence was re-established.

Five minutes after a voice, sharp and insolent, was
heard:

"The moon-roses do not please me."

"No one asked your opinion," said the Señorita
Rosa, believing that this declaration had been provoked by Marisalada.

Five minutes after, another conspirator said, on picking up her thimble which had fallen—

"I do not like white roses."

"What does it signify?" cried Rosa, whose black eye shone like a beacon. "You mock me!"

"Moss roses do not please me," said one of the smallest girls, hastily hiding under the table.

"Nor the passion roses, me."

"Nor the roses of Jericho, me."

"Nor the yellow roses, me."

The strong and clear voice of Marisalada drowned all other voices—

"I cannot bear dry roses," cried she.

"I cannot bear dry roses," repeated all the scholars in chorus.

Rosa Mistica, who at the commencement was only astonished, rose up on seeing so much insolence, ran to the kitchen, and returned armed with a broom.

At sight of this all the conspirators fled like a flock of birds. Rosa remained alone, let fall her broom and crossed her arms.

"Patience, Lord!" she exclaimed, after having done every thing possible to subdue her emotion. "I will support a sobriquet with resignation, as thou, Lord, supported thy cross; but I yet lack that crown of thorns. Thy will be done!"

Perhaps she might have decided to pardon Marisalada this escapade, but the adventure which soon after followed obliged her to send her away.

The son of the barber, Ramon Perez, a great amateur of the guitar, came every night to touch the chords of his guitar and sing amorous couplets under the strongly fastened windows of the devotee.

"Don Modesto," said she to him one day, "when you

hear this bird of night, Ramon, whose voice wounds your hearing, do me the kindness to go out and order him to carry his music elsewhere."

"But, Rosita," replied Don Modesto, "would you that I get on bad terms with this eccentric fellow, when his father (may God repay him!) has shaved me for nothing since my arrival in Villamar? And, see how it is. *I* like to listen to it, because none can deny that he draws from his voice and instrument modulations of excellent taste."

"I congratulate you," said Rosa. "It is possible that your ears are proof against a bomb-shell. If it pleases you, it is not convenient to me that he comes and sings under the windows of an honest woman. It produces neither honor nor profit."

The physiognomy of Don Modesto expressed a mute answer divided into three parts. In the first place—astonishment, which seemed to say, What! Ramon make love to my hostess! In the second place—doubt; as if he had said, Is it possible? Lastly—the certainty embodied in these phrases : The thing is sure ; Ramon is audacious.

After this reflection, Rosa continued :

"You might cool yourself in passing from the heat of your bed to the fresh sea air ; you had better remain quiet, and it is I who will say to this magpie, Do you wish to divert yourself? then buy yourself a doll."

Precisely at midnight was heard the sounds of a guitar, and a voice which sang—

> "The black of thy black hair I love,
>   Believe me, much more fully,
> Than ivory whiteness e'er can prove,
>   Or the majestic lily."

"What folly!" cried Rosa Mistica, springing out of

her bed. "See how he continues this annoyance which he sings so profitlessly."

The voice continued:

> "To thy prayers, to the church so superb,
> All resplendent thou seemest in vain;
> Tread thou gracefully then the light herb,
> For the herb will be green soon again."

"God assist us!" murmured Rosa, in putting on her third petticoat: "he mixes up the Church with his profane couplets, and those who hear him will say that he sings thus to insult me. This beardless barber! does he believe he can mock me? It required only that."

Rosa entered into the saloon, and caught a view of Marisalada, who, leaning against the shutter, listened to the singer with all the attention she was capable of. Then she made the sign of the cross, exclaiming—

"And she is not yet thirteen years old! There are no more children."

Taking her scholar by the arm, she drew her away from the window, and placed herself there at the moment when Ramon powerfully touched his guitar, and strained his throat to entone the following couplet:

> "My loved one to the window came,
> Now all around here is obscure;
> But thy bright eyes will soon illume,
> For love will be the Cynosure."*

Then the music of the guitar continued the air with more vehemence and ardor than ever.

"It is I who will lighten thee with a torch of hell!" cried Rosa Mistica, in a sharp and angry voice. "Libertine! Profaner! Everlasting and insupportable singer!"

* In poetry—the *North Star*.

Ramon Perez, recovered from his first surprise, set off to run lighter than a buck, and without casting a single look behind.

This was the decisive *coup*. Marisalada was sent back to her room, in spite of the timid efforts at reconciliation tendered in her favor by Don Modesto.

" Señor," replied Rosita to her guest, " charges are charges, and while this shameless girl is under my responsibility, I must render account of her actions to God and to men ; each one has enough of his own sins, without charging himself or herself, in addition, with those of others. You view it otherwise, she is a creature who will never follow the good path. When she is pointed to the right, she turns always to the left."

CHAPTER X.

STEIN had inhabited his peaceful retreat during three years. He had adopted the customs of the country in which he had found himself; he lived, day after day, or, in other terms, according to the counsels of his good hostess Maria, who said that the morrow should not so disquiet us as to lose the present day, and that we should occupy us with but one thing, viz., that to-day should not make us lose to-morrow.

During those three years, the young doctor had been in correspondence with his family. His parents had died while he was with the army of Navarre; his sister Charlotte was married to a farmer in easy circumstances, who had made of his wife's two brothers cultivators—not much instructed, but handy and assiduous at their work. Stein, therefore, believed himself free and sole arbiter of his fate.

He devoted himself to the education of the young invalid, who owed her life to him, and although he cultivated a soil ungrateful and sterile, he succeeded, by patience, to ingraft on her mind the elements of a preliminary education. But what surpassed his expectations was the development of the musical faculties, really extraordinary, with which nature had endowed the fisherman's daughter. Her voice was incomparable, and Stein, who was a good musician, could easily and surely direct her, as one trains the branches of the vine, which are at once flexible and vigorous, strong and elastic.

But the master had a heart soft and tender, and a craving for confidence which turned to blindness. He was devoted to his scholar, stimulated by the exalted love of the fisherman for his daughter, and by the admiration of the good Maria for Marisalada. Stein and his scholar possessed a certain powerful communicative sympathy, which could exercise its influence upon a soul frank and open, candid and good-humored as that of the young German. He then persuaded Pedro Santalo that his daughter was an angel, and Maria, that she was a prodigy. Stein was one of those men who could assist at a masked ball without convincing himself that under these absurd masks, under these caricatures of painted cardboard, there were other physiognomies and other faces—the work of nature, in one word. And if impassioned affection blinded Santalo, if extreme goodness of soul blinded Maria, both succeeded in putting a bandage over the eyes of the good doctor.

But that which bewitched, above all, our hero, was the pure, sweet, expressive, and eloquent voice of his scholar.

"It must be," he said to himself, "that she who expresses in a manner so admirable, sentiments the most sublime, must be gifted with a soul full of elevation and tenderness."

Like as the grain of corn, in the fruitful soil, germinates and takes root before the stem sprouts above the ground, so this love, so calm and true, took root in the heart of Stein: love which he felt without having yet defined it.

Marisalada, on her part, was equally attached to Stein, not because she was grateful to him for his attentions, but that she appreciated his excellent qualities, and because she comprehended his great superiority of soul and

intelligence: nor yet even because she obeyed an attractive charm which imparted love to the person who
inspired it ; but because that the musician, the master
who had initiated her in the art, felt, himself, all these
sentiments of gratitude and admiration. The isolation
in which she lived tended to put far away any other object that could excite her preference.

Don Modesto was not of an age to figure in this tour-
nament of love. Momo was not only disqualified by his
extreme ugliness, but he preserved all his hatred for
Marisalada, never ceasing to call her Gaviota, and she
had for him the greatest contempt. Certainly gallants
were not wanting in the village ; to commence with the
barber, who was obstinate in his sighs after Marisalada;
but no one would oppose Stein.

This tranquil state of things had continued three
springs and three winters, which had glided by like
three days and three nights, when that came to pass
which we will now relate.

An intrigue (who could have predicted it ?) dawned
on the peaceful village of Villamar.

The promoter and the chief (who would have thought
it ?) was the good Maria. The confidant (who will not
be astonished ?) was Don Modesto!

Although it was an indiscretion, or, the better to express it, a baseness to watch, listening to the conspirators hidden behind that orange-tree, whose trunk is still
solid, while the flowers are withering and the leaves falling—image of the resignation which rests in the heart
when joy is fled, when hopes are vanished ; listening to
a conversation, which, in reconcilable secrecy, held the
two accomplices, while brother Gabriel, who is a thousand miles off and all near to the speakers, was busy in
binding up the lettuces to make them white and tender.

"It is not an idea that I have, Don Modesto," said the instigatress, "it is a reality. Not to see it, is to have no eyes. Don Frederico loves Marisalada, who regards the doctor no more than a bundle of straw."

"Good Maria, who thinks of love?" replied Don Modesto, who, all his life, calm and tranquil, had not seemed to realize the eternal, classic, and invariable axiom of the inseparable alliance of Mars and Cupid. "Who thinks of love?" repeated Don Modesto, in the same tone as if he had said—

"Who thinks of shearing a tambourine?"

"The young people, Don Modesto, the young people; and if it were not so, the world would come to an end. But the case is thus: we must give a spur to these young folks; they get on too slowly. For two years our man has loved his nightingale, as he calls her; that is evident in his looks, and as for me, I see it clearly. You who are a considerable personage, and whom Don Frederico loves so much, you ought to brisk up a little this affair, giving him good advice for their good and ours."

"Dispense with me, Maria," replied Don Modesto. ' Ramon Perez is an obstacle; we are friends, and I would not counteract his projects. He shaves me for my good appearances, and to thwart his interests, Maria, would be, on my part, a bad action. He sees with much pain that Marisalada does not love him, and he has become so thin and yellow that he is frightful. The other day he said that if he cannot marry Marisalada he will break his guitar, and that, no longer able to become a monk, he will become a rebel. You see, good Maria, that in every way I will compromise myself if I mix in this affair."

"Señor," said Maria, "do you take for cash in hand what lovers sing? Ramon Perez, the poor little thing!

is not capable of killing a sparrow, and you believe he will attack Christians? But take this into consideration: if Don Frederico marries he will remain with us always. What a happy chance will it not be for everybody? I assure you that when he talks of leaving us I feel all over *goose-flesh*. And the young girl, what a magnificent position for her! For you must know that Don Frederico gains a great deal of money. When he attended the son of the alcalde, Don Perfecto, he gave him a hundred *reals*, which shone like a hundred stars. What a beautiful couple they will make, my commandant!"

"I do not say nay, Maria," replied Don Modesto; "but do not force me to play a part in this affair, and leave me to preserve a strict neutrality. I have not two faces, I have only that one over which the barber passes his razor—it is my only one."

At this moment Marisalada entered the garden. She was certainly no longer the young girl we had known, dishevelled and badly clothed. She came every morning to the convent, *coiffured* with great care, and neatly dressed. Neither affection for those who inhabited it, nor the gratitude she owed, attracted her to this place. It was but the desire to hear music, and to receive her lessons from Stein. Beyond this, *ennui* drove her from her cabin, where she had for society only her father who did not much divert her.

"And Don Frederico?" she said on entering.

"He has not yet returned from visiting his patients," answered Maria. "To-day he has a dozen children to vaccinate. What an extraordinary thing, Don Modesto! He draws the *pus*, as you call it, from the teat of a cow: the cows have a counter-poison to oppose the small-pox! and it must be so, since Don Frederico has said it."

"Nothing is more true," continued Don Modesto, "than that it was a Swiss who discovered it. When I was at Gaëte I have seen the Swiss who constituted the Pope's guard, but neither of them could tell me who was the author of the discovery."

"If I were his Holiness," pursued Maria, "I would reward the inventor by a plenary indulgence. Seat yourself, my dear, I am dying with desire to see you."

"No! I am going."

"Where do you wish to go?—no one loves you better than we do here."

"What am I to do when people love me? What can I do since Don Frederico is not here?"

"What is that? You only come here then for Don Frederico, little ingrate?"

"Why not? why should I come? to find myself with Momo?"

"Then you love Don Frederico much?" hazarded the good old woman.

"I love him; and if it were not for him I would never put foot inside these doors, for fear of encountering that demon Momo, whose tongue resembles the sting of a wasp."

"And Ramon Perez?" mischievously demanded Maria, as if she would convince Don Modesto that his *protégé* might give up his hopes.

Marisalada burst into an uncontrollable fit of laughter.

"If this *Raton* (*he-mouse*) Perez—Momo had given the young barber this *sobriquet*—happens to fall into the porridge-pot, I will not be the ant who will sing or weep over him: less still will I be she who will listen to his singing; for his singing attacks my nervous system, as Don Frederico expresses it, which he assures me is now more stretched than the strings of a guitar. You shall see how this Raton Perez sings."

Marisalada rapidly took a leaf of aloe, which lay on the ground among those which served brother Gabriel as screens to protect, in their first growth, the tomato plants against the attacks of the north wind. She placed this leaf between her arms in the manner of a guitar, and began to imitate with a grotesque air the gestures of Ramon Perez, with a talent most perfect for imitation ; then she sang this couplet with strong trills :

> " Young meagre Minstrel without gladness,
>> What have you there ? why this distress, why these deep sighs ?
> Is it the cause of this dire sadness,
>> That on too high a castle you have cast your eyes ?"

" Yes," said Modesto, who remembered the serenades at the door of Rosita, "this Ramon has always had grand pretensions."

The events could not persuade Modesto that these serenades were not designed for Rosita. From thence but one idea entered the head of this man ; it was, that if she fell into a love snare, he himself could not extricate her. The calibre of his intelligence was so straitened, and so invariably fixed, that as soon as an idea penetrated his brain it became set, and remained there for life.

"I go," said Marisalada, throwing the leaf of aloe in such way that it fell with force against brother Gabriel, who, on his knees, and with his back turned, attached his hundred and twenty-fifth knot.

" Jesus !" cried out brother Gabriel, turning around frightened. Then, without uttering another word, he again set to work to tie up his lettuces.

" What aiming !" said Marisalada, laughing. "Don

Modesto, take me for artilleryman when you obtain cannon for your fort."

"Such things are not gracious; they are in bad taste,
which, you must know, please me in no way," replied
Maria a little coldly. "Say to me what you like, but as
to brother Gabriel, trouble not his peace, it is the only
good left to him."

"Do not get angry," replied the Gaviota, "you well
know that brother Gabriel is not made of glass." Then,
said she, making a courteous reverence, "My commandant, say to Rosa Mistica that she transfer her school to
your fort, when it has some 24-pounders, that she may
be well defended against the snares of the demon. I
must go, because Don Frederico does not come; I am
disposed to believe that he is vaccinating all the village,
including Rosa Mistica, the schoolmaster, and the alcalde."

But the good old woman, who was accustomed to the
rather free manners of Marisalada,—which, however, did
not wound,—called the young girl and told her to sit
down near her.

Don Modesto, warned by this that Maria was about
to open her batteries,—faithful to the neutrality he had
promised,—took leave of the old woman, made a turn to
the right and beat a retreat, not, however, without having received from the monk a couple of lettuces and a
bunch of turnips.

"My daughter," said Maria, when they were alone,
"what will you not be if Don Frederico marries you?
You will be with this man, who is a St. Louis de Gon-
zague, who knows every thing, who is a good musician,
and who gains plenty of money; you will be the doctor's
wife, the happiest of women. You will be dressed like
a dove, nurtured like a duchess; and you could then,

above all, help your poor father, who is growing old; and it pains our hearts that he is obliged to be on the sea despite rain and wind, so that his child may want for nothing. Thus would Don Frederico remain among us, like an angel of the good God, consoling and taking care of all who suffer."

Marisalada listened attentively to the old woman, affecting great distraction. When Maria had ceased to speak, the young girl was silent for an instant, and then, with an air of indifference, said—

"I do not wish to marry."

"Listen then!" exclaimed the good woman. "It is, perchance, you wish to be a nun?"

"Not at all," replied the Gaviota.

"What then?" demanded Maria, really angry. "You do not wish to be either flesh or fish! One thing only I know—woman belongs to God or to man; if not, she does not accomplish her mission, either towards God or towards society."

"What would you, Maria?" replied Marisalada; "I feel that neither marriage nor the convent is my vocation."

"Then, little girl," replied the old woman, "thy vocation is that of the mule. Nothing pleases me which is out of the regular order; above all, in that which we other women regard.

"She who does not do what we all do, I would flee from, if I were a man, as one flees from an infuriated bull. In a word—my hand on my heart—you act wrong. But you are yet but a child," she added, with her habitual goodness, "there is much for you yet to learn. Time is a great teacher."

Marisalada arose and departed.

"Yes," thought she, covering her head with her hand

kerchief, "he loves me, I have known it for a long time
—but—I love him as old Maria loves brother Gabriel,
as the aged love. He would receive a shower under
my window without fearing to take cold. Now—if he
marries me, he will render my life happy I am sure; he
will let me do as I like : he will give me music whenever
I ask him, and purchase for me every thing I may desire.
If I were his wife, I would have a neckerchief of crape,
like Quela, the daughter of old Juan Lopez; and a mantle, blonde of Almagro, like that of the Alcaldesa.

"They would both die with rage; but it seems to me
that Don Frederico, agitated as he is when he listens to
my singing, thinks as much of marrying me as Don
Modesto thinks of taking for his wife his dear Rosa—
chief of all the devils."

During the whole of this beautiful mental dialogue,
Marisalada had not one thought, not one recollection of
her father, whose well-being and whose solace had been
the chief motives adduced by Maria.

CHAPTER XI.

CONVINCED that she could neither be aided nor supported by the influential man who would not join her in these matrimonial projects, Maria determined to act by herself, with the certainty of overcoming the objections of the Gaviota, and those which Stein would oppose. Nothing stopped her, neither the boldness of Marisalada, nor the stolidity of Stein, because love is persevering as a sister of charity, and intrepid as a hero ; and love was the grand spring of all this good old woman did. It was thus she said to Stein, and to the point :

"Do you know, Don Frederico, several days ago Marisalada was here, and she explained to us very clearly, and with a grace altogether natural, that she came here only on your account ?"

"How do you find this frankness ? I say that, if it be true, it was an ingratitude that my pretty nightingale was not capable of; she was no doubt jesting."

"Don Frederico, the old are more experienced than the young, and the first impulses are the best. Does it cause you much grief to learn that you are beloved ?"

"No—certainly. We are agreed upon this axiom which you repeat so often : 'Love does not speak enough.' But, good Maria, make of love constancy : I would sooner give than receive."

"They do not talk thus to me," cried the brave woman, with impatience.

"It is still true, my dear and good mother," answered

Stein, taking and pressing the hands of old Maria, "we have a running account of affection, we two, but the balance is against me. God grant that I may some day be able to furnish the proof of my attachment and my gratitude!"

"It is very easy, Don Frederico, and I am about to demand it."

"At once, my good Maria; and what is this proof? say quickly."

"Remain with us; and to that end get married, Don Frederico. You inspire us with continual uneasiness in this living in the idea of your departure, and you would then realize the proverb, 'Which is your country? That of my wife.'"

Stein smiled.

"Whom shall I marry? with whom, my good mother, with whom shall it be? With your linnet?"

Maria replied: "With her, who is in your heart an eternal spring. She is so beautiful and so graceful: she is so moulded to your habits that she could not live without you! And what would you do without her? You love each other like two turtles—this is seen in your eyes."

"I am too old for her, Maria," replied Stein, sighing and blushing in a manner to prove that, as to him at least, the old woman had spoken truly; "I am too old," he repeated, "for a girl of sixteen years. My heart is an invalid, to whom I desire to accord a sweet and tranquil existence; I would not expose it to new wounds."

"Old!" exclaimed Maria, "what nonsense! you have scarcely attained to thirty years. Come—you reason like the leg of a table, Don Frederico."

"What could I desire more," replied Stein, "than to taste with an innocent young girl the sweet and holy

felicity of domestic life, which is the only true, the only
perfect, the only real, because it is that which God has
taught us. But, good Maria, she cannot love me."

"That is too strong; she has a very delicate taste, by
my faith, she who would be ashamed of you! Say not
to the contrary; you have the air of joking. Yes, the
wife that you love will be the happiest in the whole
world."

"Do you believe so, Maria?"

"I believe it as I believe my salvation; and she who,
in such a case, does not esteem herself happy, should be
crucified alive."

The following day, when Marisalada came, she met, on
entering the court, face to face with Momo, who was
seated on a stone of the mill, breakfasting on bread and
sardines.

"You here already, Gaviota!" this was the sweet
salutation Momo gave her; "if this continues, we will find
you one day in our soup. You have then nothing to do
at home?"

"I abandon all," replied Marisalada, "to come and
contemplate your face, which enchants me, and thine
ears, which excite the envy of Golondrina, thine ass."

In so saying she took hold of Momo's ears, and pulled
them.

The young girl had the chance at the first roar which
Momo made with all the strength of his big lungs, for a
mouthful of bread and sardines had stuck in his throat,
and occasioned such a fit of coughing, that the Gaviota,
light as a fawn, escaped the talons of the vulture.

"Good-day, my linnet," said Stein, who, on hearing
Marisalada, entered the court.

"She is beautiful, this linnet!" growled Momo, in his

fit of coughing; "she is the most hoarse magpie which has sung this summer."

"Come, Maria," continued Stein, "come write, and read the verses I translated yesterday."

"I do not remember them," replied the young girl. "Were they not of that country where grow the oranges? These trees do not grow here; or they have withered: brother Gabriel's tears are not sufficient to nourish their vitality. Let the verses go, Don Frederico, and play me the nocturn of Weber which these are the words of: 'Listen, listen, my beloved! the chant of the nightingale is heard; on each branch flourishes a flower; before the nightingale ceases to sing, before the flowers wither, sing, sing, my best beloved.'"

"What ugly words," murmured Momo, "this Gaviota remembers, and which are to her like bon-bons to a clove of garlic."

"After that you have read, I will play thee the serenade of Carl Weber," replied Stein, who by this single recompense could compel Marisalada to learn that which he would instruct her in. The young girl took, with an irritated gesture, the paper which Stein presented to her, and read it fluently, although with a bad grace.

"Mariquita," said Stein, when the young girl had finished reading, "you who do not know the world, you cannot appreciate what grand and profound truth, what philosophy there is in these verses. Do you remember that I explained to you what philosophy is?"

"I recollect," replied the Gaviota, "it is the science of happiness. But in that, señor, there are neither rules nor science which can constitute it: each one is happy after his own manner. Don Modesto places his happiness in possessing cannons in the fort as ruined as himself; brother Gabriel, to see return to the convent the

holy Prior and the bells; the good Maria, that you do
not quit her; my father, to take a *corbina;* and Momo,
to do all the evil he can."

Stein laughed, and placing affectionately his hand on
Mariquita's shoulder, "And you," said he to her, "in
what do you make happiness to consist?"

Mariquita hesitated an instant before finding a reply,
raised her large black eyes, and looked at Stein; then her
eyelids fell, and her glance rested on Momo; the young
girl smiled to herself at the appearance of those ears
which were redder than tomatoes.

"And you, Don Frederico," she at last replied, "in
what would you make it to consist? To return to your
country?"

"No," sighed Stein.

"In what then?" repeated Marisalada.

"I will tell thee, my linnet; but beforehand tell me in
what thou makest thine to consist."

"To always hear you play the flute," she replied with
sincerity.

At this moment Maria came from the kitchen with the
good intention to terminate the affair; but she occasioned that which happens to a great many: excess of
zeal spoiled all.

"Do you not see, Don Frederico, how pretty Marisalada is, and what a beautifully formed woman?"

"Yes, yes," continued Stein to Maria, "she is handsome, and her eyes are the type of Arabian eyes so celebrated."

"They say of the hedgehogs, each looks at a thorn,"
growled Momo.

"And this mouth so pretty, which sings like a sera-
phim," pursued the old woman, caressing the chin of
her *protégé.*

" See there, a mouth like a basket, which knows how to speak wrong and contrary."

" And thy mouth," said the Gaviota to Momo, with a fury which this time she could not control, " and thy horrible mouth, which cannot extend from one ear to the other because that thy face is so large it is fatigued when half way over."

Momo, for his only reply, sang in three different tones—

" Gaviota! Gaviota! Gaviota!"

" Romo! Romo! Romo!" sang Marisalada in her magnificent voice.

" Is it possible," said Stein to his linnet, " that you notice what Momo says expressly to enrage you. These witticisms are stupid and gross, but without wickedness."

" It must seem to you, Don Frederico, that this must be very stupid," replied the Gaviota; " and to inform you that I have no desire to support this lout harder than a stone, I go."

Upon this, the Gaviota went away; Stein followed her.

" You are a profligate," said Maria to her grandson; " you have more spleen in your heart than good blood in your veins. You owe respect to women, villain gosling! there is not in the village one more wicked or more detested than thou."

" You are in your turn tainted," replied Momo, " with the beauty of this sea-magpie, who have put my ears in the condition you see! All others, according to your ideas, are gross people. This *agua mala* (polypus) bewitches you. See. then a *gaviota* (sea-gull) which reads and writes! Has any one ever seen that? She does not employ herself all day but to grumble as water hisses on the fire; she does not cook for her father, who is obliged to prepare his own meals; she does not take care of his linen, and it is on you falls the work. You nourish a serpent."

Stein having rejoined Marisalada, said to her—

"Of what avails it, Mariquita, that I have endeavored to tone down your spirit, if you have not learned at least to acquire the little superiority necessary to place yourself above these miseries, which are in themselves so trifling and unimportant?"

"Listen, Don Frederico," replied Marisalada: "I comprehend that this superiority ought to serve to place me above others, but not below them."

"God help me, Mariquita! is it thus you change things? Superiority teaches us not to be proud of our qualities, and not to revolt against injustices opposed to us. But," added he smiling, "these are the faults of your youth, and of the vivacity of your southern blood. You will know all that when you have gray hairs, as I have. Have you remarked, Mariquita, that I have gray hairs?"

"Yes," she replied.

"See then, I am very young, but sufferings have made my head like that of an aged man. My heart has remained pure, Mariquita, and I offer you the flowers of spring, if you do not believe you will be alarmed at the symbols of winter which circle my forehead."

"It is true," replied the Gaviota, who could not restrain the natural ejaculation, "that a lover with gray hairs would not please me."

"I have thought it would be thus," said Stein with sadness. "My heart is loyal, and the good Maria, when she assured me that my happiness was still possible, instilled in my heart some hope, but which is as the flowers of the air without roots, and as the breath of the breeze."

Mariquita, who saw that she had wounded, with her accustomed rudeness, a soul too delicate to insist, and a man so modest as to persuade himself that this sole objection annulled the other advantages, immediately said—

"If a lover with gray hairs pleases me not, a husband with such hair would not frighten me."

Stein was taken by surprise at this brusque remark of Mariquita, and above all at the decision and impassibility with which she had enunciated it. Soon he smiled at Marisalada, and said to her—

"And then you will marry me, beautiful child of nature ?"

" Why not ?"

" Mariquita, she who accepts a man for a husband, and unites herself to him to pass her life, or, the better to express it, to make of two existences one only, as in a torch two lights blended make but one flame, such a person, I say, accords to this man a greater favor than she who accepts him for a lover."

" And of what use," replied the young girl with a mixture of innocence and indifference, " of what use are the guitarists, who sing badly and play badly, if not to frighten away the cats ?"

They had arrived at the beach, and Stein begged Mariquita to sit beside him on a rock. On the part of both there was a long silence. Stein was profoundly agitated. The young girl with stoical indifference had taken a stick, and traced figures on the sand.

" How nature speaks in the heart of a man !" at last exclaimed Stein. "What sympathy reigns in all that God has created ! A pure life is like a serene day; a life of unloosed passions resembles a tempestuous day. See those sombre clouds which slowly approach to interpose between the earth and the sun, they are such as should interpose between a heart and an illicit love, and let fall on the heart their cold but pure emanations. Happy the land on which they fall not! But our felicity will be unalterable like the sky in May, because you will always love me. Is it not so, Mariquita?"

This girl, whose rude and untutored soul comprehended neither the poetry nor the elevated sentiments of Stein, did not care to answer; but as she could not withdraw herself from this obligation, she wrote upon the sand the word *siempre* (always) with the stick which distracted her idleness.

Stein, whose emotion increased, mistook *ennui* for modesty.

"Look," pursued he, "look at the sea! Listen to the murmur of the waves, murmurs so full of charms and of terrors! 'Tis said they confine grave secrets in an unknown language. The waves, Mariquita, are those dangerous and perfidious sirens, personified by the flowery and fantastic imagination of the Greeks; creatures of a rare beauty, but without hearts, as seductive as terrible, and whose sweet voices attract men to their perdition. But thy sweet voice, Mariquita, seduces not to deceive; you attract like the siren, you will not be perfidious like her. Is it not true, Mariquita, you will never be ungrateful?"

Nunca (never), wrote Mariquita on the sand. And the rising waves amused themselves in effacing the word the young girl had written, as if they would parody the waves of time, which flowing on efface in the heart what is sworn to endure thereon forever.

"Why does not thy voice reply to me, Mariquita?"

"What would you, Don Frederico? I cannot say to a man that I love him. I am unfeeling and unnatural,

Maria says, who, however, does not the less love me. I am, like my father, economical in words."

"If you were like him, I could desire nothing more, because the good Pedro—I say my father, Mariquita—has a heart the most loving that has ever beaten in the breast of a man; such hearts belong to angels, and to a few chosen men!"

"My father a superior man!" thought Mariquita, repressing with difficulty a mocking laugh. "So be it! so much the better, if he has the air of one."

"Mariquita," said Stein in approaching her, "let us offer to God our pure and holy love; let us promise Him to render ourselves acceptable by our fidelity, and by the discharge of those duties which will be imposed on us when this love shall have been consecrated at the divine altar. Now let me embrace you as my wife and companion."

"No!" cried Mariquita, drawing back suddenly, and knitting her eyebrows. "No person shall touch me."

"It is well, my pretty fugitive," answered Stein with sweetness, "I respect all your delicacy, and submit myself to your will. Is it not appropriate to say, with one of our ancient and sublime poets, that the greatest of all felicities is, to 'obey in loving?'"

CHAPTER XII.

THE gratitude which the fisherman felt for him who had saved Marisalada, was complete when he saw him so attached to his daughter: an impassioned friendship which could only be compared to the admiration excited in him by the brilliant qualities of Stein.

From thence they were devoted to each other: the brusque mariner and the man of science sympathized, because men of kindred natures and gifted with good sentiments feel, when they come in contact, such an attraction, that, scorning the distance which separates their positions, they meet as brothers.

It thus happened when Stein offered himself as the old man's son-in-law: the good father could not articulate a word, so much was he overcome with the joy which filled his heart. He besought Stein only, when taking his hand, to come and live in his cabin. Stein cordially assented. The fisherman appeared then to recover all his strength and all the agility of his youth, to employ them in ameliorating and embellishing his habitation. He cleared away the little garret to make there his personal lodging, leaving the first story for his children; he whitened and ornamented the walls; he levelled the ground, and covered it with a precious mat of palms, which he weaved for that purpose; he engaged Maria to make up for him a *trousseau* for the bride in character with the simplicity of his dwelling.

Great was the news caused by the rumored approaching marriage of Stein, to all those who knew and loved him. Old Maria was so joyous that she passed three nights without sleep. She predicted that when Don Frederico permanently established himself in the country none of the inhabitants would die except from old age. Brother Gabriel manifested so much contentment and such pleasure in seeing Maria so sprightly, that he entered into the feelings of his protectress, and ventured to say a witty thing, the first and the last in all his life; he said in a loud voice, "that the cura had forgotten the *De profundis.*"

This remark became of some consequence, inasmuch as Maria, for fifteen days, was earnest in reporting, after the usual compliments, the famous forgetfulness of the *De profundis*, which remark she considered as the glory and honor of her *protégé*. He himself was so embarrassed with the success attendant upon his innocent wit, that he vowed never again to succumb to a similar temptation.

Don Modesto was of opinion that the Gaviota had gained the first prize in the lottery, and the people of the village the second: "Because," said he, "I would never have been maimed if I had met at Gaëte a surgeon as skilful as Stein."

Dolores added, that if the fisherman had twice given life to his daughter, the will of God had twice given her happiness, in conferring on her such a father and such a husband.

Manuel observed, that there was in Heaven a cake reserved for husbands who never repented of their marriage, and which, up to this moment, no one had yet put his teeth into.

His wife said, it was because husbands never entered there!

As to Momo, he concluded that since the Gaviota had found a husband, the Plague need not lose hope of finding one also.

Rosa Mistica took the affair differently. Mariquita had, by a recent act, increased her list of evil deeds; some devotees were assembled to sing, in honor of the Virgin, couplets accompanied by a wretched harpsicord, played by an old blind man. Rosita presided at this ceremony. Not being able to ignore the aptitude of Marisalada, she silenced her ancient resentments, and thought, by the mediation of Don Modesto, to induce the fisherman's daughter to take part in the pious concert.

Don Modesto took his cane, and set out on his campaign. Marisalada replied to the old commandant a dry "*No*," without prologue or epilogue.

This monosyllable frightened Modesto more than a discharge of artillery; the negotiator knew not what to do. Don Modesto was one of those men who are sufficiently good-hearted to desire the good of their friends, but who want strength to achieve it, and imagination to find the means of obtaining it.

"Pedro," said he to the fisherman, after this peremptory refusal, "do you know I tremble in all my limbs? What will Rosita say? What will all the village say? Can you not then influence her?"

"If she will not, what can I do?" replied the fisherman.

And the poor Don Modesto resigned himself to report this ungracious message, which would not only offend, but scandalize the mysticism of his hostess.

"I would prefer a thousand times," said he, in returning to Villamar, "to present myself before all the batteries of Gaëte, than before Rosita with a *no* on my lips. In what a state she will be!"

And Don Modesto was right; for it was in vain that he essayed to ornament her answer by an exordium which merely insinuated, to comment by vague hints, to embellish by verbose paraphrases : he did not less keenly offend Rosita, who cried out in a loud tone—

"They who would not employ in the service of God the gifts they have received of Him, merit perdition."

Also, when she learned the project of marriage, she sighed, and raised her eyes to Heaven :

" Poor Don Frederico !" she said.

Momo, according to his bad habits, took pleasure in conveying the news of this marriage to Ramon Perez.

"Really !" cried the barber, in consternation.

"You are sad; I am much more sad in seeing that there are people who ought to be beaten for the absurdity of their tastes. See a little ! To be smitten of this saucebox ! but Don Frederico proves the proverb, 'Late married, bâdly married.' "

"I am not sad," replied Ramon Perez, "because Marisalada is loved by Don Frederico, but because she loves this stranger who has hair of hemp and fishes' eyes. Why does not the ingrate recollect this sentence, ' Who marries late becomes either a dupe or a deceiver.' "

" It will not be he who will be the first to deceive. For as to Don Frederico, he is a brave man, nothing can be said to the contrary; but this vixen has bewitched him with her singing, which lasts from the rising to the setting sun. I have already said to him : Don Frederico, listen to the proverb, ' Take a house with a hearth : take a wife who knows how to spin.' He has not attended to either : it is a misfortune. As to thee, Ramon Perez, they have simply made a great mistake."

"That is easily seen," replied the barber, giving so hasty a turn to the key of his guitar that the treble-string broke: " he whom we would drive from our house must be a stranger. But you ought to know, Momo, that I care for very little. The year will finish one day, and if the king is dead, long live the king!"

Then he commenced to strike his guitar with rage, singing with bombastic voice:

> "Cold creature! what of thy contempts,
>   My heart, no longer irate, is now cured;
> Stains which no mulberry exempts,
>   By the mulberry green are no longer endured.
>
>   *   *   *   *
>
> "Love is fled! three pirouettes, and then—
>   Crack! and my happy days return;
> I have gold to please young girls I ween,
>   To purchase other loves I'll learn."

12*

CHAPTER XIII.

THE marriage of Stein and the Gaviota was celebrated
in the church of Villamar. The fisherman, instead of a
red flannel shirt, wore a white shirt, irreproachably
starched, and a vest of dark blue cloth. In this gala
costume he was so embarrassed that he could hardly
move.

Don Modesto, one of the witnesses, presented himself
in all the *éclat* of his old uniform, rendered threadbare
by constant brushing, and become too large by reason of
his having grown so thin. The nankeen pantaloons which
Rosita had washed for the thousandth time, had shrunken
so as to descend only half way down his legs. His epaulets had become copper-colored. The cocked hat, which
had survived eight lustres, and had not altered its pride,
occupied dignifiedly its elevated position. But in the
mean time there sparkled on the honorable breast of the
poor soldier the cross of honor, valiantly gained on the
field of battle, as shines a pure diamond in a fine setting.
The women, according to custom, assisted, all dressed in
black during the ceremony, but they changed their toi-
lets for the *fête*.

Marisalada was all in white. The dresses which Maria
and Dolores had received as presents from Stein on the
occasion, were made of wove cotton smuggled into
Gibraltar. The design was called *scarfs of iris*, because
of the assemblage of colors the most opposite and the
least harmonizing. One would believe the manufacturer
wished to mock his Andalusian customers. In fine, every-

body thought them handsome, except Momo, who would not put himself out on this occasion, and dressed himself to look as eccentric as possible.

"This is well for you, bad droll fellow. 'The ape, though dressed in silk, is nothing but an ape.' "

" You cut a figure! You, who to be the wife of the doctor have ceased to be the Gaviota, and dress yourself in new clothes to render yourself handsomer! Oh! yes —white becomes you so well! Put a red cap on your head, and you will resemble a phosphoric match."

Then he began to sing in a false voice—

> "Oh! oh!
> Like a crow—
> You are pretty, girl, all in white,
> Coquettish, like hunger, you siren;
> Like wax with clear color at night,
> And in bulk like a thread of iron."

Marisalada immediately replied—

> "Thy mouth, ugly ape,
> Like a basket in shape,
> Therein linen to lie;
> This you cannot deny.
> And thy teeth can tell,
> They've no parallel!
> And thine ear-rings, I know,
> But three pendants can show."

After this compliment she turned her back on him.

Momo, who was never behindhand when he meditated insolence and sallies, replied bravely—

"Go—go; when they give thee the benediction, it will be the first time thou hast received it during thine whole life, and I predict that it will be the last."

The marriage was held in the village, at the house of Maria, the cabin of the fisherman being too small to contain all the assembly. Stein, who, in the exercise of his

profession, had saved some money, although in most
cases he gave his services gratuitously, desired to do the
thing in grand style, and not to restrict the invitations.
He had abundance of wine, lemonade, biscuits, and cakes,
and three guitars. The guests sang, danced, screamed,
without omitting wit and pleasantry, joyous and gay.

Maria came and went, served the refreshments, played
the part of *godmother of the wedding*, and never ceased
to repeat, "I am as content as if I were the bride ;" to
which brother Gabriel invariably added, "I am as content as if I were the husband."

"Mother," said Manuel to Maria, on seeing her pass
near him, "the color of this dress is very gay for a
widow."

"Hold your tongue," replied the mother. "Every
thing ought to be gay on a day like this. Besides, 'we
must not look a gift horse in the mouth.' Brother
Gabriel, come along, take this glass of lemonade and
this cake, and drink to the health of the newly married
couple, before returning to the convent."

"I drink to the health of the new-married couple before
I return to the convent," said brother Gabriel.

The good monk emptied his glass, and escaped before
any one, except Maria, remarked his absence.

The reunion became animated by degrees.

"Bomba!" cried the sacristan, a little humpbacked
man, crooked and lame, "Bomba!" (This is the exclamation which announces ordinarily in Spain at a dinner or
at a *fête*, a little excited, that a guest is about to propose
a toast.)

Every one was silent at this signal.

"I drink," said the sacristan, "to the health of the
bride and groom, and to this honorable company, and to
the repose of all Christian souls!"

"Bravo! let us drink! and long live La Mancha! who gives us wine in lieu of water."

"In your turn, Ramon Perez, sing a couplet, and do not keep your voice for a better occasion."

Ramon sang—

> "A happy future—all good wishes
> To the pretty wife!
> And to her husband I've no species
> Of envy or of strife."

"Bravo! well sung!" cried all the assembly. "Now the fandango and the ball!"

After the prelude to this eminently national dance, a man and a woman rose simultaneously, and placed themselves face to face. Their graceful movements accomplished, so to speak, an elegant balancing of bodies, to the sound of their gay castinets.

In an instant the two dancers yielded their places to two others, who placed themselves in front, while the first couple retired. This divertisement, according to the usages of the country, was often repeated.

The guitarist had again his song—

> "To him who weds a beauteous bride,
> And to the holy temple hied:
> She has sworn, and now stands with wedded heart:
> She enters free—in irons must depart."

"Bomba!" soon cried one of the most expert in matters of toasts. "I drink to this excellent doctor, whom God sent to our country that we might attain a greater age than Methuselah! But I add one condition, that in case of longevity to me, he will not prolong either the life of my wife, or my purgatory."

This toast provoked an explosion of applause.

"What do you say to all this?" demanded all the guests at the wedding of Manuel.

"What do I say? That I say nothing."

"Badly answered! Get along—wake up, and propose a toast."

Manuel took a glass of lemonade, and said—

"I drink to the newly married, to our friends, to our commandant, and to the resurrection of Fort St. Cristobal!"

"Long live the commandant!" cried all present. "And you, Manuel, who know how to compose couplets, sing something."

Manuel sang the following couplet:

> "Of these allurements men take care,
> Hymen's intoxication sweet:
> 'Tis done! and 'till old age, beware,
> The fright will ne'er thy bosom quit."

After some other couplets had been sung, the greatest orator of the assembly said to Manuel:

"These people only sing trifles without head or tail. You who know how to say good things, above all when the wine gets a little in your head, make a stanza of ten lines in honor of the newly married, and take this glass of wine to loosen your tongue."

Manuel took the glass of wine, and commenced:

> "Bomba!
> Viva!
> Sweet vanquisher of secret pains,
> Physician gay of blackest dreams,
> I've seen thee born between green leaves,
> And, pressed, thy bosom madly heaves:
> Give to my voice the needful force,
> To the bride and groom I'd raise my voice!
> Here's Hymen! let's our glasses drain,
> To bride and groom, again, again."

"It is your turn, Ramon the devil. Has the liquor obstructed your throat? You are more insipid than a salad of tomatoes."

Ramon took his guitar and sang:

> "She to the church and sacrifices bold
> Herself surrenders, and I am consoled;
> My lips with kisses delicately hushed,
> Press the green grass which her small feet have pressed."

This couplet having been followed by another of little value, Maria approached Stein and said to him:

"Don Frederico, the wine commences to *tell* on our guests. It is midnight, and the poor children are alone in the house with Momo and brother Gabriel. I fear Manuel raises his elbow too often. Pedro is asleep in the corner, and I think it will not be bad to sound the retreat. Our asses are harnessed, will you that we take 'French leave?'" An instant after, the three women, mounted on their asses, were on their way to the convent. The men accompanied them on foot, while Ramon, in a fit of jealousy and of chagrin, on seeing the married couple depart, struck his guitar with an insolent air and bellowed rather than sang:

> "Thou the *calabash* hast given me;
> Or rather, I my *congé* see;
> Great good this *congé* does meeting,
> The tomatoes I have eaten!
> In thy family, at which I dine,
> Admitted once, revenged I am."

"What a beautiful night!" said Stein to his wife, raising his eyes towards heaven. "See the starry firmament! See the evening star shining in its magnificence like the brightness of my happiness! My heart has now no want unsupplied, and I have nothing to regret."

"And I who amused myself so much," replied Mari-salada, impatiently, "I do not see why we have left the *fête* so soon."

"Good Maria," said Pedro Santalo, "now we can die in peace."

"Yes," replied the old woman, "but we can as well live in joy; that would be much better."

"How is it that you do not know how to restrain yourself when you have the glass in your hand?" said Dolores to her husband. "From the moment you slacken sail, there is not a cable that could bring you up."

"*Caramba!*" replied Manuel: "I am here, what would you more? Still, one word more—I live on the brim and I return to the *fête.*"

The cries of the drinkers being continually heard, Dolores held her tongue, fearing that Manuel would put his threats into execution.

"José," said Manuel to his brother-in-law, who had also been to the wedding, "is the moon full?"

"Certainly," replied the shepherd. "Can you not see with your eyes? Do you not know what it is?"

"It should be a tear," said Manuel, laughing.

"It is not a tear; it is a man."

"A man!" exclaimed Dolores, altogether convinced by what her brother had said. "And what is this man?"

"I do not know—but I know his name."

"And how is he called?"

"He is called Venus," replied José.

Manuel began to laugh: he had drank more than usual, and, as they said, he was gay.

"Don Frederico," said Manuel to the new-made hus-band, "shall I give you a piece of advice, in my quality of being older than you in this grand Confederacy?"

"Hold your tongue, for God's sake, Manuel!" said Dolores.

"Will you leave me in peace? Listen, Don Frederico; to begin—with a wife and a dog, the bread in one hand, and a stick in the other."

"Manuel!" repeated Dolores.

"Will you leave me tranquil? or I return to the wedding."

Dolores thought it prudent to hold her peace.

"Don Frederico," pursued Manuel, "wives or slaves, women are the most powerful enemies."

"Do me the favor to hold your tongue, Manuel," interrupted his mother.

"This is odd," grumbled Manuel; "we were told we were assisting at an entertainment."

"Do you not know, Manuel," remarked the shepherd, "that these witticisms of thine are not to the taste of Don Frederico?"

"Señor," said Manuel, in taking leave of the married pair, who proceeded towards the cabin, "when you repent of what you have done we will be united again, and we will together sing the same complaint."

And he continued his route towards the convent. In the silence of night he was heard singing, in his clear and sonorous voice—

> "Alas, poor wife and cherished horse !
> Who the same hour died :
> I sorely weep, but for which loss ?
> My poor horse shall decide."

"Go to bed, Manuel, and nimbly," his mother said to him, when they arrived at home.

"My wife takes care of that," he replied; "is it not true, brunette?"

"What I wish is, that you were already asleep," replied Dolores.

"Liar! how can you thus speak in opposition to your heart?"

"Do you not know how to hold your peace?" said his brother-in-law to him, laughing.

"Listen, José," continued Manuel, "have you found in the thickets of the fields, or in the grottoes, any thing which could close the mouth of a woman? If you have found it, there will not be wanting people who will pay you for the information in solid gold. As to me, I have never met with it in this world, and I have learned nothing of it in the life of God."

Thereupon he began to sing—

> " The sun's sublimest heat,
> 'Tis easier to put out,
> Than e'er with fear to worry,
> A woman in her fury.
> Try the caress, be gay;
> She with a stick will play :
> A traitress she will be,
> For good or bad, we'll see."

CHAPTER XIV.

THREE years had passed. Stein, who could sojourn among these few men who required so little, believed himself happy. He loved his wife with tenderness, and was attached more every day to his father-in-law; and as to the excellent family, those who had rescued him, a dying man, his affection for them had never wavered. His uniform and rural life was in harmony with the modesty of his tastes, and with the tranquillity of his honest soul. And, besides, the monotony wanted not for attractions: an existence always uniformly calm resembles the man who peacefully sleeps without dreaming, or those melodies composed of a few words, but which charm us with so much sweetness. Perhaps there is nothing which leaves more agreeable souvenirs than this monotony of existence—this successive enchainment of days which have nothing to distinguish one from that which precedes, or from that which follows it.

What must have been the surprise to the inhabitants of the cabin when, one morning, Momo rushed in out of breath, calling to Stein to go to the convent without losing a single instant.

"Has any one of the family fallen ill?" asked Stein alarmed.

"No," answered Momo, "it is a lord, whom they address as 'your excellency,' who has been hunting the wild boar and roebuck in the hillock with his friends; in leaping the ravine the horse missed, and both fell. The horse is slashed, the cavalier has broken as many bones

as he has in his body, and they have conveyed him to
the convent on a litter. The monastery was transformed
into a real Babylon. They believed it was the day of
judgment. People went and came like a crowd among
which a wolf had forced his way. The only one who
retained his tranquillity was he who had caused the
excitement, and who at a glance it was seen was a man
of the grand world, a real young man. There they were
all in confusion, without knowing what to do. My
grandma had told them that there was here a surgeon
like whom there were few seen: they would not believe
her; but as to obtain one from Cadiz would occupy two
days, and three more to obtain one from Seville, his
excellency said he would have the one recommended by
my grandma. It is for this I am come here. Now I
will give you my opinion. If I were in your place, at
present, when they have despised you, I would not go
to the convent if they dragged me there with two
horses."

"I am not capable," replied Stein, "of forgetting my
duties as a Christian, nor those of a surgeon. I should
have a heart of bronze to see one of my kind suffer
without alleviating his sufferings when I have the power
to do it. Beyond this, they cannot have confidence in
me, as I am unknown to them; it is not therefore an
offence, it would not even be one if they knew me."

Stein and Momo arrived promptly at the convent.
Maria, who awaited the doctor with impatience, conducted him to the wounded man, who had been placed
in the cell of the prior, where they had made up for him
the best bed possible. Maria and Stein passed through
the crowd of sportsmen and servants, by whom the
invalid was surrounded. He was a tall young man; on
his pale but tranquil face fell a profusion of black hair.

So soon as Stein looked at him he uttered a cry, and
rushed towards him; but, fearing to touch him, he suddenly stopped, and crossing his trembling hands he cried
out—-

"My God! the duke!"

"You know me?" demanded the stranger, for the
person Stein had recognized was the Duke d'Almanza.
"You know me?" repeated the duke, raising his head,
and casting his large black eyes on Stein, without power
to recall to his mind who it was that had addressed him.

"He does not recollect me," murmured Stein, while
the large tears trembled in his eyes; "that is not
strange: generous souls forget the good they confer,
preserving eternally the favors they receive."

"Wretched beginning," said one of the assistants;
"a surgeon who weeps!"

"What sad chance!" added another.

"Doctor," said the duke to Stein, "I place myself in
your hands, I confide myself to God, to you, and to my
lucky star. I am ready, do not lose time."

At these words Stein raised his head; his countenance
remained calm, and by a silent gesture, but imperative
and firm, he banished the spectators to a distance. Then
he felt the duke with an accustomed and experienced
hand. He displayed so much assurance and dexterity
that every one kept silent. No sound was heard in the
cell but the agitated breathing of the patient.

"Duke," said Stein, after having completed his examination of the sprained ankle and the broken leg, "without doubt it is here the weight of the horse has fallen.
Still, I believe I shall succeed in effecting a complete
cure."

"Will I become a cripple for life?" asked the duke.

"In my opinion, I can assure you, no."

"Prove it so, and I will say that you are the best surgeon in the world."

Stein, without stirring, sent for Manuel, whose strength and punctuality he knew. With his assistance he commenced operations which were more painful than can be imagined; but Stein seemed to take no notice of the pain the invalid felt, and whom he made almost to lose consciousness.

In about half an hour the duke reposed, suffering, but relieved.

In lieu of marks of contempt and fear, Stein received from the duke's friends congratulations and the most lively expressions of esteem and admiration ; the good doctor, restored to his natural modesty and timidity, replied politely to all.

But do you know who "took a bath of roses ?" it was Maria.

"Did I not tell you so ?" she incessantly repeated to all the sportsmen, " did I not tell you so ?"

The duke's friends, entirely tranquillized, went to attend the prayers about to be offered up. The invalid had demanded to be left alone, under the care of his excellent doctor, his old friend as he called him, and sent away nearly all his servants.

In this way the duke and his doctor could renew their acquaintance at their ease. The first was one of those men of a character, elevated, and but little material, with whom neither habit the attachment injured his physical well-being ; one of those privileged beings who knew how to come down to the level of circumstances, not by a start or caprice, but constantly, by an energetic nature, and by a firm will, an impenetrable breastplate of iron, which may be symbolized in these words— "What matters it ?" His was one of those hearts which beat under the armor of the fifteenth century, and the traces of which cannot now be met with except in Spain.

Stein related his campaigns, his misadventures, his arrival at the convent, his love, and his marriage.

The duke listened with much interest; and the recital gave him a great desire to know Marisalada, the fisherman, and the cabin which Stein preferred to a palace. Thus, on the occasion of his first going out, he directed his walk, accompanied by his doctor, to the sea-coast. Spring had commenced, and the freshness of the breeze, the pure breath of the immense element, lent its charm to their pilgrimage. The fort of St. Cristobal appeared to be ornamented with a green crown, in honor of the noble personage in regard to whom it is presented for the first time. The flowers which covered the roof of the cabin, real garden of Semiramis, crowded against each other, were agitated by the zephyrs, and resembled timid young girls who have love whispered in their ears. The sea, beautiful and calm, wafted its waves just to the feet of the duke, as if they would bid him welcome. The lark careering through space sent forth his sweet and faint notes, until he was lost to sight. The duke, a little fatigued, seated himself on a piece of rock: he was poetic, and he silently enjoyed the magnificent spectacle. Suddenly was heard a voice, simple and melancholy. The duke, surprised, looked at Stein. The doctor sighed. The voice continued to be heard.

"Stein," said the duke to him, "are these sirens on the waves or angels in the air?"

Stein, as his response, took his flute, and repeated the same melancholy strain. Then the duke saw approaching, half running, half leaping, a young woman, who stopped suddenly on perceiving him.

"This is my wife," said Stein, "my Mariquita."

"Who possesses," said the duke with enthusiasm, "the most wonderful voice in the world. Señora, I have visited all the theatres of Europe, but never have enchanting accents excited me to this point of admiration."

If the brown and lustrous skin of Marisalada could change to another color, the blush of pride and pleasure would have shown in her cheeks, when she heard these exalted praises from the lips of so eminent a person, and so competent a judge.

"You two," continued the duke, "have all that you could require to make your way in the world; and you would remain hidden in obscurity, and forgotten! This must not be. Will you not let society share in your brilliant qualities? I repeat, this cannot be, this must not be."

"We are so happy here, duke," replied Stein, "that if I make the least change in my situation I would believe myself an ingrate towards my destiny."

"Stein," exclaimed the duke, "where is that firm and calm courage which I admired in you when we were on the voyage together on board the 'Royal Sovereign?' What have you done with your love of science, the desire to consecrate yourself to suffering humanity? Have you allowed yourself to be enervated by your happiness? Can it be true that felicity renders a man selfish?"

Stein drooped his head.

"Señora," continued the duke, "at your age, and with these happy gifts of nature, can you decide to remain forever attached to this rock, and to these ruins?"

Mariquita, whose heart beat under the influence of an ardent joy and a tempting hope, replied with, however, an apparent coldness—

"What will I gain by it?"

"And your father," her husband asked of her; "do you believe he will give his consent?"

"He is a fisherman," replied the Gaviota, feigning not to understand the true sense of the question.

The duke then entered into a long explanation of all the advantages which might arise for her distinction and a fortune.

Mariquita listened with avidity, while the duke contemplated with rapture the play of this countenance, alternately cold and full of enthusiasm, alternately impassible and energetic.

When the duke retired, Mariquita pinched the ear of Stein, and said to him eagerly—

"We will go! we will go! and whatever happens, I feel called to go. Crowns are promised me, and will I remain deaf to all that? No! no!"

Stein sorrowfully followed the duke.

6*

CHAPTER XV.

WHEN they entered the convent, old Maria demanded of the noble convalescent, who always received his nurse with much kindness, how he had found her dear Marisalada.

"Is she not a beautiful creature?" she said.

"Certainly," replied the duke. "Her eyes, as a poet says, are such as an eagle only can look at."

"And her grace?" pursued the old woman; "and her voice?"

"Her voice! it is too beautiful to be lost in this solitude. You have nightingales enough, and goldfinches. Husband and wife must go with me."

The thunder had fallen at the feet of Maria; and all the other words he spoke were as nothing.

"And do they wish it?" she cried in affright.

"They must wish it," replied the duke, leaving the room.

Maria remained some moments confused and in a state of consternation. Then she went to find brother Gabriel.

"They are going," she said to him, her eyes filled with tears, "they are going!"

"Thank God!" replied the brother. "They have enough deteriorated the marble pavement of the Prior's cell. What will his reverence say when he comes back?"

"You have not understood me. Those who are going are Don Frederico and his wife."

"They are going away! It's impossible," said the brother.

"Is it true?" asked Maria of Stein, who came in.

"She wishes it," he replied dejectedly.

"That is what her father has always said," continued Maria; "and with this response he would have let her die, if it had not been for us. Ah! Don Frederico, you are so well here! You would be like that Spaniard who being well would be better."

"I hope for nothing better; I believe in nothing better in the world, my good Maria."

"One day you will repent it. And poor Pedro! My God! why has this earthquake fallen on us?"

Don Modesto entered. For some time his visits had been very rare, not but the duke would have received him most amiably, nor but that his lordship would have exercised on him the same irresistible attraction which was felt by all who approached him, but Modesto was the slave of ceremony, and he imposed upon himself the rule not to present himself before the duke, general, and ex-minister of war, but in grand and rigorous ceremony.

Rosa Mistica had told him that his grand uniform could not stand active service, and this was the cause of the suspension of his visits. When Maria learned that the duke contemplated to depart in two days, Don Modesto retired immediately. He had formed a project, and he required time to realize it.

When Marisalada announced to her father the resolution she had taken to follow the advice of the duke, the grief which attacked the poor old Pedro would have softened a heart of stone.

He listened silently to the magnificent plans of his child, without either condemning or approving them;

to her promises to revisit him in his cabin, he neither
made request nor refusal. He regarded his child as a
bird regards her offspring, when they try to quit the
nest which they may never again enter. In one word,
this excellent father wept in secret.

Next day the servants, horses, and mules which the
duke had ordered for his departure arrived.

The cries, the good wishes, and the preparations for
travel resounded throughout the convent.

Morrongo climbed upon the top of the roof and slept
in the sun, and cast a look of contempt upon the tumult
raised below him.

Palomo barked, growled, and protested so energetically against the strange invasion, that Manuel ordered
Momo to fasten him up.

"There is no doubt," said Momo, "but my grandma,
who is a *charlatan* the most skilful to be found under
the canopy of heaven, has no lover now to attract in-
valids to this house."

The day of departure arrived. The duke was ready
in his room. Stein and the Gaviota had arrived, followed by the poor fisherman, whose looks were on the
ground, and his body bent double under the weight of
his grief. This grief had made him old more than his
years, more than ocean's tempests; he let himself fall on
the steps of the marble cross.

As to Modesto, he was there also; consternation was
painted in his face. The infinitely small lock of hair on
his head fell flabby and soft on one side; profound sighs
escaped him.

"What ails you, my commandant?" asked Maria of
him.

"Good Maria," he replied, "to-day is the 15th of
June, the day of my holy patron, a day sad and memo

rable in the past of my life. O San Modesto! is it possible that you treat me thus, even on the day which the church celebrates?"

"But what new thing has happened?" asked Maria, with impatience.

"See!" said the veteran, raising his arms and displaying a large rent, across which was seen the white lining of his uniform, like a row of teeth behind a laughing mocker.

Don Modesto was identified with his uniform; in losing it, there would have vanished the last hope of his profession.

"What a misfortune!" Maria sadly sighed.

"Rosita is laid up with a cold," continued Don Modesto.

A servant entered.

"His excellency prays the commandant to have the goodness to go to him."

Don Modesto rose proudly, took in his hand a letter carefully folded and sealed, pressed as near as possible the arm nearest his unfortunate rent, and presented himself to the duke, and saluted him respectfully in the strict military position.

"I wish your excellency," he said, "a pleasant journey; and I hope that you will find the duchess and all your family in good health. I take, also, the liberty to pray your excellency to deliver into the hands of the minister of war this report, relative to the fort which I have the honor to command. Your excellency can be convinced by personal observation, of the urgency for repairs to re-establish the fort San Cristobal, now above all, when there is the question of a war with the Emperor of Morocco."

"My dear Don Modesto," the duke replied to him, "I

cannot risk the promise of success to your report, but I advise you to plant a cross upon the battlement of your fort, as upon a sepulchre. In any case, I promise to recommend you, so that you will be paid the arrears for your services."

This agreeable promise was not sufficiently powerful to efface the sad impression made on his heart by the sentence of death which the duke had pronounced against the citadel.

"Meantime," said the duke, "I pray you to accept this as the *souvenir* of a friend."

And, so saying, he pointed with his finger to a chair which was near to him. What was the surprise of this brave man when he saw exposed on that chair a complete uniform, new and bright, with two epaulets worthy to adorn the greatest captain of the age! Don Modesto, it was very natural, remained confused, astonished, dazzled at the sight of so much splendor and magnificence.

"I hope, commandant," said the duke, "that you will live to such an age that this uniform may last you at least as long as its predecessor."

"Ah! excellent señor," replied Don Modesto, recovering by degrees the use of speech, "it is far too much for me."

"Not at all," replied the duke; "how many people are there who wear more splendid uniforms than this, who do not merit it as you do! I know, also, that you have a friend, an excellent hostess, to whom you would not be sorry to convey a *souvenir*. Do me the pleasure to convey this *bijou* to her."

It was a chaplet of filigree, in gold and coral.

Then, without giving Don Modesto time to recover from his astonishment, the duke joined the family, which he had called together, to express to them his gratitude, and to leave them some gifts.

This noble lord did not confer his gifts with that disdainful generosity, and therefore wounding, which is so often met with among the rich; he conferred them knowing how to address those on whom fortune had not lavished her favors; he studied the needs and the tastes of each one. Thus all the inhabitants of the convent received what was the most necessary and the most agreeable to them. Manuel had a clock and a good watch; Momo a complete suit of clothes, a belt of yellow silk, and a fowling-piece; the women and children stuffs for their toilet and playthings; Anis, a kite of such vast dimensions that she disappeared behind this plaything as a rat would disappear behind the shield of Achilles. To the grandma Maria, the indefatigable nurse, the skilful maker of substantial soups, the duke gave a regular pension. As to poor brother Gabriel, he had nothing. He made so little noise in the world, and was so much hidden from the eyes of the duke, that he had never been seen of him. The grandma cut, at the suggestion of everybody, some ells from a piece of cloth the duke had given her; she added two cotton handkerchiefs, and went to find her *protégé*.

"Here, brother Gabriel," she said to him, "here is a little present the duke makes you; I will take care to make the shirt."

The poor brother remained as confused as the commandant. Gabriel was more than modest, he was humble.

All being ready to depart, the duke entered the court.

"Adieu, Momo," said Marisalada. "Honor to Villamar! If I have ever seen you, I have forgotten you."

"Adieu, Gaviota," replied Momo, "if everybody

weeps your departure as my mother's son weeps, they will ring the bells to the whole bevy."

Old Pedro remained seated on the steps of the cross. Maria was near him, and wept burning tears.

"Do not believe," said the Gaviota, "that I depart for China, and that we will never come back again, when I tell you that I will come back! See—one would think you were assisting at the death of Bohemians! Have you taken a vow to spoil my pleasure in going to the city?"

"Mother," said Manuel, much affected in witnessing the grief of the good Maria, "if you weep so much now, what will you do when I die?"

"I will not weep, son of my heart," replied the mother, smiling in spite of her grief; "I shall not live to weep for thy death."

The horses arrived. Stein cast himself into Maria's arms.

"Do not forget us, Don Frederico," said the old woman, sobbing: "return!"

"If I return not," replied Stein, "it will be because I am dead."

The duke, to distract Marisalada, in this painful separation, wished her at once to mount the mule which, by his orders, was destined for her use. The animal set off on a trot, the others followed, and all the *cortège* soon disappeared behind the angle of the convent. The poor father stretched out his arms towards his daughter.

"I shall never see her more!" he cried, suffocated by his grief; and he let fall his head on the steps of the cross.

The travellers continued their route, falling into a trot. Stein, arrived at Calvary, soothed his heart in addressing a fervent prayer to the Lord of Good-help, whose kind influence spread over all this country like the light around the sun.

Rosa Mistica was at her window when the travellers passed through the village.

"God pardon me!" she exclaimed, on seeing Marisalada on her mule at the duke's side, "she does not even look at me! She does not even salute me! The demon of pride has already whispered in her heart. I bet," she said, advancing nearer the window, "that she will not either salute the cura, who is below under the porch of the church; but the duke has set her the example. Hollo! he stops to speak to the pastor. He hands him a purse for the poor. He is so good, so generous a man! he does well, and God will recompense him!"

Rosa Mistica knew not yet the double surprise which was to happen to her. When Stein passed, he sadly saluted her with his hand.

"God accompany thee," said Rosita, waving her handkerchief. "He is the best of men! Yesterday on quitting me he wept like a child. What a misfortune that he remains not in the village! He would not have left if he had not espoused this fool of a Gaviota, as Momo so well calls her."

The little troop had arrived at the summit of a hill, and commenced to descend it. The houses of Villamar soon disappeared to Stein's view, who could not tear himself away from this spot where he had lived so happily and so tranquilly.

The duke, all this time, imposed on himself the useless task of consoling Marisalada, and painting to her, in colors the most flattering, the brilliant projects of the future. Stein had no eyes but to contemplate the country which he was abandoning.

The cross of calvary and the chapel of our Lord of
Good-help were lost in the distance; then the grand
mass of convent walls was effaced little by little. At
last, in all this corner of the world, so calm and so peaceful, there was soon nothing seen but the ruins of the
fort, its sombre form reflected upon the horizon of the
azure firmament, and the tower which, according to the
expression of a poet, like a gigantic finger pointed cease-
lessly to Heaven with an irresistible eloquence.

Then all vanished.   Stein burst into tears, covering his
face with his hands.

CHAPTER XVI.

July was an extremely hot month in Seville. People assembled in the delicious courts, or near the magnificent marble fountains, and the *jets-d'eau* fell behind the innumerable tufts of flowers. From the circular ceilings of the galleries were suspended large lamps incased in globes of crystal, and throwing out on every side torrents of light. The air was embalmed with the perfume of flowers. The richest furniture set off the sumptuousness of these *fêtes* every evening, which imparted a peculiar grace to the beauty of the Sevilleans, whose animated and joyous conversation rivalled the sweet murmurs of the fountains.

One evening, towards the end of July, there was a grand reunion at the residence of the young, elegant, and beautiful Countess d'Algar. It was esteemed a great favor to be introduced into this house; the mistress was so amiable, and possessed of such graceful manners, that she received all her guests with the same smile and the same cordiality.

In her eagerness, she had gathered around her all those who had been presented to her, without consulting the will of her uncle, General Santa-Maria, warlike *par excellence*, and, according to the spirit of warriors in those times, a little exclusive, absolute, and disdainful; in fine, a classic son of the god Mars, fully convinced that all relations among men consist in those who command and those who obey, and that the principal object, the sole utility of society, is to class each of its members; above all, Spanish like Pelayo, and brave like Cid.

The general, with his sister, the Marchioness de Guadalcanal, mother of the countess, and some other persons, were playing a species of game of cards called *tresillo*. Several guests were walking under the galleries discussing politics. The young people of both sexes, seated near the tufts of flowers of a thousand colors, chatted and laughed as if the earth produced only flowers, as if echo should send back only their own joys.

The countess, half reclined on a sofa, complained of a headache, which, however, did not prevent her from laughing. Her figure was small, and delicately formed. Her thick blonde hair waved in long ringlets, as worn by the English, on her alabaster shoulders. Her large brown eyes, her teeth white as ivory, her mouth, and the oval of her face were models of perfection. As to her grace, nothing could surpass it. Passionately cherished by her mother, idolized by her husband, who, without loving the world, left his wife unlimited liberty, because he knew her to be virtuous, and had full confidence in her, the countess was truly an accomplished woman, abusing none of her privileges, such was the nobleness of her character. It is true she possessed in no degree grand intellectual faculties, but she had the talent of *heart;* her sentiments were just and delicate. All her ambition was reduced to the desire to amuse and please, without effort, like the bird which flies without knowing it, and sings because she sings. This evening she mingled in the promenade, fatigued, and a little indisposed. She had replaced her rich toilet by a robe of white muslin of great simplicity. The long hanging sleeves garnished with lace, exposed her white and rounded arms. A bracelet and some jewels were the only ornaments which she had retained of her first attire. Near her was seated a young colonel recently arrived from Madrid, after having been distinguished in the war of Navarre. The countess, with her accustomed frankness, fixed on him all her attentions.

General Santa-Maria regarded them from time to time, and bit his lips impatiently.

"New fruit!" said he. "She would not be a daughter of Eve if the novelty had not pleased her. A white-beak! Twenty-four years of age, and already colonel! Has one ever seen such prodigality of rank? Here, for five or six years one goes yet to school; and here one already commands a regiment! They will tell us no doubt that he owes his grade to his brilliant actions; for my part, I say that valor does not give experience, and without experience no one knows how to command. Colonel at twenty-four years of age! I was one at forty, after having been at Roussillon, in America, and in Portugal, and I gained the scarf of a general only on my return from the North, after having fought during the war of independence. By my faith, gentlemen, in Spain we are all becoming crazy, some by what they do, and others by what they leave undone."

At this moment loud exclamations were heard. The countess herself shook off her languor, and suddenly rose up. "At last," she cried, "we again see him whom we had lost! A thousand times welcome, unfortunate sportsman, ill-treated señor! You have caused a frightful alarm! But what is it then? You stand there as if nothing had happened! Is it true, what has been told us of a wonderful German doctor starting out from the ruins of a fort, and those of a convent, in the manner of fantastic creations? Relate to me then, duke, all these extraordinary things."

The duke, after having received the congratulations which each one offered him on his happy return and cure, placed himself near the countess, and commenced the recital of events which the reader already knows.

Then, after having spoken much of Stein and Mari-salada, he finished by saying, he had persuaded them to come and establish themselves at Seville, to become known and useful, he by his knowledge, and she by the extraordinary faculties with which nature had endowed her.

"It was badly done," earnestly interrupted General Santa-Maria.

"Why so, my uncle?" asked the countess.

"Because these people were living contented, without ambition; and which once broken up will never more be the same. Do you recollect the Spanish comedy, the title of which has passed into a proverb: '*Ninguno debe dejar lo cierto por lo dudoso.*'" (Never quit a certainty for an uncertainty.)

"Do you believe, my uncle, that this woman, gifted with a voice so remarkable, can regret the oyster bank where she vegetated without glory, without profit to herself, or to society, or to the arts?"

"Come, my niece, would you seriously make us believe that human society would make much progress because a woman exhibits herself on the boards, and sings *Di tanti palpiti?*"

"Go along," said the countess, "we see very well that you are not musical."

"And I greatly thank the Lord that I am not so," replied the general. "Would you that, like so many others, I lose my judgment by this melomaniac furor, by this deluge of notes which is showered on Europe like an avalanche, according to the expression now-a-days. Would you that I go, thanks to my stupid enthusiasm, and swell the excessive pride of those kings and queens of harmony? Would you that my money serve to increase their colossal receipts, while so many good officers covered with wounds die of hunger; while so many virtuous, and meritorious women pass their lives in tears, without having bread to eat? These things cry for vengeance! Here is a veritable *sarcasm* (as they say now-a-days), and that passes unheeded, while the mouths of our hypocrites are continually uttering the word *humanity*. Shall I go, and throw bouquets at the feet of a *prima donna* whose whole recommendable qualities are reduced to 'do, ré, mi, fa, sol?'"

"My uncle is the most perfect personification of the *statu quo*. Every thing new annoys him. I will try to grow old soon, to please him."

"You will take good care of yourself, my niece; but do not require of me that I grow young to please the new generation."

"What is my brother discussing?" demanded the marchioness, who, until then occupied with her game, had taken no part in the conversation.

"My uncle," said a young officer, who had entered without saying a word, and was seated near the duke, "my uncle is preaching a crusade against music. He has declared war against the *andante*, proscribed the *moderato*, and gives no quarter to *allegro*."

The new speaker was of small form, but elegant, well proportioned, of a distinguished *tournure*, and a handsome face, too handsome, perhaps, for a man.

"Dear Raphael!" cried the duke, embracing the officer, who was his relation and his friend.

"And I," added the young officer, affectionately pressing the hand of the duke, "I who would have broken my arms and legs to spare you the painful hours you have passed! But we were speaking of the opera, and I would not be impious towards the melodrama." ·

"Well thought of," said the duke; "you had better relate to me what has passed in my absence. What do they say?"

"That my cousin, the Countess d'Algar," said Raphael, "is the pearl of women."

"I asked you what was new," replied the duke, "and not what everybody knows."

"My lord duke," continued Raphael, "Solomon has said, and many other wise men—I am of the number—that there is nothing new under the azure vault of heaven."

"God grant it!" sighed the general, "but my dear nephew Raphael Arias is a living contradiction of his axiom. Every day he brings new faces to our reunions, and it is insupportable."

"There, already, is my uncle," said Raphael, "who ever tilts against strangers. A stranger is the *blue-devil* of General Santa-Maria. My lord duke, if you had not appointed me your aid-de-camp when you were minister of war, I could not have found so many acquaintances at Madrid among foreign diplomatists, and these gentlemen would not have pressed me so with their letters of introduction. Do you believe, uncle, that it is very amusing to me to act as cicerone to every traveller? It has been my only occupation since my arrival at Seville."

"And who obliges you," replied the general, "to open our doors—open them wide—to all new-comers, and put ourselves at their orders? That is not done in Paris, and much less so is it the custom in London."

"My uncle," said the countess, "all people have their peculiar characteristics; each society its usages. Strangers are more reserved than we, and they have the same reserve among themselves: be just."

"Has any one recently arrived?" demanded the duke. "I ask you this, because I expect Lord G., one of the most distinguished men I know. Is he in Seville?"

"I think not," replied Raphael. "At present we have here, first, Major Fly, whom we call *Mosca*—it is the translation of his name. He serves in the Queen's Guards, and is nephew of the Duke of W., one of the grand personages of England."

"Yes, nephew of the Duke of W.," said the general, "as I am of the Grand Turk."

"He is young," pursued Raphael, "elegant, and a good fellow, but of colossal stature: he should be placed at a certain distance from you to have his whole form appreciated; close, he appears so large, so robust, so angular, so stiff, that he loses a hundred per cent. When he is not at table, he is always at my side, whether I am at home, or whether I am out. When my servant told him I was out, he replied that he would wait for me; and when he came in at the door, I escaped by the window. He has the habit of using his cane as a weapon: his thrusts, however, are very innocent, and wound only the air. As he has very long and vigorous arms, and as my room is small, he damages all the walls; and he has already broken, I do not know how many squares of glass. Seated on a chair, he so moves about, so tosses, and stretches himself out in such a fashion, that he has already broken four of them.

"The sight of this man is sufficient to throw my hostess into a rage. Sometimes he takes a book; and it is the best thing he could do, for it puts him to sleep. But conquest is his mania—his fixed idea—his war-horse. In it lies all his hopes, which, however, are yet in em-

7

bryo. He has for the fair sex the same illusion that the
Castilian peasant who goes to Mexico has for the hard
dollars : the poor man arrives in Mexico, believing that
he has only to present himself to grasp them. I have
tried to undeceive the major, but I have preached in the
desert. When I speak reasonably to him, he smiles with
an air of incredulity, caressing his enormous mustache.
He is in correspondence with a millionaire heiress ; and
that which is very curious, is, that this Ajax of thirty
years, who devours four pounds of beef-steak and
drinks three bottles of sherry at a single repast, makes
his betrothed believe that he is travelling for his health !
The other knave, as my uncle would call him, is a
Frenchman, the Baron de Maude."

"Baron," replied the general maliciously, "yes, a
baron as I am a pope."

"But in truth, my uncle," replied the countess,
"what reason is there that he should not be a baron ?"

"The reason is, my niece, that real barons—not the
barons of Napoleon, nor the Constitutional barons, but
the barons of good stock, neither travel nor write books
for money ; and they are not either so badly educated,
or so curious, or such fastidious questioners."

"But, uncle, he can be both a baron and a questioner.
They lose not their nobility because they question. On
his return to his country he is to be married to the
daughter of a peer of France."

"Certainly he will marry her," replied the general,
"as I will marry the Grand Turk."

"My uncle," said Arias, "is like St. Thomas ; he must
see to believe. Let us come back to our baron : we
must admit he is a very handsome man, and of noble
deportment, although he has, like me, ceased to grow.
His character is one of the most amiable ; he has it as a

man of learning and as a writer; he converses with the
same ease on music, statistics, philosophy, agriculture,
and the fashions. He is occupied at this moment in
writing a *serious* book, which may serve as a ladder by
which to mount to the Chamber of Deputies. This book
is to be entitled: 'Travels, scientific, philosophical, artistic, and geological, in Spain, formerly Iberia; with
critical observations on the government, the cooks, the
literature, the routes, the agriculture, the dances, and the
system of imposts of that country.' With an affected
negligence in his toilet, he is grave, circumspect, economical in the extreme; it is an imperfect fruit of that warm
greenhouse of public men, who give precocious products
without spring, without vivifying breezes, and without
free air—products without savor or perfume. These men
precipitate themselves into the future blindly, at the discovery of what they call a position; and it is for that
they sacrifice all: sad, tormented existences, for which
life has no aurora."

"Raphael, you talk like a philosopher," said the duke,
smiling; "do you know that if Socrates existed in our
time, you would more likely be his disciple than my
aid-de-camp?"

"I would not change my place of aid-de-camp for an
apostleship, my general," replied Arias. "But the truth
is, that were there not so many ignorant disciples, there
would not be so many bad masters."

"Well said, my good nephew," cried the old general.
"What of new masters! each one of them teaches his
dogma, preaches his doctrine more and more new and
advanced: the progress! the magnificent and inevitable
progress!"

"General," replied the duke, "to maintain the equilibrium of our globe, it is necessary that there be fluid,

that there be solid materials; these two forces ought to regard each other reciprocally as necessary, in lieu of wishing to destroy them with so much fury."

" What you advance," replied the general, "savors of the doctrines of the odious half-way, which, more than all others, have ruined us with these shameful opinions, and these discourses, as low as insipid, as the people say, who often have more good sense than the *learned* sectarians of moderatism, grand hypocrites of beautiful outward show and bad heart, adorers of the Supreme Being, who do not believe in Jesus Christ."

" My uncle," hinted Raphael, " so hates the moderate, that he loses all moderation in combating them."

" Hold your tongue, Raphael," replied the countess; "you attack and rail at all opinions, and you have none yourself, without doubt, so as to avoid the trouble of defending them."

" My cousin," said Raphael, " I am liberal; my empty purse says so."

" What have you to be liberal with ?" exclaimed the general, in a commanding voice.

" And why should I not be ? The duke is so."

" You would be liberal !" said anew the old soldier in a terrible tone, sounding like the roll of a drum.

" Well !" murmured Raphael, " one easily sees that my uncle will only accord the title liberal to the arts which bear that denomination. General," he added, excited with refined joy, " why cannot the duke and I be liberal ?"

" Because the military," replied the general, " have no right to be any thing but the supporters of the throne, the sustainers of order, and the defenders of their country. Do you understand, my nephew ?"

" But, my uncle—"

"Raphael," interrupted the countess, "do not take so much trouble: continue your recital."

"I obey. Ah! cousin, in the army which you command, I have never committed the fault of insubordination. We have still another stranger in Seville, a Sir John Burnwood. He is a young man of fifty years, somewhat fair, smiling, with hair worthy of the veriest lion of Atlas; an eye-glass unremovable—smile ditto; great talker, hullaballoo, turbulent, full of vivacity, like that German who, for a whim, threw himself out of a window; great lover of jollity, celebrated sportsman, and proprietor of vast coal-mines, which produce him an income of twenty thousand pounds sterling."

"Twenty thousand pounds of coals, perhaps," said the general.

"My uncle," replied Raphael, "resembles the frequenters of the exchange, who cause the funds to rise or fall, according to their caprice. Sir John has bet that he will appear on horseback at the Giralda, and it is the grand motive that has brought him to Seville. He is in despair, because they have not permitted him to take part in this royal pastime. Now he wishes, in imitation of Lord Elgin and Baron Taylor, to purchase Alcazar, and to carry him to his lordly residence."

"My general," said the duke, "do you not see that Raphael changes the colors of his tableaux, and that he relates to us only extravagances?"

"There are no extravagances," replied the general, "that are not possible to the English."

"You do not yet know the best!" continued Raphael, fixing his looks on a young and handsome person seated beside the marchioness, and noticing her play. "Sir John is in love with my Cousin Rita, and has asked her hand. Rita, who does not at all know how to pronounce the monosyllable *yes*, replied to him by a dry, hard *no*."

"Is it possible, Rita," said the duke, "you have refused twenty thousand pounds a year?"

"I have not refused the money," replied the young girl; "I have refused the money's master."

"You have done well," replied the general, "everybody should marry in his own country, it is the way to avoid exposing ourselves to taking a cat for a hare."

"It was well done," added the marchioness. "A protestant! God preserve us!"

"And what do you say, countess?" asked the duke.

"I am of my mother's opinion," she replied.

"And besides," said Rita, "he is in love with the dancer, Lucea del Salto; and thus, when even if he had been to my taste, I ought to have made him the same answer. I do not like to share, and, above all, with these *señoritas* of the green-room."

CHAPTER XVII.

Rita was niece to the marchioness and the general. An orphan since her birth, she had been brought up by her brother, who loved her with tenderness; and by her nurse, who adored and spoilt her,—without which she might have made a good and pious young girl. The isolation and independence in which she had passed the first years of her life, had impressed on her character the double seal of timidity and decision. Slightly brilliant, because she detested noise and *éclat*, she was proud and at the same time good; simple and capricious, a mocker and reserved.

To this piquant character was added an exterior the most beautiful and attractive. She was neither too large nor too small; her form, which had never been submitted to the precision of the corset, had all the suppleness and flexibility which French romances falsely give to their heroines, fastened in by narrow strips of whalebone. It is to this graceful suppleness of body and of movement, united to that frankness of manner, so natural and enchanting when elegance and good nature accompany it, that the Spaniards owe their charming attractions, which we may call their distinctive characteristic. Rita had the tint of unpolished white; it was of the purity and regularity of a marble statue. Her admirable head of black hair, and those large eyes of dark brown, surmounted by eyebrows which seemed painted by th hand of Murillo, were most attractive. Her mouth, of extraordinary freshness, and almost always serious, opened

from time to time to let escape, between her white teeth,
a joyous burst of laughter, which her habitual reserve
made her as soon take back; for nothing was to her more
painful than to attract attention, and when by chance
that happened she could not conceal her displeasure.
She had made a vow to the Virgin of grief to wear a
habit : it was for this she was always clothed in black, with
a belt of polished leather; and a little golden heart,
pierced with a sword, ornamented the upper part of her
sleeve.

Rita was the only woman whom her Cousin Raphael
seriously loved ; not with a passion elegiac and weeping,
which no way belonged to his character, the least sentimental the east wind ever blew upon, but of a true
affection, earnest, sincere, and constant. Raphael, an
excellent youth, loyal, judicious, as noble in manner as in
birth, and possessed of a handsome patrimony, pleased
in every way the family of Rita ; notwithstanding, the
young girl, spite of her brother's surveillance, had sur-
rendered her heart to another without his knowing it.

The object of her preference was a young man of an
illustrious origin, a handsome boy, but a gambler ; and
that was sufficient for Rita's brother to oppose her
love, and he had forbidden her to see or speak to him.
Rita, with her firmness of character and Spanish perseverance—which she could have better employed—quietly
waited, without complaint, without sighs or tears, the at-
tainment of twenty-one years of age, when she would have
the right to marry whom she pleased, without scandal,
and in spite of her brother's opposition. During this
time, her lover walked the streets, exhibiting to everybody
his national costume of *majo* (gallant), and riding superb
horses. It is useless to explain here that the two lovers
had established between them a daily correspondence.

This evening, as usual, Rita had arrived at the reunion without making any noise, and was seated in her accustomed place, near to her aunt, to witness the card-playing.

Raphael glided behind his cousin, and whispered in her ear:

"Rita, when can I demand the dispensation?"

"When I give you notice to do so," she replied, without turning her head.

"And what can I do to merit the advent of that happy moment?"

"Recommend yourself to my patron saint, who is the advocate of impossible things."

"Cruel! you will one day repent having refused my white hand. You lose the best and most grateful of husbands."

"And you—you will lose the most ungrateful of women."

"Listen, Rita," continued Arias: "our uncle, who is opposite to us, how is it that he prevents you turning your head towards those to whom you speak?"

"I have a stiff neck."

"This stiff neck is called *Luis de Haro*. Are you always occupied with him?"

"More than ever."

"And you will let me die?"

"Under my frowns."

"I will make a vow to the devil to gild his horns, if one day he will carry off Luis de Haro."

"Wish him evil! the wishes of the envious fatten."

Raphael rose up furiously.

"I know what is the matter with you, Raphael," said a young girl, before whom he passed, to him in a languishing tone.

This new speaker had arrived from Madrid.

The journey had completely *modernized* her. Reading French novels was her incessant occupation. She professed for the world a kind of worship; she adored music, and looked with contempt on all that was Spanish.

"What, then, is the matter with me?"

"A *deception*," murmured Eloise.

"A deception! I have them by hundreds; but the fact cannot be disputed," said Raphael, "that you are most beautiful with this coiffure, and that your toilet is in perfect taste."

"It pleases you?" cried the elegant Eloise, smirking.

"It is not extraordinary," continued Raphael, "that this Englishman, whom you see here opposite to you, is dying for Spain and for the Spaniards."

"What bad taste!" said Eloise, with a gesture of disdain. "He said there was nothing more beautiful in the world than a Spanish lady' with her mantle, her fan, her little feet, her black eyes, and her walk, so sprightly and so graceful."

"But does this gentleman not know that we consider ourselves as *Parias*."

"Do you seek to convert him? I will present you."

Arias left precipitately, with this thought: Eloise has a tender heart; and more, she has become very romantic. She has every quality to please the major.

The countess, during this time, asked the duke if his *Filomena* of Villamar was handsome.

"She is neither handsome nor ugly," replied the duke. "She has a tint very brown, and her features are not absolutely regular; but she has very beautiful eyes, and the *ensemble* does not differ from what you see everywhere in our country."

" Since her voice is so extraordinary," said the countess, " we must, for the honor of Seville, make her a *prima donna* at once. Can we not hear her?"

" When you like," replied the duke. "I will bring her here one of these evenings with her husband, who is himself an excellent musician, and who has been her teacher."

The hour to retire had arrived.

When the duke approached the countess to take leave, she held up her finger in sign of menace.

" What does that mean?" demanded the duke.

" Nothing," she replied. "It only says: Take care!"

" Take care of what?"

" Do not feign not to understand me. None are so deaf as those who will not hear."

" You puzzle me keenly, countess."

" So much the better."

" Will you, as a favor, explain to me?"

" I will explain myself, since you oblige me to do so. When I said to you, Take care, I meant, Do not enchain yourself."

" Ah! countess," replied the duke with warmth ; " for God's sake, let no unjust and false suspicion tarnish the reputation of this woman before any person knows her. This woman, countess, is an angel!"

" Without any doubt: one is not smitten of love by a devil."

" And yet you have a thousand adorers," replied the duke, smiling.

" I am not a devil," said the countess; " but I have the gift of second-sight."

" To go past the mark is not to attain it."

" I will give you six months, invulnerable Achilles !"

" Cease, for goodness, countess; that which on your lips

is but a light jest, would become a mortal poison in the mouths of those vipers who multiply in society."

"Have no fears; it will not be I who will cast the first stone. I am indulgent as a saint, or as a great sinner, without being either the one or the other."

This conversation did not completely satisfy the duke. Near the door he was stopped by Gen. Santa-Maria.

"Duke, have you ever seen any thing like it?"

"What thing?" replied the duke, almost irritated.

"You demand what thing?"

"Yes, and I desire a reply."

"A colonel of twenty-three years old!"

"Indeed, it is a little precocious." And the duke smiled.

"It is a blow struck at the army."

"Certainly."

"A solemn lie given to common sense."

"Evidently."

"Poor Spain!" sighed the general, pressing the duke's hand, and lifting his eyes to heaven.

CHAPTER XVIII.

THE duke had procured for Stein and his wife a board-
ing-house kept by a poor but honest family. The good
German had found in the drawer of a bureau, which
they had given him the key of when he took possession
of his apartments, a sum of money which would have
sufficed for his wants, however exaggerated. This
money was accompanied by a note thus worded : " Here
is the just tribute due to the service of a surgeon. Sincere gratitude and friendship alone can recompense the
care and the watchfulness of a friend."

Stein was transfixed with confusion.

"Ah! Mariquita," he cried, showing this writing to
his wife, " this man is grand in all he does. He is grand
by his race, grand in heart, grand in his virtues. Like
God he raises to his height the small and the humble.
He calls me his friend, I who am a poor surgeon ; he
speaks to me of gratitude, I who am overwhelmed with
benefits !"

" What is all this gold to him ?" replied the Gaviota ;
" a man who has millions, as the hostess tells me, and
whose farms are large as provinces ! And without you
would he not have remained a cripple all his life ?"

The duke entered at that moment. He cut short the
expressions of gratitude of which Stein was prodigal, and
addressed himself to Marisalada—

" I came," he said, " to ask a favor ; will you refuse
me, Maria ?"

"What could we refuse you?" quickly replied Don Frederico.

"Very well, then," continued the duke. "Maria, I have promised one of my intimate friends, that you will go and sing at her house."

Maria made no reply.

"She will go, without any doubt," said Stein. "Maria has not received from heaven a gift so precious, a voice so admirable, without incurring the obligation to let others of the same tastes participate."

"It is then a thing agreed upon," added the duke. "As you, Stein, are as good a pianist as distinguished flutist, you will have this evening a piano at your disposal, with a collection of the best gems of the modern opera. Thus you can choose those which please you the most, and study them; for Maria must triumph and be covered with glory. On this evening will depend her reputation as a singer."

At these last words a light sparkled in the eyes of the Gaviota.

"Will you sing, Maria?" asked the duke of her.

"And why not?" she replied.

"I know," said the duke, "that you have already seen all that Seville contains remarkable. Stein nourishes his enthusiasm, and he knows Seville at his fingers' ends; but what you have not yet seen is a bull-fight. Here are tickets for that of this evening. I depend on you, my friends—you will be near me: I wish to witness the impression this spectacle will produce."

They conversed together some time longer, and then the duke retired.

When after dinner Stein and his wife arrived at the place assigned for the bull-fight, they found it already filled with people. A brief and sustained animation pre-

ceded the *fête.* This immense rendezvous, where were
gathered together all the population of the city and its
environs; this agitation, like to that of the blood which
in the paroxysms of a violent passion rushes to the heart;
this feverish expectation, this frantic excitement, kept,
however, within the limits of order; these exclamations,
petulant without insolence; this deep anxiety which
gives a quivering to pleasure; all this together formed
a species of moral magnetism: one must succumb to its
force, or hasten to fly from it.

Stein, struck with vertigo, and his heart wrung, would
have chosen flight: his timidity kept him where he was.
He saw in all eyes which were turned on him the glowing of joy and happiness; he dare not appear singular.
Twelve thousand persons were assembled in this place;
the rich were thrown in the shade, and the varied colors
of the costumes of the Andalusian people were reflected
in the rays of the sun.

Soon the arena was cleared.

Then came forward the *picadores,* mounted on their
unfortunate horses, who, with head lowered, and sorrow-
ful eyes, seemed to be—and were in reality—victims
marching to the sacrifice.

Stein, at the appearance of these poor animals, felt
himself change to a painful compassion; a species of dis-
gust which he already experienced. The provinces of
the Peninsula which he had traversed hitherto, were
devastated by the civil war, and he had had no opportunity of seeing these *fêtes* so grand, so national, and so
popular, where were united to the brilliant Moorish
strategy the ferocious intrepidity of the Gothic race.
But he had often heard these spectacles spoken of, and
he knew that the merit of a fight is generally estimated
by the number of horses that are slain. His pity was

excited towards these poor animals which, after having rendered great services to their masters, after having conferred on them triumph, and perhaps saved their lives, had for their recompense, when age and the excess of work had exhausted their strength, an atrocious death which, by a refinement of cruelty, they were obliged themselves to seek. Instinct made them seek this death; some resisted, while others, more resigned or more feeble, went docilely before them to abridge their agony. The sufferings of these unfortunate animals touched the hardest heart; but the *amateurs* had neither eyes, attention, nor interest, except for the bull. They were under a real fascination, which communicated itself to most of the strangers who came to Spain, and principally for this barbarous amusement. Besides, it must be avowed, and we avow it with grief, that compassion for animals is, in Spain, particularly among the men, a sentiment more theoretical than practical. Among the lower classes it does not exist at all.

The three *picadores* saluted the president of the *fête*, preceded by the *banderilleros* and the *chulos*, splendidly dressed, and carrying the *capas* of bright and brilliant colors. The *matadores* and their substitutes commanded all these combatants, and wore the most luxurious costumes.

"Pepe Vera! here is Pepe Vera!" cried all the spectators. "The scholar of Montés! Brave boy! What a jovial fellow! how well he is made! what elegance and vivacity in all his person! how firm his look! what a calm eye!"

"Do you know," said a young man seated near to Stein, "what is the lesson Montés gives to his scholars? he pushes them, their arms crossed, close to the bull, and says to them, 'Do not fear the bull—brave the bull!'"

Pepe Vera descended into the arena. His costume was of cherry-colored satin, with shoulder-knots and silver embroidery in profusion. From the little pockets of his vest stuck out the points of orange-colored scarfs. A waistcoat of rich tissue of silver, and a pretty little cap of velvet completed his coquettish and charming costume of *majo*.

After having saluted the authorities with much ease and grace, he went, like the other combatants, to take his accustomed place. The three *picadores* also went to their posts, at equal distance from each other, near to the barrier. There was then a profound, an imposing silence. One might have said that this crowd, lately so noisy, had suddenly lost the faculty of breathing.

The alcalde gave the signal, the clarions sounded, and, as if the trumpet of the Last Judgment had been heard, all the spectators arose with the most perfect *ensemble;* and suddenly was seen opened the large door of the *toril*, placed opposite to the box occupied by the authorities. A bull, whose hide was red, precipitated himself into the arena, and was assailed by a universal explosion of cheers, of cries, of abuse, and of praise. At this terrible noise the bull, affrighted, stopped short, raised his head, his eyes were inflamed, and seemed to demand if all these provocations were addressed to him; to him, the athletic and powerful, who, until now, had been generous towards man, and who had always shown favor towards him as to a feeble and weak enemy. He surveyed the ground, turning his menacing head on all sides—he still hesitated: the cheers, shrill and penetrating, became more and more shrill and frequent. Then, with a quickness which neither his weight nor his bulk foretold, he sprang towards the *picador*, who planted his lance in his withers. The bull felt a sharp pain, and

soon drew back. It was one of those animals which in
the language of bull-fighting are called *boyantes*, that is
to say, undecided and wavering. It is for that he did
not persist in his first attack, but assailed the second
picador. This one was not so well prepared as the first,
and the thrust of his lance was neither so correct nor so
firm ; he wounded the animal without being able to
arrest his advance. The horns of the bull were buried
in the body of the horse, who fell to the ground. A cry
of fright was raised on all sides, and the *chulos* surrounded this horrible group ; but the ferocious animal had
seized his prey, and would not allow himself to be distracted from his vengeance. In this moment of terror,
the cries of the multitude were united in one immense
clamor, which would have filled the city with fright, if it
had not come from the place of the bull-fight. The
danger became more frightful as it was prolonged.

The bull tenaciously attacked the horse, who was overwhelmed with his weight and with his convulsive movements, while the unfortunate *picador* was crushed
beneath these two enormous masses. Then was seen to
approach, light as a bird with brilliant plumage, tranquil
as a child who goes to gather flowers, calm and smiling
at the same time, a young man, covered with silver
embroidery, and sparkling like a star. He approached
in the rear of the bull ; and this young man of delicate
frame, and of appearance so distinguished, took in both
hands the tail of the terrible animal, and drew it towards
him. The bull, surprised, turned furiously, and precipitated himself on his adversary, who, without a movement
of his shoulder, and stepping backwards, avoided the
first shock by a half-wheel to the right.

The bull attacked him anew ; the young man escaped
a second time by another half wheel to the left, continu-

ing to manage him until he reached the barrier. There he disappeared from the eyes of the astonished animal, and from the anxious gaze of the public, who in the intoxication of their enthusiasm filled the air with their frantic applause : for we are always ardently impressed when we see man play with death, and brave it with so much coolness.

" See now if he has not well followed the lesson of Montés! See if Pepe Vera knows how to act with the bull!" said the young man seated near to them, and who was hoarse from crying out.

The duke at this moment fixed his attention on Marisalada. Since the arrival of this young woman at the capital of Andalusia, it was the first time that he had remarked any emotion on this cold and disdainful countenance. Until now he had never seen her animated. The rude organization of Marisalada was too vulgar to receive the exquisite sentiment of admiration. There was in her character too much indifference and pride to permit her to be taken by surprise. She was astonished at nothing, interested in nothing. To excite her, be it ever so little, to soften some part of this hard metal, it was necessary to employ fire, and to use the hammer.

Stein was pale. " My lord duke," he said, with an air full of sweetness and of conviction, " is it possible that this diverts you ?"

" No," replied the duke, " it does not divert, it interests me."

During this brief dialogue they had raised up the horse. The poor animal could not stand on his legs; his intestines protruded, and bespattered the ground. The *picador* was also raised up; he was removed between the arms of the *chulos*. Furious against the bull, and, led on by a blind temerity, he would at all hazards remount his horse and return to the attack, in spite of the dizziness produced by his fall. It was impossible to dissuade him; they saw him indeed replace the saddle upon the poor victim, into the bruised flanks of which he dug his spurs.

"My lord duke," said Stein, "I may perhaps appear to you ridiculous, but I do not wish to remain at this spectacle. Maria, shall we depart?"

"No," replied Maria, whose soul seemed to be concentrated in her eyes. "Am I a little miss? and are you afraid that, by accident, I may faint?"

"In such case," said Stein, "I will come back and take you when the course is finished."

And he departed.

The bull had disposed of a sufficiently good number of horses. The unfortunate courser which we have mentioned, was taken away, rather drawn than led, by the bridle to the door, by which he made his retreat. The other, which had not the strength again to stand up, lay stretched out in the convulsions of agony; sometimes they stretched out their heads as though impelled by terror. At these last signs of life, the bull returned to the charge, wounding anew with plunges of his horns the bruised members of his victims. Then, his forehead and horns all bloody, he walked around the circus affecting an air of provocation and defiance: at times he proudly raised his head towards the amphitheatre, where the cries did not cease to be heard; sometimes it was towards the brilliant *chulos* who passed before him like meteors, planting their *banderillas* in his body. Often from a cage, or from a netting hidden in the ornaments of a *banderillero*, came out birds, which joyously took up their flight. The first inventor of this strange and singular contrast, could not certainly have had the intention to symbolize innocence without defence rising above the horrors and ferocious passions here below, in its happy flight towards heaven. That would be, without doubt, one of those poetic ideas which are born spontaneously in the hard and cruel heart of the Spanish plebeian, as we see in Andalusia the mignonette plant really flourish between the stones and the mortar of a balcony.

At the signal given by the president of the course, the clarions again sounded. There was a moment of truce in this bloody wrestling, and it created a perfect silence.

Then Pepe Vera, holding in his left hand a sword and a red-hooded cloak, advanced near to the box of the alcalde. Arrived opposite, he stopped and saluted, to demand permission to slay the bull.

Pepe Vera perceived the presence of the duke, whose taste for the bull-fight was well known; he had also remarked the woman who was seated at his side, because this woman, to whom the duke frequently spoke, never took her eyes off the matador.

He directed his steps towards the duke, and taking off his cap, said : "*Brindo* (I offer the honor of the bull) to you, my lord, and to the royal person who is near you."

At these words, casting his cap on the ground with an inimitable *abandon*, he returned to his post.

The *chulos* regarded him attentively, all ready to execute his orders. The matador chose the spot which suited him the best, and indicated it to his *quadrilla*.

" Here!" he cried out to them.

The *chulos* ran towards the bull and excited him, and in pursuing them met Pepe Vera, face to face, who had waited his approach with a firm step. It was the solemn moment of the whole fight. A profound silence succeeded to the noisy tumult, and to the warm excitement which until then had been exhibited towards the matador.

The bull, on seeing this feeble enemy, who had laughed at his fury, stopped as if he wished to reflect. He feared without doubt that he would escape him a second time.

Whoever had entered into the circus at this moment, would sooner believe he was assisting in a solemn religious assembly, than in a public amusement, so great was the silence.

The two adversaries regarded each other reciprocally.

Pepe Vera raised his left hand : the bull sprang on him. Making only a light movement, the matador let him pass by his side, returned and put himself on guard. When the animal turned upon him, the man directed his sword towards the extremity of the shoulder, so that the bull continuing his advance, powerfully aided the steel to penetrate completely into his body.

It was done! He fell lifeless at the feet of his vanquisher.

To describe the general burst of cries and bravos which broke forth from every part of this vast area, would be a thing absolutely impossible. Those who are accustomed to be present at these spectacles, alone can form an idea of it. At the same time were heard the strains of the military bands.

Pepe Vera tranquilly traversed the arena in the midst of these frantic testimonials of passionate admiration, and of this unanimous ovation, saluting with his sword right and left in token of his acknowledgments. This triumph, which might have excited the envy of a Roman emperor, in him did not excite the least surprise—the least pride. He then went to salute the *ayuntamiento;* then the duke, and the "*royal*" young lady.

The duke then secretly handed to Maria a purse full of gold, and she enveloped it in her handkerchief, and cast it into the arena.

Pepe Vera again renewed his thanks, and the glance of his black eyes met those of the Gaviota. In describing the meeting of these looks, a classic writer said, that it wounded these two hearts as profoundly as Pepe Vera wounded the bull.

We who have not the temerity to ally ourselves to this severe and intolerant school, we simply say that these two natures were made to understand each other—to sympathize. They in fact did understand and sympathize.

It is true to say that Pepe had done admirably.

All that he had promised in a situation where he placed himself between life and death, had been executed with an address, an ease, a dexterity, and a grace, which had not been baffled for an instant.

For such a task it is necessary to have an energetic temperament and a daring courage, joined to a certain degree of self-possession, which alone can command twenty-four thousand eyes which observe, and twenty-four thousand hands which applaud.

· CHAPTER XIX.

MARISALADA devoted all her time to perfecting herself in the art which promised her a brilliant future, a career of celebrity, and a position which, in flattering her vanity, would satisfy her love for luxury. Stein ceased not to admire the constancy of her studies, and was enthusiastic in his astonishment at her progress.

The introduction, however, of the Gaviota to the great world, had been retarded by the illness of the countess's son.

From the first symptoms of his malady, the countess was forgetful of every thing around her, her reunions, her engagements, her pleasures, Marisalda and her friends, and above all, the elegant and young colonel of whom we have spoken. For this mother there was no longer any world but her son. She had passed fifteen days at his pillow without sleep, in prayers and tears. The teething of her infant did not progress; the gums were inflamed and painful; his life was in danger.

The duke advised this poor mother to consult Stein, and the skilful doctor arrested the malady by means of incisions which he made in the gums. From that moment Stein became the friend of that family. The countess folded him in her arms, and the count recompensed him as if he were a prince. The marchioness said he was a saint: the general avowed that there could be good physicians out of Spain.

Rita, despite her wildness, deigned to consult him as to her headache; and Raphael declared that some day when least thought of, he would break some of his bones to have the pleasure of being cured by the *Grand Frederic.*

One morning the countess, pale and feeble, was seated at the bedside of her sleeping son. Her mother occupied a low chair, and, as a precaution against the heat, she held in her hand a fan, which she used incessantly. Rita was engaged in embroidering a magnificent altar-cloth, which she was to make in connection with the countess.

Raphael entered. "Good-day, aunt! Good-day, my cousin! How is the heir of Algares?"

"As well as we could desire," replied the countess.

"Then, my dear Gracia," continued the cousin, "it seems to me it is time to quit your retreat. Your absence is an eclipse of the sun, which has thrown the whole city into consternation. The *habituées* of the *fêtes* sigh unanimously. Soon, in sign of mourning, all the trees of our promenade, *las Delicias*, will be despoiled of their foliage. The Baron de Maude has added to his numerous collection of questions, that which regards your invisibility. This excess of maternal love scandalizes him. He says that in France they permit ladies to compose beautiful verses on this subject, but they will not tolerate a young mother who exposes her health, destroys the freshness of her complexion, by depriving herself of repose and food—forgetting, in fine, her individual well-being for love to her child."

"What extravagance!" cried the marchioness. "Can there be in the world a country where the mother leaves for a single instant her sick child?"

"The major is worse still," continued Raphael. "When he learned the sacrifices you were making, countess, he opened his eyes wider than ever, so astonished was he,

8

and declared he had not believed the Spaniards so back-ward as to be deprived of the advantages of a *nursery*."

"What is that?" asked the marchioness.

"Why, he said," pursued Raphael, "that it was the Si-beria of English children. Sir John says he will bet that you have become so thin and so frail that you will easily be taken for the daughter of Zephyr, with greater reason than the Andalusian mares, to whom they affix this origin, and who, spurred on by the prick of lances, will very soon be outrun by his English mare Atalante, when even to dis-tance her you scatter barley in her path. Cousin, the only one who is at all consoled in your absence, is Polo, who weeps for you in publishing a volume of poems. But," continued Raphael, on seeing Stein enter, and playing upon the word, "here. is the most esteemed of precious stones, stone as melodious as Momo. Don Frederico," he said, "you, who are an observer of phy-siognomy, will see that in Spain, under all circumstances of life, the equality of humor, good-nature, and even joy, are unalterable! Here we have not the *schwermuth* of the Germans, the *spleen* of the English, nor the *ennui* of our neighbors. And do you know why? It is because we do not demand too much of life, because we do not aspire to a refined felicity."

"It is," affirmed the countness, "because we are accustomed to have no other tastes than those of our age."

"And that our beautiful sky reflects the well-being of our souls," added the countess.

"I believe," said Stein, "that these are all the causes, joined to the national spirit, which makes poor Spain content with a morsel of bread, an orange, and a ray of the sun."

"You say, Don Frederico," replied the marchioness,

"that in Spain every one is satisfied with his condition. Ah! dear doctor, how much I have to regret in observing that politics—"

"Aunt," cried Rita, "if we enter upon politics I warn you that Don Frederico will fall into his German machine, Raphael into his English spleen, and that Gracia and I will become tainted with French *ennui*."

"Are you not ashamed? Hold your tongue," said her aunt, laughing.

"To avoid so great a misfortune," replied Raphael, "I propose to compose a novel among ourselves."

"Help! help!" cried the countess.

"What extravagance!" said her mother. "Will you write some *chef d'œuvre*, like those which my daughter is in the habit of reading in the *feuilletons* published by the French?"

"Why not?" demanded Raphael.

"Because no one will read them," replied the marchioness; "at least when not given as a Parisian production."

"What does it matter to us?" replied Raphael. "We will write as the birds sing—for the pleasure of singing, and not for the pleasure of being heard."

"Do not do it," observed the marchioness, "do not write up seductions and adulteries. Is it a good thing to render women interesting by their faults? In the eyes of sensible persons, nothing inspires less interest than a young inconsistent woman, and an unchaste woman who neglects her duties."

"Heaven!" said Raphael, "what eloquence! My aunt is inspired, illuminated! I will vote for her as a candidate for the Cortes."

"Dispense also," continued the marchioness, "with introducing into your novel the frightful suicide."

"Apropos of suicides, will you kill yourself if I marry Don Luis?" asked Rita of Raphael.

"I, executioner of my innocent person! God preserve me, my beautiful ingrate! I will live to see you repent, to replace Don Luis, the conqueror, if one day he takes it into his head to play a game at *monte*, in the kingdom of Lucifer, his compeer."

"My mother," said the countess, "instead of tears and crimes, make something good and amusing."

"But, Gracia," replied Raphael, "it must be acknowledged that there is nothing so insipid in a novel as virtue only. Example: let us suppose I should write the biography of my aunt. I would say she was an excellent young girl; that she was married, with the approval of her parents, to a man suited to her; and that she is the model of wives and of mothers, without any other weakness than being a little prone to things of the past, and to have a little too great *penchant* for the *tresillo*. All this is very good for an epitaph, but it is rather simple for a novel."

"Where have you discovered that I aspire to become the model of a heroine in a novel? What nonsense!"

"Then," remarked Stein, "write an historical romance. No, rather a romance on manners. At this moment you are about to have a romance composed by me—a romance which will be composed of two styles."

"The scene—will it be laid here?" said the marchioness.

"You will see, Don Frederico."

"I intend to take for my subject," said Raphael, "the life, altogether moral and honorable, of my uncle, General Santa-Maria."

"It only wanted this. You mock my brother. It seems to me that he will not lend himself to the joke. Go!"

"No, without doubt," replied Raphael. "I respect and I esteem my uncle more than I do anybody in the world ; and I know that his military virtues, pushed often to extremes, have drawn upon him the surname of Don Quixote of the army. But nothing in all this can prevent me from writing his history. Listen, then, illustrious doctor, to the history of my uncle — abridged. Santiago Léon Santa-Maria was from his birth destined for the noble career of arms, because he saw the light of day, or, to be more exact, the shades of night, when the drums, beating the retreat, passed before his paternal mansion. His *entrée* into the world, one might say, was made at the sound of the drum and fife.

"That's true," said the marchioness, smiling.

"I never lie—when I speak the truth," gravely continued Raphael. "As a most certain sign of this predestination, he came into the world with a sword, color of blood, on his breast—a sword designed in most perfect form by the hand of nature; which made all the gossips salute the future general of the army of His Catholic Majesty."

"There is nothing in all this," interrupted the marchioness. "My brother had a mark on his breast, it is true—that of a radish, a simple longing of my mother."

"Remark, doctor," continued Raphael, "that my aunt *depoetizes* the history of her dear brother, and takes away all his prestige. A radish on the breast of a hero, in lieu of a military order! Go along, aunt, there is nothing more ridiculous."

"What is there ridiculous in it," said the marchioness, "to be born with a mark on his breast?"

"Raphael," replied Rita, "I do not know all these particulars. Relate them without too much circumlocution."

"Nothing obliges us to hunt after them, dear Rita,"

replied Raphael. "One of our advantages over other
nations is, that we do not live too fast. Léon Santa-
Maria had scarcely accomplished his twelfth year when
he entered a regiment as a cadet, and from that moment
he held himself as straight as a gun : he became serious
as a sermon, and grave as a funeral. He learned his exercise, and fought valiantly at Roussillon ; then at last
this dear uncle arrived at the age when the heart sings
and sighs."

"Raphael, Raphael," cried his aunt, "do not relate
things that should not be spoken."

"Don't fear, señora. I will only speak of his platonic
loves."

"Of what loves? Are there, by accident, different
sorts of loves?"

"Platonic love," replied Raphael, "is that which is
satisfied with a look, a sigh, or a letter."

"This you say beforehand," replied the marchioness ;
"but you know that the *corps d'armée* came afterwards.
Turn down the leaf then on this chapter."

"Marchioness, have no fear. My history will be such
that, after having read it, all the world will see the portrait of my uncle, holding the sword in one hand, and in
the other the holy palm. His first love was for a pretty
daughter of Osuna, where his regiment was in garrison.
The day when he least thought of it the order arrived
to depart. My uncle said he would return, and she began to sing, 'Marlboro' goes to the war.' She would
sing it yet, if a big cultivator had not offered her his
big hand and his big farm. However, at the first she
was inconsolable ; she wept like the clouds of autumn,
and ceased not to cry day and night; 'Santa-Maria!' so
much so that a servant who slept in the adjoining chamber, believing that her mistress said the litanies, never

neglected to respond devoutly—*ora pro nobis*. My uncle received orders to go to America; he returned to Spain to take part in the war of independence, and had very little time to think of love. It resulted in his loving only the beauties he could make march to the beating of the drum; his character was soured to a point which obtained for him the surname of General Verjuice. The sobriquet remains."

"What risks you run, my nephew!"

"Aunt, I risk nothing. I only repeat what others have said. Little by little his sixtieth year arrived, bringing with it the ordinary *cortège* of rheumatisms and catarrhs, ornamented with all the appearances of an approaching chronic state. My aunt and all his friends advised him to retire from the army, and to marry and live tranquilly. You see that my noble relation felt himself led near to homœopathy."

"This new system," demanded the marchioness, "which orders stimulants to refresh? Do not believe in them, doctor, and never give that kind of remedy."

"Then, as I said," continued Raphael, "there was here a young lady of a mature age, who would not marry to please her father, and her father would not allow her to marry according to her taste. The father, who is very haughty, saw that his child, called Donna Panaracia Cabeza de Vaca (head of a cow)—"

"Well! that noble part of the animal—"

"Laugh away if you will, Raphael," interrupted the marchioness; "but know, Don Frederico, that this name, so ridiculous in the eyes of my nephew, is one of the most illustrious and most ancient in Spain; it owes its origin to the battle of *Las Navas de Tolosa*."

"Which occurred," added Raphael, "in the year 1212, and was gained by the king Alphonse IX., surnamed the Noble, father of the Queen Blanche of France, who was the mother of Saint Louis. This battle delivered Castile from the yoke of the Saracens."

"In fact," replied the marchioness, "I have heard all this related by my sister-in-law. Miramamolin (sovereign prince of the Moors), as my sister also stated, had retreated to a spot where he had deposited all his treasures, in a kind of intrenchment formed of iron chains. A river separated this commanding position from the Christian army: the king, who was unable to cross it, was in despair. Then an old shepherd, covered with a sort of capuchin mantle, came to him, and pointed out the spot where he could, without any difficulty, cross the stream at a ford indicated by the head of a cow which the wolves had devoured. Such was the importance of this information, that the king Alphonse gained the memorable battle of Tolosa. The grateful monarch ennobled him who had rendered him so great a service, and conferred on him and on his descendants the name of Cabeza de Vaca. My sister-in-law said that the statue of the patriotic shepherd, and the chains of the camp of Miramamolin, are still preserved in the cathedral of Toledo."

"Six hundred years of nobility," said Raphael, "is a bagatelle in comparison with ours; for you should know, doctor, that the name of Santa-Maria eclipses all the Cabeza de Vacas, if even their genealogical tree came from the horns of the cow which Noah had in his ark. Learn that we are related to the Holy Virgin—nothing less. And to prove it, I will tell you that one of our noble ancestors, when he counted his beads before his servants, according to the good Spanish custom—"

"A custom which is daily falling into disuse," sighed the marchioness.

"Did not neglect to say," pursued Raphael, "'God save you; our lady and cousin protect thee!' and the servants replied: 'Holy Mary, cousin and lady of his excellency.'"

"Don't say such things before strangers," replied the countess: "they are enough prejudiced against us to credit them; or, without believing, they have enough bad faith to repeat them. That which you have related is known to everybody here. It is a poor joke invented to mock the exaggerated pretensions of our family as to the antiquity of our nobility."

"Apropos of what strangers say: do you know, cousin, that Lord Londonderry has written, in his *Travels in Spain*, that there is but one beautiful woman in Seville, the Marchioness of A., concealing without doubt her name in a manner the most whimsical."

"He is right," replied the countess, "no one can be more beautiful than Adèle."

"Very handsome, cousin, but the only one! It is a frightful extravagance. The major is furious, and intends to institute a process for calumny, with full powers from the Giralda, who believes herself, and gives out, that she is the most beautiful person in all Seville."

"That is to be more royalist than the king," said Rita, with a gesture of disdain; "and you may assure the major, in the name of all the Sevillians, that we are very indifferent as to whether this lord finds us handsome or ugly. But continue your history, Raphael; you have yet to tell us of the preliminaries of your uncle's marriage."

"Above all," said the marchioness, "I will inform Don Frederico that the nobility of our family dates back as far as the year 737. One of our forefathers killed the bear which had taken the life of the Gothic king

Favila; it is for this that we have a bear on our family escutcheon."

At these words Raphael burst out into a laughter so boisterous that he broke the thread of his aunt's narrative.

"Let's see," said he, "here's part second of Santa-Maria, our Lady and cousin! The marchioness possesses a collection of genealogical facts, the one as truthful as the others. She knows by heart all the history of the dukes of Albe, history which rivalled that of Perou."

"If you will have the goodness to relate them to me, Señora Marchioness," remarked Stein, "I will be infinitely obliged to you."

"With much pleasure," replied the marchioness; "and I hope you will accord more credit to my words than this child Raphael, who pretends to know more than those who were born before him. I declare at the outset that nothing ennobles a man so much as courage."

"According to this," said Rita, "José Maria, the celebrated bandit, would be noble, and something more—grandee of Spain of the first class."

"My nephews and nieces seem fond of contradiction," replied the marchioness, with some impatience. "Well, yes! José Maria might have been noble, if he had not been a robber."

"Since you are talking of José Maria," added Raphael, "I will relate to Don Frederico a trait of the courage of this man. I have it from a good source."

"We do not wish to know the exalted deeds of the hero of the carbine," said the marchioness. "Raphael, you speak wrong, and out of place."

"Listen to my history of José Maria. A robber, elegant, heroic, a gentleman, gallant, and distinguished, is a fruit which can grow only on our soil. You foreigners

may have many dukes of Albe, but assuredly you cannot have a single José Maria."

"What say you?" interrupted the marchioness, "that
foreigners may have many Dukes of Albe? Yes, then,
it is an easy thing! Listen, Don Frederico: When the
pious King Ferdinand was before the walls of Seville,
seeing that the siege was prolonged, he proposed to the
Moorish king—"

"Who was named Axataf," interrupted Raphael.

"His name is of no consequence," continued the marchioness. "He then proposed to him, as I said, to decide
the fate of the besieged city by a singular combat—a
duel—between the two monarchs. The Moorish king
had the shame to refuse the defiance. King Ferdinand
had concealed from everybody his resolution, and when
the designated hour arrived, he went out of his camp
alone, and wended his way towards the place designed
for the combat. A soldier of his guard who saw him
depart, had some suspicions of his plan; fearing that the
king might fall into an ambuscade, he armed himself,
and followed at a distance. When the monarch arrived
at the spot which is called to this day the *King's Fountain*, and which was then a desert spot, he stopped,
waiting the approach of the Moor. But while he waited
for his enemy, the Moor had no thought of presenting
himself at the rendezvous. Ferdinand passed the night
there: at the dawn of the day he arose to retire, when
he heard a noise among the foliage.

"'Who are you?—show yourself!' he cried out.

"It was the soldier;—he obeyed.

"'What are you doing here?' demanded the king.

"'Sire, I saw your Majesty leave the camp, and I
divined your intention. I feared a snare, and I am come
to defend you.'

" ' Alone ?'

" ' Sire, your Majesty and I, are we not sufficient to vanquish two hundred Moors ?'

" ' You left my camp a soldier, you will return as *Duke of Albe.*' "

" You see, Don Frederico," remarked Raphael, " that this popular legend arranges duels at midnight, and creates dukes by the word of mouth."

" Hold your tongue, Raphael, for the love of God," said the countess, " and leave us this belief. Besides, this history pleases me."

" Yes," replied Raphael ; " but the Duke of Albe will not be very grateful to your mother for the *illustration* which she would confer upon him. You will see if I am not right."

Upon this, the young man left precipitately, and soon returned, carrying a folio volume in parchment which he had taken from the library of the count.

" Here," said he, " are the origins, privileges, and antiquities of Castilian titles, by Don José Barni y Catalo, advocate to the Royal Councils. Page 140—
' Count of Albe, now duke. The first was Don Fernando Alvarez de Toledo, created Count of Albe by Juan II., in 1439. Don Enrique IV. was created duke in 1469. This illustrious and noble family is of royal blood. It has always occupied the first employments in Spain, whether in war or in politics. The Duke of Albe commanded in chief the army during the conquest of Flanders, and during that of Portugal, where he did wonders. This celebrated family shines with so much distinction, and possesses so much merit, that one must write volumes to enumerate them.'

" You see, aunt, that your history, however good, is not the less apocryphal."

"I do not know from whence this word comes, I believe from the Greek," continued the marchioness; "but to return to Santa-Maria, this name was given them because that—"

"Aunt! aunt!" said Rita, "stop, I pray you, our genealogical history. Have we not had enough of the Cabeza de Vaca, and the Dukes of Albe? When you think of entering upon a second marriage you can parade these glorious genealogies before your favorite."

"The family name of the Dukes of Albe is Alvarez," said Stein, "and it is also that of my host, a brave and honest retired merchant. I find it astonishing that in this country names the most illustrious are equally common to classes the most elevated, and to those the most infamous. It is for this strangers ask, Do all Spaniards believe themselves of noble blood?"

"It is a confusion of ideas," answered Raphael, "as with every thing that regards Spain. Thus there is not a single foreigner who does not write in good faith respecting us, that all laborers wear at their side the sword of a gentleman. The same names of families are, without doubt, very common in Spain; but that arises in a great degree from the fact that formerly lords who possessed slaves gave their names to them on their emancipation. These names, which the free Moors already adopt, multiply, and more particularly those of great lords in proportion to the number of the slaves emancipated. Some of these new families became illustrious, and were ennobled, because many among them descended from Moors of noble race; but the grandees of Spain, who bear these names, need not be confounded with these families any more than with those of artisans whom they find in the same condition. We may also remark that many of these families have taken the names

of places from whence they came; thus we have hundreds
of Medina, Castillo, Navarre, Toledo, Burgos, Aragones,
&c. As to these pretensions to nobility, so rife among
Spaniards, I declare that the remark is not without foun-
dation : it is certain there is in our country a great deal
of pride joined to delicacy and an innate distinction;
but we must not confound this salient point of the
national character with the ridiculous affectations of nobility which we have seen in our time. The Spanish people
do not aspire to embellish themselves with rags, or to
quit the sphere in which Providence has placed them ;
but they attach as much importance to the purity of their
blood as to their honor; above all in the northern provinces, where the inhabitants glory in not having any
Moorish blood in their veins. This purity is lost by an
illegitimate birth, by an alliance more or less doubtful
with Moorish or Jewish blood, as also by their employment as mule-drivers, or public criers, and by ignominious
penalties."

"Dear me !" said Rita, " how tedious you are with your
nobility! Will you, Raphael, do me the pleasure to
continue the history of my uncle ?"

"Again !" said the marchioness.

"Aunt," replied Raphael, "I know of nothing more
tiresome than an obstinate story-teller. Then, Don
Frederico, Santa-Maria and Cabeza de Vaca united like
two doves. Very often I have heard said that my aunt,
the marchioness here present, has wept with joy and
tenderness on seeing a union so well assorted. But he
who was much astonished, as was everybody, and more
than everybody, was my dear uncle, when, after due
time, the Cabeza de Vaca gave birth to a little Santa-
Maria as large as a fan, and who appeared to be the fruit
of a union of an X and a Z. The Cabeza de Vaca was

more proud than was Jupiter at the birth of Minerva. They had on this occasion a grand matrimonial discussion. The señora wished the sweet fruit of their love to be named Panoracio, a name which, since the battle of the plains of Tolosa, had been that of the first-born of the family. My uncle was obstinate, and wished that the future representative of the venerable Santa-Marias should have no other name than that of his father—a name sonorous and warlike. My aunt reconciled them by proposing to baptize the creature with the names of Léon Panoracio; and so the father has always called him Panoracio."

This recital was suddenly interrupted by the general, who entered the saloon pale as death, his lips closed, and his eyes inflamed with anger.

" Powerful God !" said Raphael, in an under-tone, " I wish I were a hundred feet under ground, with the Roman statues which served the Moors to construct the foundations of the Giralda."

" I am furious," said the general.

" What is the matter, uncle ?" the countess, red as a pomegranate, asked of him.

Rita lowered her head on her embroidery, and bit her lips to stifle her desire to laugh.

The marchioness had a face longer than that of Don Quixote.

" It is worse than the mockery of the world," continued the general, in a voice of thunder; "it is an insult !"

" My uncle," said the countess, softening her voice as much as possible, " where there is no bad thought, where there is only trifling which makes one giddy, with the disposition to laugh—"

" Disposition to laugh !" exclaimed the general. " Laugh

at me! laugh at my wife! By my life, that will never happen again. I go, this instant even, to lodge my complaint with the police."

"The police! are you in your sound senses, brother?" cried the marchioness.

"If I can happily get out of this," said Raphael to Rita, "I vow to St. Juan the Silent to imitate him during a year and a day."

"My dear Léon," pursued the marchioness, "do not clothe this childishness with too much importance. Calm yourself. I know that he loves and respects you. Would you create scandal? Family complaints should never be made public. Come, Léon, let this be kept among ourselves."

"What family complaints are you talking about?" replied the general, approaching his sister. "Is it a family affair to witness the unheard-of insolence of this ill-bred Englishman, who insults the people of the country?"

On hearing these words, the sister and all the others breathed as if a stone was taken from off their hearts; the history, then, had *not* been heard by the inflexible general, and Raphael demanded in the most severe tone he could give to his voice—

"What has he then done, this great amphibious animal?"

"What has he done? I will tell you. You know that, unfortunately for me, this man resides opposite to me. Well! at one o'clock at night, when everybody is enjoying his best sleep, the *master* opens his window, and begins to play on his trumpet!"

"I know he has a passion for that instrument," said Raphael.

"Besides, he plays horribly bad, and the breath from

his powerful chest brings notes from the instrument capable of waking the dead for twenty miles around ; in such a manner too that all the dogs in the neighborhood set up a horrible barking and yelling. You will by this have an idea of the nights we have to pass."

All the efforts which the auditors had made up to this moment to contain themselves now proved ineffectual. The burst of laughter was so instant, so loud, that the general was instantly mute, and cast on them an indignant look.

" It wanted but this, my friends ! It wanted only one such audacious insolence, and one such contempt of honest people to create for you a subject for laughter. Laugh! laugh! we will soon see if your *protégé* will laugh also, Raphael."

He said this, and left the saloon, as furious as he had entered it. He went to lay his complaint before the police.

Rita laughed till her neck stretched.

" My God, Rita," said the marchioness, " this is not a thing to make you so joyous. You have done wrong."

" My aunt, I would laugh if I were even in my coffin. I promise you, to revenge my uncle, that when the Major *Grande Mosca* (big fly) comes to me to jabber his twaddle, I will not content myself with turning my back on him, but I will say to him, ' Save your powerful breath to blow your trumpet with.' "

" You would do better," replied Raphael, " to imitate foreign young ladies, who blush in saying ' Good-day,' and turn pale when they would say ' Good-evening.' "

" With all this," added Stein, persevering like a German, " you have promised me, Señor Arias, to relate to me a trait of courage of José Maria."

" That will be for another day, Don Frederico. Here

is my general-in-chief," he said, taking out his watch; " it is three o'clock less a quarter, and I am invited to dine with the captain-general at three o'clock. Doctor, were I in your place I would offer the aid of my art to my aunt Cabeza de Vaca, in the critical state she is thrown into by the major's trumpet."

CHAPTER XX.

After the complete re-establishment of the health of the countess's son, came the evening fixed upon to receive Maria. Some of the persons invited had already assembled, when Raphael entered precipitately.

"My cousin," he said, "I come to ask a favor. If you refuse I will take to my bed, under the pretext of a horrible headache."

"Jesus!" replied the countess, "how can I obviate so great a misfortune?"

"You shall know immediately: yesterday I received a letter from one of my comrades at the embassy, Viscount St. Leger."

"Take away the St. and the Viscount, and leave the Leger only," remarked the general.

"Well," said Raphael, "my friend, who, according to my uncle, is neither saint nor viscount, introduced an Italian prince to me."

"A prince! Well," phlegmatically remarked the general, "why do you not call things by their proper names? He will prove, probably, to be one of the Carbonari, a propagandist, a veritable scourge. And where is this prince?"

"I am ignorant," replied Raphael. "All I know is, that the letter says, 'I will feel under a thousand obligations if you will have the goodness, my friend, to introduce to the person I now present to you the most beautiful and the most amiable of your ladies, your most

choice reunions, the most remarkable antiquities of
' Seville, the beautiful,' this 'garden of Hesperides.' "

"The garden of Alcazar he should rather have said,"
observed the marchioness.

"It is probable. When I saw myself charged with
the accomplishment of this task, without knowing to
which saint to address myself, I caught the luminous
idea to address myself to my cousin, and to ask her permission to bring the prince to her *soirée ;* because, in this
way he can make the acquaintance of ladies the hand-
somest and most amiable, society the choicest, and," he
added, in a low voice, pointing to the *tresillo* table, " antiquities the most notable in Seville."

"Take care, my mother is there," murmured the
countess, laughing secretly. " You are an insolent fellow. And," she added, in a loud voice, "I will have
much pleasure in seeing your *protégé.*"

"Good! very good!" exclaimed the general, striking
the cards violently. " Take care of them, open to them
wide the doors, place them all at their ease; they will
accept all this pleasure at your house, and finish by
mocking you."

" Believe me, uncle," replied Raphael, "that we have
our revenge. It is true they pretend admirably. Some
foreigners arrive among us with the single object of
searching for adventures, persuaded that Spain is the
classic land for this. Last year I had one of these mo-
nomaniacs in my care. He was an Irishman, related to
Lord W."

"Yes, as I to the Grand Turk," said the general, sar-
castically.

"The spirit of the hero of La Mancha," continued
Raphael, "took possession of my Irishman, whom I will
call *Green Erin,* in default of his true name, which I

have forgotten. An extraordinary affection for robbers had brought him to Spain. He wished to see them in all their strength. The pleasure of being robbed was his fixed idea, his caprice, the object of his travels. He would have given six thousand sacks of potatoes to see at his side Don José Maria, in his magnificent Andalusian costume, splendidly mounted, with buttons of doubloons. He brought, at all risk for José, a poignard, with handle of gold, and a pair of pistols."

"To arm our enemies?" cried the general. "This is his great desire. Always the same."

"He wished to go to Madrid," continued Raphael; "but knowing that a diligence might have the bad taste to escort him, he decided to depart in the carriage of a courier. All my arguments to dissuade him were useless. He went, in fact; and a little beyond Cordova his ardent desires were realized: he encountered the robbers, but not the robbers of *bon-ton*—not *fashionable* robbers like Don José, who sparkles like a piece of gold, mounted on his fiery chestnut horse. They were little robbers, marching on foot, common and vulgar. You know what it is to be vulgar in England? There is no pestilence, no leprosy, which inspires so much horror in an Englishman as that which is vulgar. Vulgar! at this word Albion is covered with her densest fog; the dandies have spleen of the blackest dye; the ladies have the blue-devils; the misses have spasms; and dressmakers become nervous. Thus it is forbidden as if a lion approached. He did not fight, however, for his treasures, for these he had confided to me until his return. What he valued the most was a branch of willow from the tomb of Napoleon, the satin shoe of a danseuse, scarcely as big as a nut, and a collection of caricatures of his uncle, Lord W."

"Here is detail enough to paint the man," interrupted the general.

"But I do nothing but chatter," said Raphael. "Adieu, cousin; I go, but I will soon return."

"How, you go away leaving the poor Erin in the hands of the robbers. You must finish your history," said the countess.

"I will then tell you, in two words, that the exasperated robbers ill-treated him, and fastened him to a tree. He was discovered by an old woman, who transported him to her cabin, where she took a mother's care of him during all the illness which his misadventures had brought on him. I was for some time without any tidings from my friend, and recollecting the Spanish saying, '*Que la esperanza era verde y se la comió un borrico*' ('Hope is green; an ass might feed on it'), I began to believe that some accident had happened to Green Erin, when I received a letter from my Irishman, containing all the details of his romantic history. He instructed me to give six thousand reals to the woman who had nursed and saved him, so she could not doubt the state of his fortune: then the toilet left him by the robbers was simply that which he wore when he came into the world. As you see, the recompense was becoming. Let us be just; no one can deny the generosity of the English. But here comes Polo, with an elegy in his eyes. The prince waits for me. I will make up for being late by running, at the risk of breaking my nose." And Raphael disappeared.

"Jesus!" said the marchioness, "Raphael is so restless, he gesticulates so much, he is witty with such volubility, that I lose half of what he says."

"You do not lose any great things," growled the general.

" Well," said the countess, " I could love Raphael for the pleasure which he affords me, if I had never before had a love for every thing that is good."

" Here, dear Gracia," said Eloise, entering and embracing the countess, " here is Alexander Dumas' ' Travels in France.' "

The countess took the book. Polo and Eloise engaged in a long dissertation upon the works of this writer. Our readers will dispense with our reporting it here.

" How well the French know how to write !" said Eloise, resuming this literary dissertation.

" What do they not know how to do, these sons of liberty ?" replied Polo.

" But, señorita," replied the general, " why do you not read Spanish books ?"

" Because every Spanish book bears the seal of a coarse stupidity," replied Eloise. " We are deplorably in arrears."

" What do you think, then, should constitute a writer of merit in this detestable country," added Polo, a little piqued, " if we attain eminence in nothing, if we know only how to plagiarize ? How would you that we revise our country and our manners, if there is to be found nothing good, nothing elegant, nothing characteristic ?"

" At least," said Eloise, " you do not extol, like the Germans, the orange-tree, with its flowers and fruits ; like the French, the boléro ; and, like the English, the wine of Jerez (sherry)."

" Ah ! Eloisita," cried Polo, enthusiastically ; " here is a *spirituelle* sally ! If she is not French, she deserves to be." And thus speaking, Polo, as usual, was himself but a plagiarist : he repeated one of the set phrases of France as an axiom.

The general had the good fortune not to hear this
dialogue ; they summoned him to the card-table. Raphael entered, accompanied by the prince, whom he presented to the countess. She received the stranger with
her usual amiability, remaining seated, according to
Spanish usage. The prince was tall and slender, and he
appeared to be about forty-five years of age ; but, beyond his noble title, he possessed no distinction, either
of person or of manners. The society was then complete. All waited for the *cantora*, with an impatience
mixed with some doubt as to the real value of her
talent.

Major Fly threw himself affectedly into a chair near
some young ladies, and cast on them glances as homicidal as the thrusts of a fencing-foil. Sir John held his
eye-glass bent on Rita, who paid no attention to him.
The baron, seated near an old councillor, asked him if
the Moors whitened their houses with chalk.

"I have no documents on this subject," replied the
magistrate. "This point has not had the advantage of
having received the attention of our historians."

"What ignorance !" thought the baron.

"What a silly question !" thought the magistrate.

"You have a very beautiful cousin," said the prince to
Raphael.

"Yes," he replied ; "*she is the Ondine of perfumed
waters.*"

"And the general whom I see so attentive to the
game, and who has an air so distinguished ?"

"He is the retired Nestor of the army. You have
not at Pompeii an antiquity better preserved."

"And the señora with whom he is playing ?"

"His sister, the Marchioness of Guadalcanal, a species
of escurial, a solid assemblage of devout and monarchial

sentiments, with a heart which emanated from the Pantheon of kings without thrones."

There was suddenly heard a great noise. It was the major, who, on rising to join Raphael, had upset a vase of flowers. And Raphael cried out, "The major announces his arrival; without doubt he comes to sigh, like the pipe of an organ, over the little note the ladies take of his person."

"They must be very difficult to please," remarked the prince; "the major has a handsome figure."

"I do not say to the contrary. He is a Samson in strength. But, to begin with, he has his Delilah, who will soon be legitimately his, thanks to the millions which tea and opium cast into the coffers of his father. She waits in the midst of the fogs of his isle, while he amuses himself under the beautiful sky of Andalusia. Foreigners who visit Spain are all of one accord in anticipating the pleasures they propose to themselves: the beauty of the climate, the bull-fights, the oranges, the boléros, and, especially, their love conquests. What complaints have I heard from those who came here like Cæsar, and left like Darius!"

During this dialogue, the baron had approached the table, and regarded the game.

"Madame," said he to the marchioness, "is the mother—"

"Of my daughter? Yes, sir," replied the marchioness.

Rita impulsively burst into a fit of laughter.

Raphael, who had stolen away from the major, mixed in the groups of guests, and soon found himself among some young ladies, of whom several were his relations. He had in this feminine squad a large party; but seeing that he had neglected them to devote his attentions to the strangers who were his cousin's guests, this evening introduced by him, were all leagued against him, and had made up their minds to be revenged.

"Am I transformed to the head of Medusa, that you do not know me?" demanded Arias.

"Ah! is it you?" said one of the conspirators.

"It seems to me so, Clarita," replied the young man.

"It is so very long since I have seen you, I did not recognize you again. How have you been able to tear yourself away from your strangers?"

"My strangers! I renounce the property."

"Is it the torments and fatigues these *protéges* of thine cause thee, which has given thee already the appearance of old age?"

"Señoritas," exclaimed Raphael, "is this a declaration of war, a conspiracy? What have I done?"

As an only response, he was overwhelmed with appeals, which burst forth in rapid succession, like an explosion of fireworks.

At this moment, the guests who found themselves assembled near the door of the court separated to permit the duke, leading in the Gaviota, to enter. Stein followed.

CHAPTER XXI.

MARISALADA, instructed in her toilet by her hostess, presented herself accoutred in a manner the most ridiculous. She wore a dress of silk, handkerchief pattern, too short, and blending colors the most extravagant; her coiffure was most ungracefully intermingled with red ribbons of unheard-of stiffness; a mantle of tulle, white and blue, garnished with Catalan lace, exceeded the black of her tint. The *ensemble* of this *parure* could but necessarily produce, and did produce, the most pitiable effect.

The countess in making some steps towards the Gaviota passed near to Raphael, and whispered in his ear, applying to the circumstance the fable of La Fontaine—

> "Sans mentir, si son ramage
> Se rapporte à son plumage."

"How many thanks we owe you," said the countess to Maria, "for your goodness in wishing to satisfy our desire to hear you! The duke has paid you so brilliant a compliment!"

The Gaviota, without saying a word, let herself be conducted by the countess to a seat which had been destined for her between the piano and the sofa.

Rita, to be near her, had abandoned her ordinary place, and was seated beside Eloise.

"My God!" she said, on seeing the Gaviota, "she is blacker than a mole."

"One could swear," added Eloise, "that it was her greatest enemy who has dressed her. One would say a

Judas of Holy Saturday. How does it seem to you, Raphael?"

"This wrinkle which she has between her eyebrows," replied Arias, "gives her the appearance of a unicorn."

During this time, in this assembly so numerous and so brilliant, no symptom of politeness or good feeling was shown towards Maria; who not the less preserved all her *aplomb* and her unalterable calmness. Thanks to her look, always investigating and penetrating, to her quick intelligence, and the exquisite tact of a Spanish woman, two minutes sufficed her to remark every thing, and to judge of it all.

"I already understand," she said to herself, in resuming her observations, "that the countess is good, and desires my success; the young elegants make fun of me and of my toilet, which must be frightful; for these strangers look at me disdainfully, as I am only a simple country girl: for the old I am a nullity; the others remain neuter. In consideration of the duke, who is my protector, they will neither praise nor criticise until after an opinion favorable or the contrary is formed of me."

For her part, the good and amiable countess tried to enter into conversation with the Gaviota, but her laconic responses neutralized all her good intentions.

"Does Seville please you much?" asked the countess.

"Sufficiently," replied Maria.

"And what do you think of our cathedral?"

"It is too large."

"And our beautiful walks?"

"Too small."

"And what then interests you the most?"

"The bulls."

The conversation stopped here. It was resumed by the countess after a long pause—

"Allow me to pray your husband to place himself at the piano."

"Whenever it pleases you."

Stein took his place at the piano. Maria, whose hand the duke had taken, and conducted her, placed herself at the side of her husband.

"Do you tremble, Maria?" Stein asked of her.

"And why should I tremble?" she replied.

There was profound silence. They could then easily distinguish the various impressions she reflected on the countenances of those present; with the greater part of whom it was curiosity and surprise; with the countess a sweet good-nature; around the gaming-tables, which Raphael called the upper house, there was nothing remarkable but complete indifference.

The prince smiled with disdain; the major opened his eyes, as if that would help him to hear; the baron closed his.

Sir John profited by this moment of interval to take off his eyeglasses, and rub them with his handkerchief.

Raphael fled into the garden to smoke a cigarette.

Stein played without affectation or flourishes the prelude of *Casta Diva;* but the pure, limpid, and powerful voice of the Gaviota made her so well heard, that the spectators seemed touched as by a magic wand. On every countenance was painted astonishment and admiration. The prince allowed an approving exclamation to escape him.

When the Gaviota had finished singing, a storm of bravos was sent forth from all the assembly: the countess set the example by applauding with her beautiful and delicate hands.

"God preserve me!" said the general, stopping his

ears; he really thought he was in the place where bulls are kept.

"Let them alone, Leon," said the marchioness; "let them divert themselves. It is better to be amused than to speak ill of one's neighbor."

Stein acknowledged on all sides his respectful thanks.

Mariquita resumed her seat, as cold and impassive as before. She sang in succession several variations most difficult, where the melody disappeared in the midst of trills and cadences. Surmounting without effort every obstacle, she elicited more and more admiration.

"Countess," said the duke, "the prince desires to hear some Spanish songs which have been much spoken of to him; Maria excels in this species of song; will you procure a guitar for her?"

"With great pleasure," replied the countess. And she complied at once with the request.

Raphael was seated near to Rita, after having taken care to place the major beside Eloise, who tried to persuade the Englishman that the Spaniards were becoming day by day more desirous of putting themselves on a level with foreigners, above all in that which relates to affectation and affected airs; for we know that in servile imitations, it is always defects which are the more readily imitated.

"What beautiful eyes!" said Raphael to his cousin. "These long black lashes are magnificent. Her look has truly the attraction of love."

"It is you who are the lover of strangers," said Rita. "Why have you placed the major near Eloise? Listen to the nonsense he is telling her. I warn you, my cousin, that each day you take the aspect and the attractions of a dictionary."

"There it is, raillery, and raillery again," cried Raphael,

striking with his fist the arm of the chair. "You stray from the question, I speak to you of my love for yourself, Rita, of my love which will endure eternally. Know it well, my cousin, a man never loves seriously but one woman in his lifetime. The others—they pretend that they love them."

"That is what Don Luis has repeated to me often, my cousin; but do you know, in your turn, that you are becoming fatiguing, *ennuyant*, like a repeating watch."

"What does this signify?" cried Eloise, seeing a guitar brought in.

"It appears she is to sing some Spanish songs, and I am rejoiced. These songs divert me much."

"Spanish songs!" sighed Eloise indignantly. "What horror! They are good for the common people, but not in society where *bon-ton* reigns. What then is Gracia thinking of? Here then is it why foreigners rightly think we are behind other nations; because we will not adopt their manners and their tastes as our models, because we through obstinacy will dine at three o'clock, and because we never will persuade ourselves that all that is Spanish is stupid."

"But," said the major in a gibberish sort of Anglo-Andalusian, "I believe *indeed*, that they do very well to be as they are."

"If this is a compliment," replied Eloise with emphasis, "it is so much exaggerated that it resembles mockery."

"It is the Italian lord," said Rita, "who has asked for these Spanish sonnets. He likes them, and understands them; that's one proof that they merit being heard."

"Eloise," added Raphael, "the *barcarolles*, the *tyroliennes*, and the *ranz des vaches* are the popular songs of other countries; why will we not admit in the society

of distinguished people our *boleros* and the other songs
of the Spanish people ?"

" Because it is more vulgar," replied Eloise.

Raphael shrugged his shoulders, Rita laughed out-
right, and the major comprehended nothing of it.

Eloise got up, and under pretext of a headache left,
accompanied by her mother, to whom she said in de
parting—

" Let them know at least that there are in Spain young
ladies sufficiently distinguished and sufficiently delicate
to fly from such buffooneries."

"How unfortunate will be the Abelard of this Heloise !"
said Raphael, on seeing her retire.

Maria, beyond her beautiful voice and excellent
method, possessed, as a daughter of the common people,
the infusing of science in the songs of Andalusia; and
that grace, that charm which a stranger could not understand nor value, without having resided a long time in
the country, without having, so to speak, become identified with the national character. There is in these songs,
as well as in the airs of the dances, a richness of imagination, an attraction so powerful, an enchainment of sur-
prises, complaints, bursts of joy, of languor, and of exal-
tation, that the audience, at first astonished, soon finish
by being captivated and intoxicated.

Thus when Maria took the guitar, and sang—

> " Si me pierdo, que me busquen
> Al lado del Mediodia,
> Donde nacen las movenas,
> Y donde la sal se cria," *

admiration became enthusiasm. The young people
marked the measure by clapping their hands, repeat-

* See note 1.

ing "Good! Good!" to encourage the singer; the cards fell from the hands of the players; the major could no longer contain himself, and beat the measure in the wrong time; Sir John swore that the song was even better than "God save the Queen;" but that which was the triumph of the Spanish music was, that it smoothed the brow of the general.

"Do you remember, brother," the marchioness smilingly asked him, "the time when we sang *el Zorengo* and *el Tripili ?*"

"What is that, the Zorengo and the Tripili?" asked the baron of Raphael.

"They are," replied Arias, "the fathers of *Sereno* and of *la Cachucha*, and the forefathers of *la Jaca de Terciopelo*, of *Vito*, and other songs of the day."

These particulars of songs and of national dances, of which we have spoken, may seem in bad taste, and they would certainly be so in other countries. But to abandon one's self without reserve to sentiments which instigate our songs and our dances, one must have a character like ours; it must be that grossness and vulgarity be, as they are with us, two things unknown, two things which do not exist. A Spaniard may be insolent, but rarely will he ever be gross, because it is not in his nature. He lives according to his inspiration, which will never efface in him the stamp of a special distinction. This is what gives to Spain, despite of an education but little nourished, that finish of manner and frank elegance which render their intercourse so agreeable.

Mariquita left the hotel of the countess as pale and as impassible as she had entered it.

When the countess was alone with her friends, she said with a triumphant air to Raphael—

"What think you now, my dear cousin ?"

9*

"I think," replied the young man, "that 'the warbling is better than the plumage.'"

"What eyes!" cried the countess.

"One might say, two black diamonds in a casket of Russia leather."

"She is grave," said the countess, "but not haughty."

"And timid as a woman of the common class," said Raphael.

"But what a voice!" added the countess; "what a divine voice!"

"There should be engraven on her tomb," replied Raphael, "the epitaph which the Portuguese composed for their celebrated singer Madureira—

> " Aqui yaz o senhor de Madureira,
> O melhor cantor do mundo:
> Que movieu porque Deus quiseira,
> Que si naon quiseira naon.
> E por que lo necisitó na sua capella,
> Dijole Deus : canta-cantou cosa bella !
> Dijo Deus á os anjos : id vos á pradeira,
> Que melhor canta o senhor de Madureira."*

"Raphael," said the countess, "you are an eternal railler, and nothing escapes your love of fun. I will go and order your portrait under the figure of a mocking-bird."

"In that case," replied Raphael, on going away, "I will make a beautiful masculine Harpy that would have the advantage of being able to propagate his species."

* See note 2.

CHAPTER XXII.

It was at the close of summer, in the month of September. The weather was still warm, but the evenings were already long and cool. Nine o'clock had struck, and there remained at the countess's only the family and intimate friends, when Eloise entered.

"Sit down here near me on the sofa," said the mistress of the house to her.

"I am very much obliged to you. Notwithstanding, you will agree with me, Gracia, that our sofas in Spain are stuffed only with tow and horsehair. Nothing is harder or less comfortable."

"But also nothing is more fresh," said Rita, near whom Eloise had seated herself, in a studied attitude.

"Do you know what they say?" asked this last of the poet Polo, playing with his yellow gloves, and stretching out his leg, to exhibit his beautiful patent-leather shoes; "they say that Arias is named town-major, but I believe it is a splendid puff."

"Village gossip, for Seville resembles a village," replied Eloise, smirking. "Raphael merits better than that. He is a man who is very spiritual, very fashionable, and a brave officer."

"What do you say, señorita?" demanded the general, who had vaguely understood something of the conversation.

"I say, sir, what everybody repeats who knows it."

"Town-major! one should have patience," cried the general, striking his cards.

"What can excite so violently the bile of our uncle?" asked Raphael, on entering, of his cousin Rita.

"The report which is circulated."

"What report?"

"That which names you town-major. Our uncle believes it is a joke."

"He is right, I would not aspire to that honor. But I bring some news which has a thousand claims to be placed in the first circle."

"News! news belonging to us all? Then relate it to us quickly."

"Know then," said Raphael, raising his voice, "that the *Grisi* of Villamar is ready to be heard on the stage of Seville."

"Oh! what joy!" cried Eloise. "Here, then, is a veritable event, which will break up monotonous Seville from its ordinary routine, in which it has vegetated since San Fernando founded it."

"The *Conquest*," her friend Polo whispered.

But Eloise continued without listening: "In what piece will she first appear?"

"In a piece written expressly for her, and for Stein, her husband," replied Raphael.

"Has any one ever seen the like!" exclaimed the marchioness.

"Do you not see, mother," said the countess, "that Raphael is jesting, according to his very laudable and very ordinary habit?"

"Since *Lucretia, Angelo, Antony y Carlos, el Hechizado*, have been played, there is nothing in the world I do not believe possible."

"The theatre is the *School of Manners*," remarked the general, ironically, "where they raise to their level those whom they would adopt."

"How right the French are in saying that Africa commences beyond the Pyrenees!" murmured, during this time, Eloise in the ears of Polo.

"Since they occupy a part belonging to the sea-shore," he replied, "they speak of it no more; that would be too great a pleasure to us."

Eloise restrained a fit of laughter by biting her little handkerchief trimmed with lace.

"Here are two who conspire," announced Rita to Raphael. "Polo has an infernal machine between his eyes and his eye-glass, and Eloise hides in her handkerchief, which she conveys to her mouth, a whole world of engines destined to fight against a cursed and stationary Spain."

"Why, these are not conspirators," replied Raphael.

"What are they then, eternal contradictor?"

"They are— I will tell you, so that you can judge them in all their sublimity."

"Finish! tiresome fellow."

"They are," said Raphael, solemnly, "incomprehensible regenerators."

Several evenings after what we have just related, the vast galleries of the hotel the countess inhabited were deserted. There was seen only the playing of *tresillo.*

"How late they are!" said the marchioness. "It is already half-past eleven, and they do not come."

"Time does not seem long at the theatre," added her brother; "when they are at the opera, they are amused like so many fools."

"Who would have believed," continued the marchioness, "that this woman could have been so studious, and so determined, as to walk the boards so soon?"

"As to the study," said the general, "when one knows how to sing, it does not require so much study as

you think. As to her determination, I would be satisfied with a regiment of grenadiers like her to besiege
Numance or Saragossa."

"I will tell you what occurred," then remarked one of
the players. "When three months ago the Italian company arrived, our future prima donna became a sub-
scriber, and chose a box the nearest to the stage. She
did not miss a single recitation, and she even obtained
permission to assist at the rehearsals. The duke directed
the Italian prima donna to give lessons to his *protégé*,
which made her accepted afterwards by the director;
but he would engage her only as second, which Maria
refused haughtily. By one of those chances which always favor the audacious, the prima donna fell danger-
ously ill, and the *protégé* of the duke offered herself to
replace her. We well know how she has acquitted herself of the task."

At this moment the countess, animated and brilliant
as the light, entered, accompanied by several invited
guests.

"Mother, what a delightful evening we have had!
What a triumph! What a beautiful and magnificent
thing!"

"Will you tell me, my niece," replied the general,
"what importance it could have, and what effect produced by this new arrival having a fine voice and singing
well on the stage, that she has excited in you the same
elevation, and even the same enthusiasm, which the
recital of a great fact or of a sublime action would inspire
in you."

"Think then, uncle, what a triumph for us! What
glory for Seville, to be the cradle of an artist whose
renown will fill the whole world!"

"Like the Marquis de la Romana!" replied the general. "Like Wellington, or like Napoleon! Is it not true, my niece?"

"What, sir," replied the countess; "the renowned, is she not a war-trumpet? How divinely this woman, without a rival, sings! With what ease and good taste she walks the stage! She is a prodigy! And what enthusiasm and admiration seized all the audience! My own pleasure was redoubled when I saw the duke so satisfied, and Stein dumb with emotion."

"The duke," interrupted the general, "should find his joy in things of a different nature."

"General," remarked one of the guests, "these are human weaknesses. The duke is young—"

"Ah!" cried the countess, "there is nothing more frightful than suspicion, and to suspect evil where it does not exist. The world dishonors him who would be culpable of such infamy. Do you not all know that the duke does not only give himself up to the study of the fine arts, but that he patronizes the artists, the learned, and all whom he can happily influence in the progress of intelligence? And besides, Maria, has she not for her husband a man to whom the duke owes much?"

"My niece," replied the general, "all this is very beautiful and very Christianlike; but do not destroy the appearances which permit the suspicion. In this world it is not sufficient to be at the shelter of the critic; we must still be careful of propriety. For this same reason, as you are young and handsome, you will do well not to take in hand the defence in certain causes."

"I have not the ambitious pretension to pass myself off as perfect," replied the countess, "nor to establish in my house a tribunal of justice; but what I desire, is to be a loyal and sincere friend, when I defend and make respected those who honor me with their friendship."

Raphael and Arias entered at this moment.

"Ah, Raphael," she said to him, "do you still mock this fair enchantress?"

"My cousin, to please you, I am brilliant with enthu- siasm, in imitation of the public. I have been a wit- ness to the imperial ovation awarded to this eighth wonder."

"Relate it to us," said the countess; "relate it to us."

"When the curtain fell, I thought for an instant that we were going to witness a second edition of the Tower of Babel. Ten times they encored the *diva ;* and they would have encored it twenty times, if the insolent and irreverent lustres of the opera house, fatigued by the length of their services, had not begun to sparkle and go out. The friends of the duke were eager to go and congratulate the heroine ; we all precipitated ourselves at her feet—and we prostrated ourselves, our faces to the earth."

"You also, Raphael?" asked the general. "I thought you had more sense under your apparent giddiness."

"If I had not been where all the others went, I would not now have had the pleasure to paint to you the re- ception which we gave to this Queen of Molucca, this Empress of Bernol. (A flat, in music.) To begin : she arranged all her answers in a species of chromatic scale, according to her usage, and which again close the fol- lowing demi-tones : to begin, the calm, which is called also indifference ; then the supineness; and, to finish, the disdain. I was the first to offer her the tribute of my homage. I showed to her my hands, bruised with ap- plauding, and swore to her that the slight sacrifice of the surface of the skin was well due to her incomparable talent—happy rival of that of the illustrious Madureira. She replied only by a superb inclination of the head worthy of the goddess Juno. The baron entreated her to come to Paris, the only city where bravos are of any value, because the Paris success resounds throughout the universe. And Maria replied coldly: ' You see that it is not necessary that I go to Paris to be applauded : bravos for bravos, I like better those of my country than those of France.' "

" She said that ?" demanded the general. " There is much good sense in this woman."

" The major, ' *Grande Mosca*,' " continued Raphael, " said to her, with his usual awkwardness, that of all the singers he had ever heard, one only, Grisi, sang better than she.

" ' Since Grisi sings better than I,' coldly replied the *artiste*, ' you were wrong to listen to me in lieu of going to hear her.'

" Then came Sir John, shaking hands with and treading on everybody's feet.

" ' Señora Maria,' he said to the Gaviota, ' your voice is wonderful : if you wish to sell it, I will pay you fifty thousand pounds for it.'

" ' I do not sell my voice,' said Maria, disdainfully."

" All this is beautiful and good, dear cousin ; but what think you of the mystery which surrounds this affair ?"

" Of what mystery do you speak ?" demanded the baron, who just appeared.

" Of this brilliant *début*," replied Arias ; "of this *début*, bursting among us like a bombshell, at a moment when no one thought of it. I understand certain things now : the interviews of the duke with the *impressario;* the assiduity of this Norma at the theatre."

" Ah, here comes Señorita Rita," exclaimed the baron. " Señorita, I believe that I had the honor to see you this morning, in the street Catalans."

"I did not see you," replied Rita.

"It is a misfortune," observed Raphael, "which never happens to our cathedral, nor to Major '*Grande Mosca.*'"

"I saw you," continued the baron, "near to a large cross placed against the wall. I asked what this cross meant, and was informed that it is called the cross of the negro. Can you tell me, señorita, from whence comes this strange denomination?"

"I do not know. Probably some black person was crucified on it."

"It is probable. But can you also tell me," added the baron, with that insupportable irony which approaches so near to the familiar insolence of the incredulous, when they speak to those whom they know to be credulous, "why there is a crocodile suspended from the vault of this gallery of the cathedral, which surrounds the court of orange-trees, on entering by the right of the Giralda? The cathedral with you, does it serve also as a museum of natural history?"

"This large crocodile," said Rita, on walking away, "is there, because it was taken on the roof of the church."

"Ah," cried the baron, laughing, "all is wonderful in your cathedral—every thing, including the crocodile."

"This is a popular belief," said the countess; "here is the truth: this crocodile was presented to King Alphonse, the wise, by the famous ambassador sent by the Sultan of Egypt. At the side of this crocodile there is still the tooth of an elephant, a stick, and a bridle—symbols of strength and of moderation. For six hundred years have these symbols been placed at the entrance to the church, as an inscription which the people comprehend without knowing how to read."

The baron seemed much to regret he could not adopt Rita's version. The cruel countess had deprived him of the pleasure of writing an article critical, burlesque, satirical, and humorous. Who knows if the crocodile has not been called to fill the part of a holy spirit of a new species in the pleasant recital of this Frenchman, endowed with the advantage of having been born malicious?

During this time the marchioness scolded Rita for the sham she had passed off on the baron, respecting the crucified negro.

"You had better have told him the truth," said the marchioness.

"I do not know that—and then the baron bores me."

"You must avow your ignorance. Do you not know that this man is capable of publishing your answer in his 'Travels in Spain?'"

"What does it matter to us?"

"It matters, my niece, that I do not like that they speak evil of my country."

"Yes," interposed the general, with bitterness, "arrest the stream that overflows. It is not astonishing that foreigners calumniate our country, when we are the first to slander it, without remembering the proverb: 'It is vile to believe one's self vile.' Marchioness, my sister, you ought also to reprimand this fool of a Raphael, for having replied to the baron—who put to him a question of the same kind, relative to the cross of the robbers, near to the Cartago—that this cross bore that name because it was there the robbers came to pray to God to bless their enterprises."

"And the baron believed it?"

"As firmly as I believe that he is not a baron."

"It was poor wit. This cross was raised in memory

of a miracle which led to the conversion of a troop of
bandits. I will severely reprimand this crackbrain." And
she called Raphael, to whom his cousin Gracia said :

"I am full of joy. What delightful moments we are
to pass with this Mariquita !"

"It will not be for long, countess," said the colonel.
"They assure me that the duke is to take the new
Malibran to Madrid."

"And what *nomme de théâtre* has she taken ?" asked
the countess. "It will not do to call her Marisalada, I
suppose. The name is pretty, but it is not sufficiently
imposing for an *artiste*."

"She will perform, without doubt, under that of
Gaviota," said Raphael: "one of the duke's servants
told mine that it was the name given her in the village.
She might take the name of her husband."

"What horror !" said the countess; "she must have
a euphonious name."

"She might take that of her father—Santalo."

"No, señor ; it must be a name ending in *i* ; better
still if it were *d'i*."

"In that case," said Raphael, "name her Mississippi."

"We will consult Polo," said the countess. "Eh, but
where then is he hid, our poet ?"

"I would willingly bet," said Raphael, "that at this
instant he is confiding to paper the poetic inspirations
which the divinity of the day has born in his soul. To-
morrow, without any doubt, we will read in 'Il Sevil-
lano' one of those compositions, which, according to my
uncle, if they do not raise up easily to Parnassus, they
will infallibly precipitate into Lethe."

The marchioness again called to Raphael.

"I am sure," he said to his cousin, "that my aunt
does me the honor to call me now to have the pleasure

of scolding me. I see a sermon trembling on her lips: her knit eyebrows announce a terrible admonition, and the quivering nostril already sends to my ears the sound of harsh reprimand. But what lucky chance!—here is a shield," and he glided his arm within that of the baron, and led him along with him near to the card-table. The marchioness, although furious, deferred her rebuke to a more favorable occasion. Rita felt a great desire to laugh, and the general struck the floor with the heel of his boot, which gave indication of his impatience.

" Is the general indisposed ?" asked the baron.

" He is afflicted with a nervous movement," replied Raphael, in an under-tone.

" What a misfortune !" cried the baron. "It is *tic-douloureux*. Whence this evil? Some tendon injured in the wars, perhaps, dear Raphael ?"

" No ; a strong moral impression—"

" It must be very terrible. And what was the cause ?"

" A word of your king Louis XIV."

" What word ?" asked the alarmed baron.

" The celebrated word: ' *There is no longer the Pyrenees.*' "

They talked much of the new singer at all the reunions; but they were ignorant, above all, of a significant fact which passed with her on the same evening. Pepe Vera had not ceased to follow Marisalada. In his quality of a favorite with the public, it was not difficult for him to cross the threshold of the temple consecrated to the muses, despite the animosity they had sworn to the bull-fights. Maria left the stage amid a torrent of applause, when she met Pepe Vera and some other young men face to face.

"How blessed is she !" said the celebrated bull-fighter, spreading his mantle as a carpet for the *artiste ;* "how blessed is this voice, capable to make all the nightingales of May to die with envy!"

" What blessed eyes!" added another, " which wound more Christians than all the poniards of Albacete."

The Gaviota passed on, as always, impassible and disdainful.

" She does not even deign to look at us," said Pepe Vera. " Listen then, my beautiful: a king is a king, and yet he can look at a cat. See, caballeros, she is, nevertheless, a very beautiful girl, although—"

" Although what ?"

" Although she squints."

Marisalada, on hearing these words, could not repress an involuntary movement. She fixed on the group her large, astonished eyes. The young men set up a loud laugh, and Pepe Vera sent her a kiss at the ends of his fingers.

Marisalada understood at once that this word *squint* was addressed to her merely to make her turn her head : she could not resist smiling, and then went on her way, having let her handkerchief drop. Pepe picked it up, and approached her as if to hand it to her.

" I will deliver it to you to-night, at the grating of your window," he said to her hurriedly, in a low voice.

At midnight Mariquita left her bed with precaution, after being convinced that her husband slept profoundly. Stein indeed slept, a smile on his lips, intoxicated with the praises lavished that evening on his wife—his scholar, the beloved of his heart. During this sweet sleep a blackness had rested against one of the gratings of the window. It was impossible to distinguish any feature, for an officious hand had previously extinguished all the lights on the street.

Seville had become already a theatre too confined for the ambition and the thirst for ovations which devoured the heart of Marisalada. Besides, the duke, obliged to return to the capital, desired himself to present this phenomenon, whose reputation had preceded her to Madrid. Pepe Vera, on the other hand, engaged to appear at the *Corrida* in Madrid, urged Maria to make the journey: she made it. The triumph which she obtained at her *début* on this new stage, surpassed what she had achieved in Seville. The happy times of Orpheus and Amphion, the wonders of the mythological times, seemed to be brought back again. Stein was confused, the duke was in a state of complete intoxication. Pepe Vera said one day to the *cantora*: "*Caramba!* (hah!) Mariquita, they applaud you neither more nor less than if you had killed a bull seven years old."

Marisalada was surrounded with a numerous court, at which strangers of distinction, present in Madrid, made part. Among them were those of high rank, either from personal merit or from birth. What were the powerful motives which moved them? Some visited the singer to give her a *ton*, according to modern custom. And what is this *ton?* It is a servile imitation of what others do. Some were guided by the same sentiment which prompts children to examine closely the secret springs of a plaything which amuses them.

Marisalada required to make no effort to feel at ease in the midst of this brilliant circle. She had in nothing reformed her cold and haughty indolence; but her person was more elegant, a better taste presided at her toilet;—material conquests, all exterior, which, in the eyes of certain persons, could supply the want of intelligence, tact, and distinction. At evening, on the stage, when the reflection of the lights rendered her paleness more transparent, and her large black eyes more brilliant, the Gaviota was really beautiful.

The duke was so fascinated with this woman, whose triumphs touched him some little, for they had confirmed his prophecies; and such was also the enthusiasm which her singing excited in him, that he thought it not improper to beg her to give lessons to his daughter. Notwithstanding he remembered very well the prediction of his amiable friend in Seville, and he trembled in thinking over the delay fixed by the lovely countess.

Then he formed the decision to respect the innocent woman, whom he had himself led into the brilliant and dangerous career she was now embarked in, and he thought of the duchess. The duchess was a virtuous and beautiful woman. Although she had passed her thirtieth year, the freshness of her complexion and the candid expression of her face made her appear much younger. She belonged to a family as illustrious as that of her husband. Leonore and Carlos had loved each other almost from their infancy, with that truly Spanish affection, affection profound, constant, which never leaves the heart, which never grows cold. They were married very young, and at eighteen years of age Leonore gave a daughter to her husband, who was himself then just twenty-two years of age.

The family of the duchess, like many families among the great, was entirely devotional; Leonore had been educated in the same spirit. Her modesty and her austerity kept her away from the pleasures and the noise of the world, for which, indeed, she felt no desire. She read little, and her hand never opened a novel. She was quite ignorant of the dramatic effects of the grand passions; she had never learned, neither at the theatre, nor from looks, the interest inspired by adultery, which she regarded as a crime as abominable as homicidal. She could never be made to believe, as had been told her, that there was adopted in the world a standard under which to proclaim the emancipation of women. Never could she comprehend this pretension; no more than she could comprehend much of other women who, nevertheless, did not live so retired, and did not adopt a reserve so strict as the duchess. If she had heard said that there are apologists for divorce and for detractors of marriage, she would believe she dreamt; she would think the end of the world had come. Loving and devoted as a daughter, generous and sure friend, tender and devoted mother, a wife consecrated to her husband even to blindness, the Duchess of Almansas was the type of the woman whom God loves, of whom poets sing, society admires and venerates, and who should take the place of those *amazons* who possess nothing of the exquisite delicacy of woman.

The duke submitted himself for a long time to the attractive influence Marisalada exercised over him, without the slightest cloud arising to trouble that peace, calm and pure as heaven, which reigned in the heart of his wife. He, however, until then so affectionate, neglected the duchess each day more and more. The duchess wept, but she was silent. Later she learned that this *Cantora*, who upset all Madrid, was protected by her husband, who passed his life in the house of this woman. The duchess shed fresh tears, and still doubted. One day the duke conducted Stein to his house, to give lessons to his young son; and soon he wished, as we have said, that Marisalada should also give lessons to his daughter, a beautiful creature, eleven years of age. Leonore energetically opposed this last wish of the duke, alleging that she could not permit a woman of the

theatre the least contact with her child. The duke,
accustomed to the easy compliances of his wife, saw in
this opposition a doctrinal scruple, a want of the habits
of the world, and he persisted in his idea. The duchess
yielded, in obedience to her confessor : a double motive, which, if comprehended, would cause bitter
tears.

She received, then, Marisalada with excessive circum-
spection, extreme reserve, cold politeness. Leonore, who,
according to her tastes, lived very retired, received but
few visits, and these chiefly those of her relations. Her
other visitors were priests, and some few persons in whom
she had full confidence. She followed the lessons of her
daughter with a perseverance which never tired, and she
devoted so much care as not to separate her child from
her maternal regards : so the system of surveillance could
not give offence to the susceptibility of Marisalada. The
duchess's visitors had but a cold salute for the mistress
of song, and never addressed a word to her. All this
rendered very humiliating, in this noble and austere
house, the position of this woman whom the public of
Madrid adored. The Gaviota felt it, and her pride daily
became indignant : but how to complain ? The duchess
always practised an exquisite politeness; never a smile
of disdain had passed over the serenity of her calm and
beautiful countenance ; her eye had never shown a
haughty look. On the other hand, the duke, so full of
dignity and of delicacy, would he have permitted a complaint against his wife ? Marisalada was endowed with
sufficient penetration and taste to know that silence was
necessary on her part, and that she could lose neither
the friendship of the duke, which flattered her ; nor his
protection, which was indispensable ; nor his presents,
which enchanted her. She must bear her trials until a

proper occasion should present itself to put an end to this painful position.

One day when, all decked out in silk and velvets, resplendent with bijoux and diamonds, enveloped in a rich mantle of lace, she entered the duchess's drawing-room, she met there her grace's father, the Marquis of Elda, and the bishop of ——. The marquis was an old and austere man, one of the partisans of the olden time, a Catholic Spaniard and pure royalist. He lived near the court since the death of the king, whom he had faithfully served since the war of independence.

There was a great deal of coldness in the relations of the marquis with his kindred, whom he reproached with conceding too much to the ideas of the present times. This coldness increased when this virtuous and severe old man heard the public rumors which accused the duke of being the protector of a singer of the theatre.

When Maria entered the drawing-room, the duchess rose with the intention of thanking her, and giving her *congé* for this day; but the bishop, ignorant of what was passing, manifested the desire to hear his little grand-daughter sing. The duchess resumed her seat, saluted Marisalada with her accustomed politeness, and called her child, who came immediately at the request of her mother. She had hardly executed the three measures of the prayer of Desdemona when there were heard three taps on the door.

"Quick, quick," said the duchess, showing by her earnestness that she knew the person by this manner of knocking; and with a vivacity which Marisalada had never given her credit for, she rose to get away before the visitor could enter.

Maria was more astonished at the sight of the new personage. She was an ugly woman, at least fifty years

old, and of common aspect. Her clothes were as coarse
as strange. The duchess received her with the greatest
mark of consideration and cordiality, the more remarkable when contrasted with the icy reserve which she
always observed towards the mistress of song. The
duchess took the old woman by the hand, and presented
her to the bishop. Marisalada knew not what to think.
She had never seen such a costume, never had she met
a person in a position less in harmony with the people of
distinction where she was received.

After a quarter of an hour's animated conversation the
old woman rose. It rained. The marquis insisted that
she accept his carriage; but the marchioness said to
him—

"My father, I will order mine."

So saying, she approached the new arrival, who
took leave, and obstinately refused to use a carriage.

"Come, my child," said the duchess to her daughter,
"come, with the permission of your mistress, and salute
the good friend."

Maria could not believe what she saw and heard. The
child embraced her whom her mother had called her
good friend.

"Who is this woman?" Marisalada asked of the child
when she came to her.

"She is a sister of charity," replied the child.

Marisalada was annihilated. Her pride, which rose
in array against all superiority which defied the dignity
of the nobility, the rivalry of artists, the power of authority, and even all the prerogatives of genius, to bend
before the grandeur and elevation of virtue!

She rose to retire. It still rained.

"You have a carriage at your disposal," said the
duchess, saluting her.

Marisalada, on arriving in the court, remarked that they had taken away the horses from the duchess's carriage. A lackey respectfully let down the steps of a hired hack, and Maria was driven off, swelling with rage. Next day she declared to the duke that she had ceased giving lessons to the young duchess. She took great care to hide the true motive for this decision. The duke, as blind by his enthusiasm for Maria as by the dangerous means he had adopted to make her celebrated, supposed that his wife was the cause of this resolution, and he appeared before her colder than ever.

CHAPTER XXIII.

THE arrival in Madrid of the celebrated singer Tenorini raised the glory of Maria to its height, not only
because of the admiration this colossal lyric displayed,
but because of the earnestness she showed in wishing to_
unite her voice to a voice so worthy of hers. Tononi
Tenorini—*alias* the great—came from nobody knew
where. Some affirmed that, like Castor and Pollux, she
was couched in an egg—not the egg of a swan, but the
egg of a nightingale. Her splendid and brilliant career
commenced at Naples, where she had eclipsed Vesuvius.
Then she passed to Milan, to Florence, St. Petersburg,
and Constantinople. She had now arrived from New
York, passing through Havana, with the purpose of
appearing in Paris, where the inhabitants, furious in not
having yet consecrated this gigantic reputation, had
gotten up a resolution to assuage their anger. From
thence Tenorini designed to go to London, where the dilet-
tanti were dying of longing and of spleen, and where the
season promised to be dull, if that celebrated notability
and *artiste* should not take pity on them.

Strange thing, and which surprised all the *Polos* and
all the *Eloisitas*, this sublime *artiste* did not arrive in
Madrid borne on the wings of genii. The dolphins of
the ocean were too badly educated and too little melo-
dramatic to carry her on their back, as they had before
done for Amphyon, in happier times, those of the Medi-
terranean. Tenorini came by the *diligence.* Horror!
And that which was more horrible still, she brought a

carpet-bag with her. They formed a plan to celebrate her arrival by ringing all the bells at the same moment, to illuminate the houses, and to raise an arch of triumph for her, with music from all the instruments of the circus orchestra. The alcalde would consent to nothing of the kind.

While Marisalada shared with the grand singer the unbridled ovation of a discerning public, who fell on their knees in all humility, a scene of a character altogether different passed in the poor cabin which she had quitted scarcely a year ago.

Pedro Santalo was dying on his pallet. Since the departure of his daughter he had not raised his head. He kept his eyes constantly closed, and opened them only to look at the chamber of Mariquita, which was separated from his by a narrow passage which led to the garret. Every thing remained in the state his daughter had left it : the guitar was hung on the wall, by a ribbon once rose-colored, and which now hung without form like a forgotten promise, and faded like a recollection extinguished. A handkerchief of India was thrown on the bed, and there could yet be seen on the chair a pair of her little shoes. Old Maria was seated at the bedside of the invalid.

"Come! come! Pedro," said the good old woman, "forget that you are a Catalan, and be not so stubborn. Let yourself be governed for once in your life, and come to the convent. You know you will want for nothing there. There at least you can be better cared for, and you will not be abandoned in a corner like an old broom."

The fisherman made no reply.

"Pedro, Don Modesto has already written two letters, and has sent them by the post. They say it is the most sure and prompt way to insure their arrival."

"She will not come!" murmured the invalid.

"But her husband will come; and, for the moment, that is of the greater importance."

"She! she!" cried the poor father.

An hour after this conversation Maria set off for the convent, without having been able to decide the obstinate Catalan to let her conduct him to her home. The old woman rode upon Golondrina, the peaceful Dean or the chapter of asses of the country.

Momo, now become a man, without having lost any of his native ugliness, conducted the ass.

"Listen, grandma," said he; "these visits to the old sea-wolf, will they continue for a long time yet? These daily walks fatigue me."

"Certainly they will still continue, since Pedro will not come to the convent. I fear for the death of this brave man if he does not see his daughter."

"I will never die of that disease," said Momo, with a sardonic laugh.

"Listen, my son," pursued the old woman; "I have not much confidence in the post, although they say it is sure. Don Modesto has not much faith in it either. Then, that Don Frederico and Marisalada learn of the danger Pedro is now in, there is but one means to employ, and that is that you go to Madrid, and tell them; for indeed we must not remain here with our arms folded, and see the father die calling on his daughter with all his soul, and do nothing to bring her to him."

"I go to Madrid, and to seek the Gaviota again!" exclaimed Momo horrified. "Are you in your right senses, grandmother?"

"I am so much in my sound senses, that if you will not go, I will go myself. I have been to Cadiz without losing myself, and without any thing happening to me; it will be the same if I go to Madrid. My heart breaks when I hear this poor father calling on his child. But you, Momo, you have a bad heart, I say so to you with pain. And I do not know truly from whence you get this wickedness; it is neither from your father nor from your mother; but so it is: in every family there is a Judas."

"The devil himself could not better torment a Christian to damn him," murmured Momo. "And that is not the worst; you get this extravagance into your head, you push it just to its end, and as the only good result, I will be deprived of my arms and legs for an entire month."

And Momo, to vent his anger, struck a heavy blow with his stick on the side of the poor Golondrina.

"Barbarian!" cried his grandmother, "why do you beat the poor animal?"

"Animals are made to be beaten," replied Momo.

"Who has preached to you such a heresy?"

"Your misfortune, grandma, is, that you resemble the celestial vault, you protect everybody."

"Yes, son, yes. And may it please God that I never witness a grief without sympathizing with it—that I may never be one of those people who listen to a complaint as if they were listening to the dropping of rain!" ..

"That which you tell me applies only to our neighbor, grandmother; but the animals, the devil!"

"The animals, and do they not suffer? Are they not creatures of the good God? Here below we suffer the punishment due to the sin of the first man. The Adam and Eve of asses, what sin have they committed?"

"They have, at least, *eaten the parings of the apple*,"

10*

said Momo, with a laugh which sounded like a detonation.

They then met Manuel and José, who returned with them to the convent.

"Mother," asked Manuel, "how is Pedro?"

"Ill, my son, ill. My heart bleeds to see him so low, so sad, and so lonely. I asked him to come to the convent, but it would be easier to remove the fort of San Cristobal than this obstinate man. A twenty-four-pounder would not move him. Brother Gabriel must go, and stay with him, and Momo go to Madrid and bring here Don Frederico and the daughter of this poor father."

"Let Momo go," said Manuel; "he will thus see the world."

"I!" cried Momo anew; "how can I go to Madrid?"

"In putting one foot before the other," answered his father. "Are you afraid of being lost? or do you fear being eaten up on the way?"

"It is this, that I have no desire to go," replied Momo exasperated.

"Well! I have here a branch of olive which will give you that desire, scapegrace."

Momo was quiet, inwardly cursing old Pedro and his family. He commenced his journey in the company of the muleteers of the mountain of Aracena, who came to lay in a stock of fish at Villamar. He arrived at Valverde, and from there passed by Aracena, Oliva, and Barcarota to Badajoz, where he took the diligence for Madrid from Seville, and arrived at Madrid without stopping.

Don Modesto had written in big letters the address of Stein, which he had sent when he arrived in Madrid with the duke. Momo commenced to walk through the city with this paper in his hand, reciting for the benefit of the Gaviota a litany of imprecations always new.

We will leave him in search of his enemy, and come back to Villamar.

It was afternoon ; old Maria, more grieved than ever, came from visiting Santalo.

"Dolores," said she to her daughter-in-law, "Pedro is going. This morning he rolled up his sheet ; that is to say, he made up his parcel for the journey from which he will never return, and our dog Palomo has *howled the death*. And yet these people do not arrive! I am on hot coals. Momo ought already to be returned. He has been ten days gone."

"The road is long to measure from here to Madrid, mother," replied Dolores. "Manuel assures me that Momo cannot be here before four or five days yet."

What was the astonishment of the two women when they saw, all of a sudden, the frightened face of Momo himself, Momo dismayed, fatigued, and harassed.

"Momo!" both cried out at the same moment.

"Himself, in body and soul," replied Momo.

"And Marisalada?" asked the old woman with anxiety.

"And Don Frederico?" asked Dolores.

"You may wait for them until the Last Judgment," said Momo. "Thanks to you, grandmother, I can boast of having made a famous journey."

"What is it? what has happened?" asked at the same time both grandmother and mother.

"That which you will soon hear, so that you will admire the judgments of God, and who blesses you, inasmuch as He has permitted me to return safe and sound, thanks to the excellent legs he has given me."

The old Maria and Dolores remained silent on hearing these words, symptoms of grave events.

"Speak, for the love of heaven ; what has happened ?"

cried again both the women. "Do you not see that our souls are drawn out to a thread?"

"When I arrived in Madrid," commenced Momo, "when I saw myself alone in the midst of this world, I was seized with vertigo. Each street appeared to me a soldier, every place a patrol. I entered into a public house with the paper of the commandant, and which was a paper that spoke. There I encountered a species of drunkard, who conducted me to the house indicated on the paper. The servants told me that their master and mistress were absent, and they were about to shut the door in my face; but they knew not, these imbeciles, whom they were dealing with. 'Ha!' said I to them, 'pay attention to whom you are speaking, if you please. Do you know that it was at our house we rescued Don Frederico when he was dying, and that without us he would have been altogether dead?'"

"You said that, Momo!" exclaimed the grandmother, "one never speaks of these things. What mortification! what will they think of us? Remind one of a favor! who has ever seen the like?"

"Well! what? I ought not to have said it? Let's see then! I spoke much stronger: I said it was my grandmother who had brought their mistress to our house when she was ill, running and crying herself hoarse on the rocks like a gull as she was. These profligates looked at each other, and mocked me; they told me I was mistaken, that their mistress was the daughter of a general of the army of Don Carlos. Daughter of a general! do you understand? Is there in the world a lie more shameful? to say that the good old Pedro is a general! old Pedro, who has never served the king! At last I told them that my commission was very pressing, and that what I wished was, to depart immediately, and lose sight of them, their masters, and Madrid. ' Nicholas,' then said a girl, who seemed to wish to be as shameless as her mistress, ' conduct this peasant to the theatre, he may see the señora there.' Remark well that she spoke of me, this viper's tongue, as a *peasant;* and that she said *señora*, in speaking of this bad Gaviota. Can you believe that? It is what can only be seen in Madrid! It is confounding. Then the servant took his hat, and conducted me to a grand building, high, and constructed like a species of church. In lieu of tapers and candles, one only sees lamps which light up like suns. This large room was furnished all around with seats, upon which I have seen more than a thousand women seated all in *fête* dresses, stiff as sticks, and ranged like vials on an apothecary's shelves. The men were so numerous that one might believe he saw an ant-hill. Jesus! from whence can so many Christians have come! 'That is nothing,' said I to myself, ' it is the quantity of bread they must consume in this city of Madrid!' But prepare yourself for the saddest. All this world was there—why? to hear the Gaviota sing!"

" I see nothing in all this to oblige you to come back so promptly and so amazed," said the grandmother.

" Wait! wait! I cannot go faster than the music. I relate things as they happened. Then listen well to this. Then suddenly, without anybody giving command, more than a thousand instruments commenced playing at once. There were flutes, trumpets, and violins big as *Golon-drina*. What an uproar! It was enough to assemble together all the blind in Spain. There is something more wonderful still : without knowing how or why, a kind of garden which was in front of us disappeared suddenly ; and, the devil mixing in it without doubt, replaced the garden by the stairs of a palace covered with a magnificent carpet. Then I saw a woman admirably dressed; she was covered with more velvet, silk, gold, and jewels than the Virgin of Rosaire. 'It is Isabella the Second,' said I to myself. No, my people, it was not the queen. Do you know who it was? Neither more nor less than the Gaviota, the wicked Gaviota, who went about among us with naked legs and feet. Yes, the devil had thus taken her, and made her a princess. I was stunned, when, at a moment when no one thought of it, a gentleman, very well dressed, came forward. He was in a frightful rage! What fury! He rolled his eyes! ' *Caramba!*' thought I, 'I would not be in this Gaviota's skin.' That which astonished me the most was that both recited their anger in *singing*. 'Good!' said I, 'it is perhaps the usage among people of high rank.' Nevertheless, I did not understand a word of what they were saying. All that I could discover was, that the gentleman was a general of Don Carlos, that the Gaviota said he was her father, and that he would not recognize her as his daughter, although she supplicated him on her knees. 'That's well done!' I cried at this impudence."

"Why did you mix yourself up with it?" asked the old woman.

"Because that I knew her, and that I could prove it. Do you not know that he who is silent approves? But it appears that where I was it is forbidden to speak the truth, because my neighbor, an *employé* of the police, said to me, ' Will you hold your tongue, my friend!' 'I have no desire to do so,' I replied, and I made my cry ring to the roof, 'This man is not her father.' 'Are you mad, or do you come from another world?' said the policeman to me. 'I am not the one, nor do I come from the other, insolent,' I replied. 'I know better than you, and I come from Villamar, where her legitimate father resides, her true father, the old Pedro Santalo.' 'You are an imbecile,' replied the policeman. I kicked, and was about to inflict on him a blow, when Nicholas caught my arm in time, and led me away to take a drink. 'I have understood it all,' I said to Nicholas; 'this general is he whom~this cursed Gaviota wishes to have for her father. I have heard talk of many villanous things, of murders, thefts, piracies, but I have never yet heard spoken of one who would deny her father.' Nicholas held his sides in laughing: at Madrid such indignities affright no one. When we re-entered, it is believed that the general had ordered the Gaviota to take off that beautiful attire, for she was entirely dressed in white, and appeared overwhelmed with sadness. She began to sing, and accompanied herself on an immense guitar which she had placed immediately before her on the floor, and which she pinched with her two hands. (Of what is she not capable, this Gaviota?) But here comes the interesting part. Suddenly there appeared a Moor."

" A Moor ?"

" But what a Moor! blacker and more cruel than Mohammed himself. He held in his hand a poniard, large as a sabre."

" Jesus, Maria!" cried Maria and Dolores.

"I demanded of Nicholas who was this proud Moor, and he told me that he is called *Telo*. To make a finish of my story, the Moor said to the Gaviota that he was about to kill her."

" Holy Virgin!" exclaimed the old woman, " it was the public executioner !"

" I do not know if it was the executioner or a paid assassin," replied Momo; " but of this I am sure, that he seized her by her hair, and stabbed her several times with the poniard. I saw it with my own eyes, those eyes which will one day be in the land of death, and I can affirm it."

Momo placed his two fingers on his two eyes with such rigorous force, that it seemed as if they would start from their sockets.

The two good women raised a frightful cry. Old Maria sobbed and rung her hands with grief.

"But what did the spectators do?" asked Dolores, shedding abundance of tears; "was there no one to arrest this scoundrel?"

"That is what I do not know," answered Momo. "For on seeing this, I took to my legs, and in the fear that they would call upon me to depose, I did not cease running until I had put some leagues between the city of Madrid and the son of my father."

"We must," said the poor old Maria, amidst her sobs, "conceal this misfortune from Pedro. What griefs! what griefs!"

"And who could have courage enough to tell him?" replied Dolores. "Poor Marisalada! she was well, and would be better. See what has happened to her!"

"Each one gets what they merit," said Momo. "This bad daughter should end badly—it could not be otherwise. If I were not so fatigued, I would go on the instant, and relate it all to Ramon Perez."

CHAPTER XXIV.

The news spread quickly through the village that the daughter of the fisherman had been assassinated. Thus this egotist, this rustic, this stupid Momo, thanks to his evil spirit, and his bad instincts, took what he saw at the theatre for reality, and he not only made a useless journey, because he had not accomplished his mission, but his folly led all the good people into an error.

The face of Don Modesto lengthened amazingly. The cura said a mass for the soul of Marisalada. Ramon Perez put a black ribbon on his guitar.

Rosa Mistica said to Don Modesto—

"God pardon her! I predicted that she would end badly. Do you remember that the more pains I took to make her go the right way, the more obstinate she was in going the wrong?"

Old Maria, calculating that this catastrophe prevented the arrival of Don Frederico, decided to confide the cure of Pedro to a young physician who had taken the place of Stein at Villamar.

"I do not know much of his science," she said to Don Modesto, who recommended this Esculapius to her; "he knows only how to order medicinal drinks, and there is nothing which more weakens the stomach. For nourishment he prescribes chicken broth. Will you tell me what strength such a beverage can give? All is topsyturvy, my commandant. But all this will come right in the future, and experience will always be experience."

The doctor found Pedro very ill; he declared he was anxious to prepare for his death.

Maria could not hear this news without weeping bitterly; she called Manuel, and charged him with the painful mission to announce his approaching death to Pedro, with every possible precaution.

"Believe me," she said, "I would never have the courage to do it."

Manuel set off to visit the patient.

"Hallo! Pedro," he said to him, "how are you?"

"I am sinking, Manuel," replied the invalid: "if you have any commands for the other world, tell me immediately: I am about to weigh anchor, my son."

"Come! Pedro, this is not so. You will live longer than I; and, as the proverb says—"

"Do not finish, Manuel," replied Pedro without moving. "Say to your mother that I am ready. It is now a long time since I have felt my last moment approaching. I think only of that—and of *her!*" he added, in a broken voice.

Manuel went away with his eyes filled with tears, although he had seen, during his military life, much bloodshed, and painful agonies.

The following day there was one of those terrible storms which the equinox usually brings. The wind whistled in every variety of tone. One could believe he heard the seven heads of the hydra breathing all at once. It beat against the cabin, which seemed to complain and moan. The invisible element sent its doleful sounds through the resounding vaults of the ruins of the fort; it struck furiously across the forest, became softer in the orchards, and vanished in a long murmur in the deserted plain, as gradually disappears the shadow of a landscape on the horizon.

The sea dashed its waves angrily, as fury agitates serpents among the leaves. The clouds piled themselves up without pause, and their black flanks opened to emit their torrents on the earth. All was shivering, all trembling, all complaining. The sun had fled, and the color of day was dark as the pall of death.

Although the cabin was protected by the rock, the tempest had swept away a part of the roof during the night. To prevent its complete destruction, Manuel, aided by Momo, had stayed it with some wood and some stones of the ruins.

"You do not wish to shelter your host?" said Manuel. "Wait at least for it to fall down, and then there will be no more need of you."

If any other look than that of God could through the tempest penetrate the desert, he would have seen some men following along the margin of the sea, braving the fury of the storm, enveloped in their mantles, wrapt and silent, their bodies bent towards the earth, and their heads bowed down. He would have seen an old man, grave, and wrapt in meditation, like those who followed him, his arms crossed on his breast, in the manner of Orientals, and preceded by a child ringing a bell. There could be heard at intervals, despite the roaring of the tempest, the tranquil and sonorous voice of this old man, saying, " *De profundis clamavi ad te, Domine,*" and of the men who responded, " *Domine, exaudi vocem meum.*"

The rain fell in torrents, the wind blew furiously, and the men continued their onward, impassible march, their step at once grave and slow.

They were the cura and some pious parishioners, who, conducted by Manuel, went to carry to the dying fisherman the last consolations of a Christian.

The priest approached the invalid, whose poor dwelling had been metamorphosed, thanks to the attentions of old Maria and of brother Gabriel. They had placed on the table a crucifix, surrounded with lights and flowers.

"Light and perfume," said the good old woman, "are the exterior homage which we ought to offer to the Lord."

After the ceremony, the priest, Maria, and brother Gabriel alone remained near the dying man. Pedro was calm. After a few moments he opened his eyes—

"Is she not come?" he asked.

"My good Pedro," replied Maria, while streams of tears prevented her from seeing the invalid, "it is far from this to Madrid. She wrote she would set out, and we will see her arrive very soon."

Santalo again fell into a lethargy. An hour passed, and then he came to himself. He fixed his look for a long time on Maria, and said to her—

"Maria, I have implored of my Divine Saviour that he will deign to come and visit me; that he will pardon me, that he will make you happy, and recompense you for all you have done for us."

Then he swooned. He again revived, opened his eyes, in which already one could read death, and he murmured—

"She has not come!"

His head fell on the pillow, and he exclaimed—

"Pity, Lord!"

"Let us repeat the *Credo*," said the priest, taking in his hands those of the dying man, and approaching his mouth to his ears, to make him understand the last words of faith, hope, and charity. A majestic and imposing silence reigned in this humble retreat, which death had come to penetrate.

Without, the tempest raged in all its terrible power; within, all was peace and repose: because God takes from death all its fears, and all its horror, when the soul springs to heaven at the cry of pity!

CHAPTER XXV.

The world is composed of contrasts: nothing is more true than this eternal verity.

It was thus that, when the poor fisherman presented to his humble and pious friends the sublime spectacle of the death of a believer, his daughter rendered the public of Madrid enthusiastic even to frenzy. *A prima donna* without a drop of Italian blood in her veins, eclipsed the grand Tenorini herself. The impression produced by the singer was so great, so general, that the *employés* deserted their offices, and the students the benches of their classes.

This enthusiasm manifested itself one evening at the door of the theatre, in a group of young men, who sought to make two strangers, recently landed, share their admiration. They commented, they analyzed the quality of the voice, the suppleness of her throat, the superiority of her method of the *Diva*, without forgetting to eulogize her physical advantages. A young man, covered up to his eyes in a cloak, remained immovable and silent some paces from this group; but when they boasted of the physical advantages of the singer, he stamped his foot with anger.

"I will bet a hundred guineas, dear viscount," said our friend Sir John Burnwood, who, not having obtained authority to carry off Alcazar, proposed to himself to ask leave to take Escurial—"I will bet that this woman will make more noise in France than Madame Lafarge; and in England, more than Tom Thumb; and in Italy, than Rossini."

" I do not doubt it," replied the viscount.

" What magnificent black eyes!" added a new admirer.

" What an elegant and subtle form! As to her feet, one does not see them, and we can only guess: the Magdalen would envy her her hair."

" I am impatient to hear this wonder," said the viscount; " let us enter, gentlemen."

The mysterious young man had disappeared.

Maria, in the costume of Semiramis, came on the stage. The man in the mantle, who was no other than Pepe Vera, entered at this moment, approached the actress, and without any person hearing him, said to her—

" I do not wish you to sing."

And he went on his way, cold and indifferent.

Maria at first turned pale, then the blush of indignation mounted to her face.

" Come!" said she to her waiting-woman; " Marina, arrange the folds of this mantle. We are about to commence." And she added in a loud voice, so that Pepe, who was far off, heard her, " We do not play for the public."

The boy of the theatre came to her, and said—

"Señora, shall we raise the curtain ?"

" I am ready."

But she had scarcely pronounced these words when she uttered a sharp cry.

Pepe Vera had come and placed himself behind her; he laid hold of her arm violently, and said to her a second time—

" I do not wish you to sing."

Vanquished by her grief, Maria seated herself on a chair, and wept.

Pepe had disappeared.

"What is it? what has happened?" asked those who were present.

"I feel ill," answered Maria, who continued to weep.

"What is the matter, señora?" asked the director, who had been informed of what had occurred.

"It is nothing," said Maria, rising, and drying her tears. "It is already passed. I am ready. Come!"

Pepe Vera, pale as a corpse, then came and interposed between the director and the artist.

"This is cruelty," said he, with an imperturbable calmness, "to force on to the stage a woman who can hardly support herself.

"What!" cried the director; "are you ill, señora? Since when? it is but a moment since I saw you very joyous!"

Maria was about to reply, but she dropped her eyes, and could not open her lips. Pepe's look fascinated her.

"Why not avow the truth?" he said, without losing any of his calmness. "Why not say it is impossible for you to sing? would it be a great crime? Are you a slave, that they can oblige you to do more than you can?"

The public was impatient, the director knew not what to do. The authorities sent to demand the cause of the delay, and while the director recounted the incident which had occurred, Pepe Vera, who had approached Maria as if to offer his attentions, seized her arm as if he would break it, and said to her in a firm voice—

"Caramba! is it not enough to tell you I do not wish it?"

Maria must decide. When she was in her room with Pepe her anger broke out.

"You are an insolent, an infamous fellow," she cried,

suffocated with fury. " What right have you to treat
me thus?"

" I love you."

" Cursed be your love!"

Pepe began to laugh.

" You curse my love, and you cannot live without it.
We will see! we will see! I will never again appear
before you until you summon me."

" I would sooner call a demon."

" You may call him, I am not jealous."

"Go then! quit me."

" Be it so," said the *toreador*. "I depart, and go to
Lucia del Salto."

Marisalada was very jealous of this woman, a dancer,
whom Pepe had courted before he knew Maria.

" Pepe! Pepe!" screamed Maria, "traitor! add per-
fidy to insolence."

" That," said Pepe, without moving, "that will not
make me do but what I choose. You are too grand a lady
for me. If then you wish that we get along well together,
it must be that every thing is done as I wish. I will
command, and you obey. You have enough of dukes,
ambassadors, and serene excellencies at your feet."

So saying, he made some steps towards the door.

"Pepe! Pepe!" called Maria, tearing in pieces a
mantle richly garnished with lace.

" Call sooner the demon."

" Pepe! remember this well: if you ever go near
Lucia I will accept the love of the duke."

" You dare do that?" said Pepe, starting with a gesture of menace.

" I dare every thing, for revenge."

Pepe placed himself in front of the Gaviota, his arms
crossed, and darting on her the most terrible looks.

Maria sustained them without flinching. These brief moments sufficed for these two characters to study and know each other.

They comprehended that both were powerful in pride and in energy. This combat could no longer continue ; it must be broken or suspended. With mutual and tacit accord each renounced the triumph.

"Come, Mariquita," said Pepe, who was the culpable one, " let us be friends. I will not go near Lucia, but in exchange, and to have confidence in each other, conceal me this evening at your house, in such a manner that I can convince myself that you do not deceive me."

"That cannot be," replied Maria haughtily.

"'Tis well. I go where I go in leaving you."

"Infamous! you put the knife to my throat," cried Maria, doubling her fists with fury. "Depart!"

An hour after this scene Maria was half reclining on the sofa, and her husband was feeling her pulse. The duke was seated near her.

"It is nothing, Maria," said Stein. "It is nothing, duke. A nervous attack, already dissipated. Her pulse is perfectly tranquil. You need only repose, Maria. Work is killing you. It is already some time that your nerves have been extraordinarily irritated. Your nervous system rebels against the zeal you devote to the study of your characters. I am in no way uneasy, and now I go to attend a patient, who is in a dangerous condition. Take the prescription which I will order for you, and some orgeat on retiring; and to-morrow when you rise some ass's milk. Duke, I leave you with regret, but duty obliges me : *à dios!*"

After the departure of Don Frederico, the duke gazed on Maria for a long time ; her face was altogether changed.

" Are you fatigued, Maria?" asked he, with that penetrating sweetness which love alone knows how to give
to the voice.

" I will repose myself," replied Maria coldly.

" Do you wish that I retire ?"

" If it so pleases you."

" That would pain me."

" Remain then."

" Maria," said the duke, after a short silence, taking
out of his pocket a paper, " when I cannot talk to you I
sing your praises ; here are some verses which I have
written for you; to-night, Maria, I will have agitating
dreams, without sleep. Sleep has fled from my eyelids
since peace fled from my heart. Pardon me, Maria,
if this avowal which escapes from my heart offends the
purity of your sentiments, but I have suffered from your
sufferings, and—"

" You see," said Maria, smiling, " that my sufferings
are already ended."

" Would you like, Maria, that I read these verses to
you ?"

" Be it so."

The duke read his sonnet in honor of the *Diva*.

" Your verses are very beautiful, duke," remarked
Maria with more than animation. " Will you have them
published in the *Heraldo ?*"

" Do you wish it ?"

" I think they merit it."

The duke at this reply let his head fall on his hands.
When he raised it again, he saw as it were a light pass
in the look which Maria fixed on the glass door of her
alcove. He turned his head to that side, but saw nothing.

He had, in his abstraction, rolled the paper on which
the verses were written, and which the singer had not

taken into her possession. She asked him if he intended
to make a cigarette of her sonnet.

"Then, at least," said the duke, "it would serve for
something."

"Give it to me; I will keep it."

The duke passed the roll of paper to her in a magnificent ring.

"What! the ring also, my lord duke?"

Maria placed the ring on her finger, and let fall the
paper on the carpet.

"Ah!" thought the duke, "there is no love in that
heart, there is no poetry in that soul, no blood in these
veins. And yet heaven is in her smile, hell in those
eyes, and her voice chants all the harmonies of earth and
heaven. Repose yourself, Maria," he said, rising; "leave
your soul in its happy quietude, and do not give entrance
to the importunate idea that others grow old and suffer
because of you."

The duke departed.

CHAPTER XXVI.

HARDLY had the duke closed the door of the saloon, when Pepe Vera came out of the alcove, laughing.

" Will you keep quiet ?" said Maria, occupied in lighting the fire with the precious production of the duke.

" No, my dear, I cannot; I would stifle if I did not laugh. I am no longer jealous, my Mariquita, no more than the sultan in his seraglio. Poor woman! if you had not me to love you ardently, what could you do with a husband, who proves to you his love by his prescriptions—with a bashful lover, who courts you in reciting to you his verses? Now that one of them has gone to *dream without sleeping*, and the other *wishes to sleep*, we will go, you and I, and sup with the gay companions who wait for us."

" No, Pepe, I am not well. The disorder you have caused me, the cold I felt on leaving the theatre, has injured me. I am chilly."

" You do the princess! Come with me, a good supper will cure you sooner than ass's milk. Come, let us go."

" I will not go out. We have one of those north winds, which, while it would not extinguish a candle, kills a man."

" It is well! if it pleases you, so let it be. Since you wish to pamper yourself, pamper thyself, and—good-evening !"

" How! you are going to supper? You leave me? You leave me alone, and ill, as you see, and ill because of your fault !"

"Well! what? Do you wish I put myself on diet? No, no, my beauty. They are waiting for me, and I go; you lose some hours of pleasure."

Maria seemed to regain courage. She rose, went out, and slammed the door with anger. Pepe Vera laughed. An instant after she came back, dressed all in black, her face hidden under a thick mantle, and enveloped in a large shawl. Thus disguised she went out with Pepe Vera.

On entering his house, well advanced in the night, Stein received from his servant a billet, which he read as soon as he was in his chamber. It ran thus—

"Señor Doctor,

"Do not believe that this is an anonymous letter; I act frankly, and I tell you my name at the commencement—*Lucia del Salto*. It seems to me it is a name sufficiently known.

"Husband of the Santalo, one must be as simple as you are, not to have perceived that your wife is the mistress of Pepe Vera, who was my lover; I may say so, because I am not married, and deceive no one. If you wish that the scales fall from your eyes, go to-night to No. 13 —— street, and there you will do as St. Thomas did."

"Can one be guilty of such an infamy?" cried Stein, letting the letter fall from his hands. "My poor Maria has those who are envious of her, and without any doubt they are the women of the theatre. Poor Maria! she is ill! and now perhaps she is sleeping in a sweet slumber. But let us see if she is calm. Last evening she was not well. Her pulse was agitated and her voice was hoarse. Affections of the chest are common now in Madrid. Let us see!"

Stein took a light, went out, and walked on tiptoe
through the rooms which led to his wife's apartment.
Arrived near to the chamber, he redoubled his precau-
tions; he softly approached the bed, drew aside the cur-
tains—the bed was empty!

A man as loyal, as confident as Stein, could not easily
convince himself of the possibility of such treason.

"No," said he, after some instants of reflection, "no,
it is impossible! Her absence at such an hour is from
some other cause, some unexpected circumstance. Still,
I cannot remain in the dark, with a doubt in my heart.
I must have the power to reply to that calumny, not
only with contempt, but with irrefutable proofs, with a
formal contradiction without reply."

He went out.

Thanks to the night watchmen, he arrived easily at the
place indicated in the letter.

The house designated had no porter. The street door
was open, and Stein entered. He climbed the first flight
of stairs, and, arriving at the first landing-place, he knew
no longer how to direct his steps, nor where to go.

Recovered from his first movement, he commenced to
feel ashamed of his action. "To spy," said he to himself, "is a base action. If Maria knew what I am doing,
she would be irritated, and she would be right to feel so.
O my God! suspect her whom I love, is it not to call
down the cloud which will obscure the heaven of our
love? I a spy! This has happened from the contemptible letter of a woman more contemptible still. Yes, I
will return home. To-morrow I will demand of Maria
what I desire to know. It is the way the most simple,
and the most natural. Come—no more suspicions, no
more doubts!"

Stein sighed so deeply that it seemed to suffocate him, and he wiped the sweat from his forehead.

"Oh, suspicion!" he cried—"suspicion, which makes the most confident heart believe treason to be possible. Infamous suspicion, the fruit of bad instincts and wicked insinuations! For a moment this monster had vanquished my soul, and now I dare no more look at Maria without being ashamed of myself."

Stein was at last about to depart when a door, which communicated with the landing-place where he was, opened. This door, when opened, let forth the sound of glasses clashing, joyous songs, and bursts of laughter.

A servant who came out from within, his hands full of empty bottles, moved to make room for Stein to pass, whose appearance and costume inspired him with a sort of respect.

"Enter," he said to him, "although you come late, and they have already supped;" and he descended without saying any thing more.

Stein found himself in a little antechamber which communicated with the adjoining room: he approached. Hardly had his look penetrated into the interior of this room than he stopped motionless, struck with stupor—Maria was there!

What must he have suffered when he saw his wife, with naked shoulders, seated at table on a stool, and having at her feet Pepe Vera, who sang, accompanying himself on the guitar—

"Una mujer andaluza
Tiene en sus ojos el sol :
Una aurora en su sonrisa,
Y el Paraiso en su amor."*

"Bravo! bravo! Pepe," cried the company. "Now

* See note 3.

it is Mariquita's turn to sing. Come, sing, Mariquita! We are not the gents of yellow gloves and varnished boots, but we have, as well as grand lords, ears to listen. Come, Mariquita, sing; sing, and so that your country-men can understand you. The gold-laced, embroidered, and decorated world knows only how to sing in French."

Mariquita took the guitar, which Pepe presented to her on his knees, and sang—

> " Mas quiere un jaleo pobre,
> Y unos pimientos asados,
> Que no tener un usia
> Desaborio á mi lado."*

This couplet was received by a storm of vivas, bravos, and applause, which made a concussion among the glasses.

Shame, more than indignation, caused Stein to blush.

"This Pepe was born with a *caul*," said one of his companions; " he has more happiness than he wants."

"I would not change my condition for an empire," said the *toreador*.

" But what will the husband say to all this ?" asked a *picador*, the oldest in the band.

"The husband !" replied Pepe, " I only know him to render him my duty. Pepe Vera associates only with valiant bull-fighters."

Stein had disappeared.

* See note 4.

11*

CHAPTER XXVII.

The day following these events, the duke was seated in his library, absorbed by his thoughts.

The door slowly opened, and near the window appeared the pretty ringleted head of a lovely child.

"Papa Carlos," he said, "are you alone? may I enter?"

"Since when, my angel, have you had need of permission to enter here?"

"Since you have ceased to love me so much," replied the lovely creature, seating himself on his father's knees. "Do you know, papa, I am very wise. I study well with Don Frederico, and I already speak German."

"Really!"

"I know already how to say, 'God bless my good father and my good mother:' I say, ' *Gott segne meinen guten Vater und meine liebe Mutter!*' Now kiss me. But," said he suddenly, "I forgot to tell you that Don Frederico wishes to speak to you."

"Don Frederico?" asked the duke in surprise.

"Yes, papa."

"Go, and ask him to come in, my son; his time is precious, and he must not lose it."

The duke folded the paper on which he had traced some lines, and Stein entered.

"My lord duke," he said, "I will no doubt astonish you: I come to take your orders, to thank you for all your goodness, and to announce to you my immediate departure."

r

"Your departure?" said the duke, overcome with astonishment.

"Yes, señor, to-day."

"And Maria?"

"She does not go with me."

"Come, Don Frederico, this must be a piece of fun; this cannot be."

"That which cannot be, duke, is that I remain an instant longer in Madrid."

"What motive?"

"Do not ask me, I cannot tell you."

"I cannot imagine even the motive of such folly."

"The motive must be very powerful to oblige me to adopt so extreme a course."

"But, Stein, my friend, once more, what is the motive?"

"It cannot be spoken. And the silence which I impose on myself is very painful to me, for I deprive myself of the only consolation that remains: to open my heart to a noble and generous man, who has held out to me his powerful hand, and has deigned to call me his friend."

"And where do you go?"

"To America."

"It is impossible, Stein; I tell you again, it is impossible." The duke rose in an agitated state. "There is nothing in the world," he continued, "that can oblige you to abandon your wife, to separate yourself from your friends, and to quit your patients, of whom I am one. You have then ambition? Are you then promised great advantages in America?"

Stein smiled bitterly.

"Advantages, my lord duke! Has not fortune disappointed all these hopes of your poor fellow-traveller?"

"You confound me, Stein. Is it a caprice—a sudden thought—an act of folly?"

Stein was silent.

"In any case, Don Frederico, it is ungrateful."

These bitter, and at the same time affectionate words, caused Stein the utmost emotion. He covered his face with both hands, and his long-repressed grief burst forth in sobs.

The duke approached him.

"Don Frederico," said he to him, "there is no indiscretion in confiding one's griefs to a friend. In the grave circumstances of life, every thing obliges those who suffer to receive the good counsel of those who are interested in their happiness. Speak to me, my friend, open your heart to me. You are too much agitated at this moment to act with coolness. Your reason is too much troubled to allow you to be directed wisely. Let us sit down. Listen to me: let me guide you in circumstances which appear to me grave, imperious, and receive my advice as I would receive yours under like circumstances."

Stein was vanquished. He took a seat near to the duke, and both remained for a long time silent. Stein broke through it at last.

"My lord duke," said he, "what would you do if the duchess preferred another man?—if she practised infidelity towards you?"

"Doctor! this question—"

"Answer me!" supplicated Stein, a prey to the most intense anxiety.

"By heaven! both should die by my hand."

Stein bowed his head.

"I," said he, "I will not kill them. *I* will die."

The duke began to suspect the truth, and an involuntary trembling shook his limbs.

"Maria?" cried he.

"Maria," said Stein, without raising his head, as if the infamy of his wife pressed on him with all its weight.

"You surprised them?" asked the duke, scarcely able to articulate these words, his voice was so stifled with indignation.

"In a veritable orgie, as gross as licentious : in an atmosphere of wine and tobacco, and where Pepe Vera, the matador, boasted of being her lover. O Maria! Maria!" he continued, letting his head fall on his hands.

The duke, like all energetic men, had great command over himself; he was immediately calm, and replied with but one word to Stein—

"Go!"

Stein rose, pressed in his hands those of the duke. He desired to speak, but his sobs prevented.

The duke opened his arms.

"Courage, Stein," he said to him, "and to a happier meeting."

"Good-by, and—forever," murmured Stein.

And he departed.

The duke, now quite alone, walked about for a long time. As he calmed down from the agitation which Stein's revelation had caused him, a smile of contempt played on his lips, for he was not one of those men who, possessed of those gross desires for which the misconduct of women, far from being a motive of repulsion, serve on the contrary to stimulate their brutal appetites. His character, full of elevation and nobleness, could not admit of love joined to contempt. The woman, whom he had sang in verse, who had fascinated him in his dreams, had become completely indifferent to him.

"And I," he said to himself, "I who adored her as one adores an ideal being which he has created; I who

honored her as virtue is honored, and who respected her
as one respects the wife of a friend! I, who blindly
absorbed by her, estranged myself from the noble woman
who was my first and my only love, the pure and chaste
mother of my children—my Leonore, who has so much
suffered, without ever a complaint escaping from her
lips!—"

By a sudden movement, yielding to the powerful
influence of these last reflections, the duke left his
library, and went to the apartment of his wife. On
arriving near the saloon where the duchess was accustomed to remain during the day, he heard his name
pronounced; he stopped.

"Then the duke has become invisible?" said a voice.
"It is now fifteen days since I arrived in Madrid, and my
dear nephew has not deigned to come and see me yet,
and I have seen him nowhere."

"My aunt," replied the duchess, "he is no doubt
ignorant of your arrival."

"Ignorant of the arrival in Madrid of the Marchioness
Gutibamba! It is impossible! He would be the only
person of the court who knew not of it. I will tell you,
besides, you have had time to inform him of it."

"That is true, my aunt, I am culpable for having forgotten it."

"But that is not astonishing," said the voice. "What
pleasure can he find in our society, and that of persons
of his rank, he who only frequents actresses?"

"It is false!" replied the duchess.

"Are you blind, or consenting?" said the marchioness
exasperated.

"What I would never consent to is this calumny,
which is at once an insult to my husband, here, in his
house, and to his wife."

"It would be wiser," continued the voice, angrily, "to prevent the duke, your husband, from giving credit by his conduct to the thousand scandals he has given birth to in Madrid, than to defend him, and driving away from your house your best friends with your ungracious answers—dictated, without doubt, by your confessor."

"My aunt, it will be also wiser to consult your own as to the language you ought to hold to a married woman, who is your niece."

"'Tis well," said the Gutibamba; "your reserved character, austere and gloomy, has already lost you the love and the heart of your husband: it will finish by your losing the affection of your friends."

And the Marchioness de Gutibamba departed, enchanted with her peroration.

Leonore remained seated on the sofa, her head bowed, and her face bathed in tears long suppressed.

Suddenly she uttered a cry—she was in the arms of her husband. She still wept, but these tears were sweet; she comprehended that this man, always frank and loyal, returned her love, a love which no one could henceforth dispute.

"My Leonore, can you, will you pardon me?" asked the duke on his knees before his wife, who put both her hands on the duke's mouth, and said to him—

"Would you disturb the happiness of the present in calling back the memories of the past?"

"I wish that you know my faults, which the world has judged too severely; I wish to justify myself and repent."

"And I, I wish to make a compact with you," interrupted the duchess; "never speak to me of your faults, and I will never speak to you of my sufferings."

Angel entered at that moment.

"Mamma weeps! mamma weeps!" he cried, sobbing.

"No, my child," replied the duchess; "I weep for joy."

" And why?" asked the child, whose smile had already succeeded to his tears.

" Because that, to-morrow, certainly," said the duke, taking him in his arms, " we depart for our country-seat in Andalusia, which your mother desires to visit."

Angel gave vent to a cry of pleasure, and, casting his arms around the necks of the duke and the duchess, he drew their heads together, and covered them with kisses.

The Marquis of Elda entered, and became a witness of this charming family *tableau*.

"Papa Marquis," said the child, "to-morrow we all depart."

" Truly?" asked the marquis of his daughter.

" Yes, my father, and our happiness will be complete if you come with us."

" My father," said the duke, " can you refuse any thing to your daughter, who would be a saint, if she were not an angel?"

The marquis looked at his daughter, whose face was radiant with happiness; then at the duke's, whose ecstasy was visible. A sweet smile illuminated his countenance, naturally austere, and, taking the hand of the duke, he said to him—

" Since I am necessary to complete your happiness, count on me."

CHAPTER XXVIII.

The state of the Gaviota, already ill before she went to take supper with Pepe Vera, was made sensibly worse, and on the morrow she was seized with a violent fever.

"Marina," she said to her maid, after an agitated sleep, "call my husband ; I do not feel well."

"The señor has not come in," replied Marina.

"He has remained to attend some sick person. So much the better ; he would have prescribed for me a dose of physic, which I abhor."

"You are very hoarse, señora."

"Yes, 'tis true. I require care. I will remain at home to-day. If the duke calls, tell him I sleep. I do not wish to see anybody. My head is on fire."

"And if some one presents himself at the door privately ?"

"If it be Pepe Vera, you can let him come in : I have something to say to him."

The servant left ; but she returned immediately.

"Señora," she said, " here is a letter which the señor, my master, has sent to you by Nicolas."

"Go along with your letter ; there is no light to read here, and I wish to sleep. What is it he says : ' The path where duty calls him.' What does this communication mean ? Leave the letter on the round table, and go away at once."

Marina a few moments after again entered.

"You here again ?" groaned the Gaviota.

"It is because the señor Pepe Vera wishes to see you."

" Let him enter."

Pepe Vera entered without ceremony, opened the
blinds, threw himself on a chair, without abandoning his
cigarette, and gazed at Maria, whose inflamed cheeks
and swollen eyes indicated a serious illness.

" How beautiful you are!" he said to her · " and your
husband ?"

" He has gone out."

" So much the better! and may he follow his path like
the wandering Jew until the last day. I come, Mariquita, on my way to visit the bull destined for the course
this afternoon. They will give this *corrida* to annoy
me. There is one bull which they call *Medianoche*
(midnight), who has already killed a man in the pas-
ture."

" Do you wish to frighten me, and render me still
more ill? Close the blinds, I cannot stand this glare of
light."

" Nonsense!" replied Pepe. " Pure childishness! the
duke is not here, my dear, so that you might fear that
too much light may glare on you; nor your *mata sanos*
of a husband, to dread a draft of air on his beloved. One
inhales here the infernal odors of musk, lavender, and all
the stench of perfumery; these are the drugs which make
you ill. Let the air into your room, that will do you
good. Tell me, my dear, do you go this evening to the
corrida ?"

" I am perhaps in a state to go !" replied Maria. " Shut
that window, Pepe, I pray you; the cold and the light
make me ill."

Pepe arose, and threw the window wide open.

" That which makes you ill, is affectation. You moan
too much for such a trifle. Do they not tell you, you are
about rendering up your soul? Señora Princess, I go to

order your coffin, and afterwards to kill *Medianoche*, in honor of Lucia del Salto, who, *gracias á Dios*, cannot but be more amiable."

"Still this woman!" screamed Maria. "This woman, who is going off with an Englishman! Pepe, you will not do as you say. It would be infamous!"

"Do you know what would be an infamy?" said Pepe, placing himself in front of the Gaviota; "it would be, when I go to risk my life, that you, in lieu of sustaining my courage by your presence, remain at home to receive the duke freely."

"Always the same fear! Will it not content you to be concealed here in my alcove, and act as a spy upon me, and to be convinced with your own eyes that there exists nothing between the duke and me? Do you not know that that which pleases him in me is only my voice, and not my person? As to me, you know too well—"

"What I do know is, that you fear me; and, by the blood of Christ! you have reason to fear me. But God only knows what may happen if I leave you alone, and certain not to be surprised by me. I have faith in no woman, not even my mother."

"I have fear? I?" said Maria, "I have fear?"

"But do you believe myself so blind," interrupted Pepe, "as not to see what is passing? Do I not know, from a good source, that you put on a good face before the duke, because you have got it in your head to obtain for your imbecile husband the position of surgeon to the queen."

"'Tis a lie!" cried Maria.

"Maria, Pepe Vera does not mistake bladders for lanterns. Know that I understand as well the *ruses* of the rude bull of the mountains as those of the less ferocious bull of the plains."

Maria began to weep.

"Come!" replied Pepe, "dry your tears, the *refugium peccatorum* of women. You know the proverb which says, 'Make a woman weep, and you vanquish her;' but, my beautiful, there is another proverb, 'Confide not either in the barking of dogs, or in the tears of women.' Keep your tears for the theatre; here we do not play comedy. Look well to yourself. If you deceive me, you make me incur the danger of death; I do not prove my love by the recipes of the apothecary, nor by dollars. I am not satisfied with grimaces, I must have acts. If you do not come this afternoon to the bull-fight you will repent of it."

And Pepe Vera went away, without even saying *à Dios* to his mistress. He was at that moment borne down by two opposite feelings which required iron nerves to conceal them, as he did, under appearances the most tranquil, under a countenance the most calm, and the most perfect indifference.

He had studied the bulls he was about to fight with; never had he seen any so ferocious. One of them strangely preoccupied him; as often happens to men of his profession, who, without caring for the other bulls, believe themselves saved if they can conquer the one which causes their anxiety. Besides, he was jealous. Jealous! he who knew only how to vanquish, and be cheered by bravos. He was told that they mocked him, and in a few hours he went to find himself between life and death, between love and treason. At least he believed so.

When he had quitted Maria, she tore the lace trimmings of her bed, unjustly scolded Marina, and shed abundance of tears. Then she dressed herself, called one of her maids, and went with her to the bull-fight, where she seated herself in the box which Pepe had reserved for her.

The noise and the heat increased her fever. Her cheeks, ordinarily pale, were inflamed, and a feverish ardor shone in her large black eyes. Anger, indignation, jealousy, offended pride, terror, anxiety, physical pain, combined in vain to force a complaint, even a sigh, from that mouth closed like a tomb. Pepe Vera perceived her: he smiled; but his smile in no way moved the Gaviota, who, under her icy countenance, swore to revenge her wounded vanity.

One bull had already bitten the dust under the blow of another *toreador.* This bull had been *good:* he had been well fought.

The trumpet again sounded. The *toril** opened its narrow and sombre door, and a bull, black as night, dashed into the arena.

"It is *Medianoche !*" cried the crowd.

Medianoche was the *bull of the corrida;* that is to say, the king of the *fête.*

Medianoche was in no way like an ordinary bull, who at once seeks his liberty, his fields, and his deserts. He would, before every thing, show them they were not playing with a contemptible enemy; he would revenge himself, and punish. At the noise made by the cries of the crowd, he stopped suddenly.

There is not the least doubt of the bull being a stupid animal. Nevertheless, whether it be the sharp anger, or intelligence the most rebellious, whether it be that he has the faculty to render clear instincts the most blind; it is the fact that some bulls can divine and baffle the most secret *ruses* of the course. The *picadores* attracted, at first, the attention of the bull. He charged the one he

---

* The place where they excite the bulls before the combat.

found nearest to him, and felled him to the earth; he did the same with the second, without leaving the spot, without the lance being able to arrest him, and which inflicted but a slight wound. The third *picador* shared the fate of his comrades.

Medianoche, his horns and front bloody, raised his head towards the seats whence came cries of admiration at such bravery.

The *chulos* conveyed the *picadores* outside the arena. One of them had a broken leg; they took him to the infirmary, and the other two changed their horses.

A new *picador* replaced the wounded, and while the *chulos* occupied the attention of the bull, the three *picadores* resumed their places, their lances in rest.

The bull divided them, and after a combat of two minutes all three were overthrown. One had fainted from having his head cut open; the furious animal attacked the horse, whose lacerated body served as a shield to the unfortunate cavalier.

There was then a moment of profound stupefaction. The *chulos* searched in vain, at the risk of their lives, to turn aside *Medianoche*, who appeared to have a thirst for blood, and quenched his rage upon his victim.

At this terrible moment a *chulo* rushed towards the animal, and covered his head with his cloak. His success was of short duration.

The bull disengaged himself promptly; he made the aggressor fly, and pursued him; but, in his blind fury, he passed him; the *chulo* had thrown himself on the ground. When the animal suddenly turned round, for he was one of those who never abandon their prey, the nimble *chulo* had already risen, and leaped the barrier amid the acclamations of the enthusiastic crowd for so much courage and agility.

All this had passed with the rapidity of light. The heroic devotion with which the *torreros* aid and defend each other, is the only thing really noble and beautiful displayed in these cruel, immoral, inhuman *fêtes*, which are a real anachronism in our times, so much vaunted as an age of light.

The bull, full of the pride of triumph, walked about as master of the arena. A sentiment of terror pervaded all the spectators.

Various opinions were expressed. Some wished that the *cabestro** be let into the arena, to lead out the formidable animal, as much to avoid new misfortunes as to preserve the propagation of his valiant race. They sometimes have recourse to this measure; but it frequently happens that the bull withdrawn does not survive the inflammation of blood which had provoked the fight. Others insisted that his tendons be cut, thus killing the bull easily. Unfortunately the greatest number cried out that it would be a crime not to see so beautiful a bull killed according to all the rules of art.

The alcalde did not know which party to side with. To preside over a bull-fight is not an easy thing.

At last, that which happens in all similar cases occurred in this: victory was with those who cried the loudest, and it was decided that the powerful and terrible *Media-noche* should die according to rule, and in possession of all his means of defence.

Pepe Vera then appeared in the arena, armed for the combat.

He saluted the authorities, placed himself before Maria, and offered her the *brindo*—the honor of the bull. He was pale.

* The bull who leads the troop, and which they introduce into the arena to make the animal retire, when they would finish the combat.

Maria, her countenance on fire, her eyes darting from their sockets, breathed with difficulty. Her body bent forward, her nails forced into the velvet cushions of her box, contemplated this young man, so beautiful, so calm before death, and whom she loved. She felt a power in his love which subjugated her, which made her tremble and weep; because that this brutal and tyrannical passion, this exchange of profound affection, impassioned and exclusive, was the love which she felt: as with certain men of a special organization, who require in place of sweet liqueurs and fine wines the powerful excitement of alcoholic drinks.

Everywhere reigned the most profound silence. A gloomy presentiment seemed to agitate every soul. Many arose and left the place.

The bull himself, now in the middle of the arena, appeared valiant: he proudly defied his adversary.

Pepe Vera chose the spot which seemed to him the most favorable, with his habitual calm and self-possessed manner; and designated it to the *chulos*, by pointing with his finger.

"Here!" he said to them.

The *chulos* sprang out like rockets in a display of fireworks; the bull had not for an instant the idea of pursuing them. They disappeared. *Medianoche* found himself face to face with the *matador*.

This situation did not last long. The bull precipitated himself with a rapidity so sudden, that Pepe had not time to put himself on guard. All he could do was to dodge the first attack of his adversary. But the animal, contrary to the habits of those of his species, took a sudden spring, and, turning suddenly, he came like a clap of thunder on the *matador*, caught him on his horns, furiously shook his head, and threw at a distance from him the body of Pepe Vera, which fell like an inert mass upon the ground of the arena.

A cry, such as the imagination of Dante alone could conceive, broke forth from a thousand human breasts, a cry profound, mournful, prolonged, and terrific.

The *picadores* rushed towards the bull to prevent his returning to his victim. The *chulos* also surrounded him.

"The *medias lunas!* the *medias lunas!*" (long partisans by which sometimes the tendons are cut) cried the crowd.

The alcalde repeated the cry of the crowd.

Then were seen to appear these terrible weapons, and soon *Medianoche* had his tendons cut; he was red with rage and with pain.

At last he fell under the ignoble poniard of the horse-killer.

The chulos raised up the body of Pepe Vera.

"Dead!"

Such was the cry which escaped from the lips of the group of *chulos;* and which, passing from mouth to mouth throughout the vast amphitheatre, brought mourning to all hearts.

Fifteen days had fled since this fatal bull-fight. In a bedchamber, from which the luxurious furniture had disappeared, on an elegant bed, but whose furniture was soiled and torn, was lying a young woman, pale, meagre, and broken down.

Nobody was near her.

This woman seemed to have awakened from a long sleep; she seated herself on her bed, let her astonished looks ramble around the chamber, and resting her forehead on her hands, sought to collect her ideas.

12

"Marina," she called in a voice harsh and feeble.

A woman entered; it was not Marina. It was an old woman bringing in a beverage she had prepared.

The invalid gazed on her attentively.

"I know that face!" she said, surprised.

"It is possible, my sister," replied the woman with sweetness; "we render our services equally to the rich and to the poor."

"But where is Marina?"

"She ran off with the servant, carrying with them all they could take."

"And my husband?"

"He has gone away. No one knows where he has gone to."

"My God! my God! And the duke? you ought to know him, for it was at his house I believe I saw you."

"At the Duchess of Almanzas? Indeed, this lady sometimes commissioned me to distribute her charities. She has departed for Andalusia, with all her family, and her husband."

"Thus, I am alone, abandoned by all," cried the invalid; "but the recollections of the past come back in a crowd on my memory."

"Am I not here?" said the good sister of charity, entwining her arms around Maria; "if they had let me know sooner, your present condition would have been less grave."

A hoarse cry escaped from the breast of the Gaviota.

"Pepe! The bull! Medianoche! Pepe! Dead! Ah!"

And she fell back on her pillow broken-hearted.

CHAPTER XXIX.

Six months after, the Countess de Algar was in her saloon with the marchioness, her mother, occupied in putting a ribbon on her son's straw hat, when General Santa-Maria entered.

"See, general, how well a straw hat becomes a boy at that age."

"You spoil this child."

"What matters it?" said the marchioness. "Do not we all spoil our children, who nevertheless become serious men? Our mother spoilt you also, my brother, and that did not prevent you from becoming what you are."

"Mamma," said the child, "wilt thou give me a biscuit?"

"What is this?" cried the general. "Your child *tutear's* you? You adopt then, after the French fashion, this *te* and *tu*, which corrupts our manners. The grandees of Spain formerly obliged their children to call them ' excellency.' It was in the good old time. The *tutear*, in imitation of the French *tutoies*, makes children lose the respect they owe to their parents."

"Eh! general—this innocent creature! Can he distinguish between *thou* and *you ?*"

"It is taught him."

"I acknowledge that my children *tutear* me; and if I had done the same to my mother, I had not less respected nor less loved her."

"You have always been a good daughter; but the exception proves nothing."

" General, in spite of your severity, your countenance seems joyous."

" It is because I have a good piece of news to announce to you. The corvette *Iberia*, from Havana, has arrived at Cadiz, and to-morrow morning, most probably, we will embrace Raphael. He is fortunate, this Raphael! Hardly had he written us that he desired to revisit Spain, when a magnificent occasion presents itself, and he comes home charged with important dispatches confided to him by the captain-general of Cuba."

The marchioness and the countess had scarcely time to rejoice at this good news, and to give expression to their happiness, when the door opened, and Raphael threw himself into their arms.

" How happy I am again to see you, my good, dear Raphael!" said the countess to him.

" Jesus!" added the marchioness, " thanks to our lady of Carmen, you are here returned to us. But what idea have you had, you who are rich, to travel by sea, as if it were but a river? I bet you have been sea-sick."

" That is the least of it; it is nothing but an unpleasant voyage, and I have suffered more from delay and my uneasiness for those I love. I do not know if it be because Spain is a good mother, or because we Spaniards are good sons, but we cannot live far away from our country."

" It is for both reasons, my dear nephew; it is for both," repeated the general with ardent satisfaction.

" Cuba is a rich country, is it not, Raphael?" demanded the countess.

" Yes, cousin. Cuba is rich, and it knows how to be so, like a great lady, who has always been one, without ostentation, and parading everywhere its benefits."

" And the women, do they please you?"

"As a general rule, all women please me : the young, because they are so; the old, because they have been so; and the little girls, because they will be so."

"Do not generalize so ; be more precise."

"Cousin, the Cuban ladies are charming feminine *lazzaroni*, covered with muslins and lace, and whose little satin shoes are useless ornaments for the little feet they are destined for, as I have never seen an Havana lady on foot. They speak like nightingale's singing, live on sugar like bees, and smoke like the chimneys of a steamboat. Their eyes are poems, and their hearts mirrors, without tin-foil. The doleful drama is not written for this country, where the women pass their life lying in a hammock balanced amidst flowers, and fanned by their slaves with fans fringed with flowers of a thousand colors."

"Do you know that public rumor announces your marriage ?"

"Dame Rumor, my dear Gracia, arrogates to herself the royal buffooneries of the olden time. Like them, she tells all that passes in her head without inquiry into the truth. But public rumor has told a lie."

"They add, that your future wife brings you a fortune of two millions of *duros*."

Raphael burst into a fit of laughter.

"Indeed, I remember that the captain-general wished to make me indorse this bill of exchange."

"And who was to be my future cousin ?"

"She was ugly as mortal sin: her left shoulder approached too conspicuously the ear on the same side, while the right shoulder was separated from the ear, its neighbor, by a distance too marked. I therefore refused the indorsement."

"You were wrong," said the countess, "above all,

knowing that—" She did not finish. She had seen pass over the frank and open countenance of her cousin the expression of a bitter recollection.

"Is she happy?" he demanded.

"As much as one can be in this world. She lives very retired, since above all she expects soon to be a mother."

"And he?"

"Entirely changed, since the marriage. He is a model of a husband. The family have received him as a returned prodigal son."

"And Eloisita?"

"Hers is a lamentable history. She secretly espoused a French adventurer, who called himself cousin of the Prince of Rohan, coadjutor of Alexander Dumas, and sent by the Baron Taylor to purchase artistic curiosities, and who, unfortunately, is called Abelard. She saw in the name of her beloved and in her own the decree of destiny commanding their union; and in this man, at the same time literary, artistic, and of princely family, she believed she saw the ideal being who had appeared to her in her beautiful dreams of gold, and a happy future. She regarded her parents, who opposed this union, as the tyrants of a melodrama, of ideas retrograde, and filled with obscurity."

"And of *Spanishism*," added the general, ironically. "And the learned señorita, nourished by novels and poetic flowers, united herself to this grand swindler, already twice married, as we learned later. After the lapse of some months, after having dissipated the money she had given him, he abandoned her at Valence, where her unfortunate father went to seek her, and to take her back, dishonored, but neither married, nor widow, nor maid. You see, my nephew, to what leads this mad love of *strangerism*."

" And our A. Polo, our eternal point of exclamation, what has become of him ?"

" He has become a political man," replied Gracia.

" I know it," replied Raphael; " I know also that he has written an ode against the throne, under the pseudo name of *Tyranny.*"

" Poor tyranny," said the general, " all the world make fagots of the fallen tree."

" I know, besides," pursued Raphael, " that he wrote another poem against Prejudice, in which he compre-hended the fatal presage of the number thirteen, the infallibility of the Pope, the upsetting of a salt-cellar, and conjugal fidelity. If I do not cite the text, I cite at least the spirit of this *chef-d'œuvre*, which public opin-ion will class among—"

" Among ?"

" We will see, when they have destroyed this society, with what they will replace it."

" I know indeed that our A. Polo has composed a satire (he felt himself carried towards this point, and for a long time he has felt growing on his forehead the horns of Marsias), a satire, I say, he declares it to be an act of hypocrisy, all claims of tithes, or the rights of convents."

" Eh! Well, my dear nephew," said the general, " these lucubrations will give him sufficient merit to be received in an opposition journal."

" I understand that much, general, and I can imagine what will happen ; it is a comedy played every day : he made of his pen the jaw-bone of an ass, and, armed with this jaw-bone, he will bravely attack the Philistines of power."

" You have been a good prophet," affirmed the gen-eral ; " I do not know how he will get on. But at present he is a personage; he has money, he gives the *ton*, he is strong."

"And the duke, will I meet him at Madrid?"

"No, but you may see him, on your way, at Cordoval, where he is at this moment with his family."

"The duke has finished by following my advice," said the general; "he has abandoned public life. Everybody of slight importance ought to-day, like Achilles, to retire within their tents."

"But, my uncle, is it then the fashion to retire?"

"They say that the duke," interrupted the countess, "is entirely devoted to literature. He writes for the theatre."

"I bet that the title of his first piece will be, 'The goat returns always to the mountain,'" said Raphael, in the ear of his cousin, alluding to the loves of Maria and Pepe Vera, which everybody knew.

"Hold your tongue, Raphael," said the countess, "we ought to act with our friends as the sons of Noah did with their father."

"And Marisalada, has she mounted to the capitol in a chariot of gold, drawn by her fanatical admirers?"

"She has lost her voice, caused by a severe attack of pleurisy; did you not know that?"

"I was so far from knowing it that I bring her magnificent offers from Havana. What does she do?"

"Now, when she can no longer sing," replied the general, "she will follow without doubt the counsels of the ant: she will learn to dance."

"But where is she?" repeated Raphael, insisting; "I have a letter to deliver to her from her husband."

"From her husband!" cried at once the marchioness, the countess, and the general.

"Have you seen him?" demanded the marchioness, with interest.

"He embarked in the same vessel with us for Havana. How he was changed! how sad he was! you would not have recognized him. A little time after our arrival he died of yellow fever."

"He died! poor Stein!" said the countess.

"The death of this good man," said the general, "will fall entirely on the conscience of this accursed singer."

"I, who believe myself invulnerable," replied Raphael, "and without ever having had the epidemic, I went to see him so soon as I learned he was ill. The attack was so violent that I found him almost at his last extremity; always calm, always filled with serene goodness, he thanked me for my visit, and said to me that he was happy in seeing, before he died, a loved face. He asked me for paper and a pen, and, almost dying, he traced some lines which he asked me, as the last request of a dying man, to convey to his wife. The vomiting soon followed, and he died with one hand clasped in those of the priest, the other in mine. I confide to you this letter, my dear Gracia; send it by a trusty man to Villamar, where, I suppose, Marisalada will have retired near to her father. Here is this letter, which I have often read, as one reads a holy hymn."

The countess opened the paper, and read—

"Maria, thou whom I have loved, and who I love still; if my pardon can save you from remorse, if my benediction can render you happy, receive them both. I send them to you from my death-bed.

"FRITZEN STEIN."

12*

CHAPTER XXX.

IF the reader, before quitting us perhaps forever, will follow us, we will revisit Villamar, after the lapse of four years, that is to say in the summer of 1848, this pretty and tranquil village placed on the border of the sea; and we will narrate to him the grave events, public and private, which have happened during all that time.

We commence by recounting the vicissitudes of the unlucky inscription which gave so much trouble to the alcalde, and which was almost effaced by one of those showers of Andalusia, more calculated to submerge the earth than to fructify it.

The alcalde, fearing that his patriotism, like that of the inscription, might be effaced, would revive a noble sentiment, and he believed he would attain his object in giving to the street known as the *Calle Real*, the name of *Calle de los Hijos de Padilla*.

This change brought about the following *émeute*:

One of the inhabitants of this street, named Cristobal Padilla, had died, and his children continued to inhabit the house of their father; but the Lopez, the Perez, and the Sanchez were living in the same street, and they protested against the preference accorded to Padilla. The alcalde hastened to explain to them that the *Sons of Padilla* formed, in former times, an association of freemen, and that it was named in honor of them. They answered, that they were also as much *freemen* as the Padillas, and that, if the alcalde persisted in his idea, they would appeal for justice to the government. The alcalde sent them all to the devil. Then, after a second *émeute*, an *émeute* of women this time, led by Rosa Mistica, equally on account of the change of name, he wrote under the signature of *El Patrioto Modelo*, to a leading journal of the capital, an article, in which, after having praised his own civic rule and his courage, he spoke of the harvest of melons and calabashes.

To return to our narrative : The tower of the fort San Cristobal was in ruins, and with it the hopes of Don Modesto, who had always nourished the idea of one day seeing his fort placed on a scale with that of Gibraltar, Brest, Cadiz, Cherbourg, Malta, and Sebastopol.

But nothing so much astonished our friends at Villamar as the change brought about in the shop of the barber Ramon Perez. Ramon, some time after the death of his father, which happened a month or two after the departure of the Gaviota, could not resist the desire to proceed to Madrid, to follow the ingrate, who had sacrificed him for a stranger.

He went, and was absent two weeks.

These two weeks passed, he returned, and with him brought—

1st, An exhaustless supply of lies and bragging.

2d, An infinite variety of songs and Italian scraps, horrible to listen to.

3d, An assumption of the *fashionable*, impudent airs, and a free-and-easy manner capable of provoking the unfortunate inhabitants of Villamar, whose ears and jaws, more unfortunate still, retained for a long time the traces of these dangerous acquisitions.

4th, The most absurd tendencies to copy the king of barbers, *Figaro*, whom, unfortunately, he had seen represented at the theatre of Seville.

Ramon Perez had also brought from his journey one

thing which he revealed to nobody: a magnificent *kick*, which was bestowed upon him one evening, under the windows of Marisalada.

Thanks to one circumstance, which we learned later, the barber had come into possession of a considerable sum of money. Then his *souvenirs* of Figaro and of Seville rose up in his mind more intensely. He embellished his shop with Asiatic luxury, associated with disorder the most ridiculous. He hung against the walls three engravings: a Telemachus, large as a drum-major; a Mentor, with a full beard; and a lank Calypso. He believed and affirmed that they were St. Peter and the Magdalen. The wags said that every thing was remodelled at Ramon's except his razors; but Perez said that the device of the age was, "Appear, rather than be."

He had a sign painted of such huge dimensions that he was obliged to construct two pillars to sustain it.

Now that the reader knows what had passed at Villamar, let us follow with him the thread of actualities.

One day, Ramon sang, accompanying himself on the guitar. It was not a song of the country, but a melancholy romance entitled *Atala*. It was a frightful thing to hear the trills, the cadences, the flourishes of all sorts, which he resorted to, to render the music unnatural. Don Modesto, moved by a sentiment of gratitude towards the man who shaved him for nothing, alone listened to Ramon's singing, when suddenly the door of the back shop was opened wide, and there was seen going out a woman, with an infant in her arms, and another who followed her weeping. This woman, pale, meagre, and of coarse manners, was dressed in a robe of light muslin, and an old barege shawl, and her long hair escaped from her comb, descending in disorder to her feet. Her feet were dressed in satin shoes, worn down at the heels. And she wore in her ears large gold ear-rings.

"Hush! hush! Ramon," she cried in a coarse voice, "do not stun my ears. I would rather prefer to hear the croaking of all the ravens on the coast, and the mewing of all the cats in the village, than to hear this mutilation of serious music. I have already told you to sing only the songs of the country. Your voice is sufficiently flexible, and it is always good for that; but there is not a living soul who could support your pretensions to the graces of an artist. I tell you this, and you know if I am competent or not to express an opinion. You so bore me with your stupid vocalization, that, if you continue it, I will quit this house, never to return to it. Be silent!" she added, striking the infant, who had begun to cry, "you *bray* like your father."

"Go, then, by all the saints!" replied the barber, wounded in what his *amour propre* cherished as most dear. "Go, run away, and never return until I recall you: in this way you will run for a long time without stopping."

"Dare you speak to me thus, you beardless chin!— to me, whom the grandees of Spain, ambassadors, and the entire court recall to their memory."

"If all the world saw you to-day, be sure they would not desire to listen to you, or think of you."

"Why have I married this booby, who, after having spent the allowance I had from the duke, now insults me—me, the celebrated Maria Santalo, who made such a noise in the world?"

"It will be better for you if you make no more," said Ramon.

At these words the woman sprang upon her husband, who, filled with fear, had not time to save himself.

In going out he ran against a new personage, whom he upset. Hardly had Maria perceived the ludicrous *rencontre* when her anger gave place to the loudest laughter.

This personage was Momo, whose cheeks were bandaged with an old handkerchief, and frightfully swollen. He had come to Ramon, who to his quality of barber joined that of dentist, to have a tooth extracted.

"What horrible vision!" cried Maria. "You would frighten fear itself. Have you come to exhibit yourself for money?"

"I came to have a tooth taken out, and not to be insulted. But Gaviota you have been, Gaviota you are, and Gaviota you will be."

"If you have come here to have extracted that which is really bad, Ramon must commence with your heart."

"See then, who speaks of heart! A daughter who left her father to die in the arms of strangers, without sending even the slightest assistance!"

"And whose fault?" replied Maria. "Yours, ugly peasant, who left Madrid without delivering your message, and spread everywhere the report of my death, because you mistook a theatrical representation for a reality. In consequence of which, on my arrival here all Villamar took me for a spectre from the other world."

"Theatrical representation! yes, you have always so said. But if Telo had not missed you, and if your husband had not cured you, you would long ago have been food for worms, for the repose of honest people who know you."

"You do not enjoy this repose; and you will not enjoy it for a long time to come. I will live a hundred years to torment you."

Momo, as his only reply, shrugged his shoulders with contempt, and in a sententious voice pronounced—

" Gaviota you have been, Gaviota you are, and Gaviota you will be."

When Don Modesto, stunned by the noise of the quarrel, heard the laughter which succeeded the tones of violent anger, he profited by the occasion to sneak away from the battle-field. He had scarcely escaped from the dispute between Momo and Maria, when new terrors assailed him, at the sight of the single eye of Rosita, an eye full of severity and of menace. Don Modesto went, and seated himself in a corner, and, like a bird, who sees a storm approaching, hides his head under his wing, he bent down his head, and waited.

" It was very becoming," said Rosita, " and very dignified, in a man of your age, and of your importance, one of the first authorities of the place, a man who has seen his name printed in large letters in the Gazette, to go near these people, near these brainless fools, not to say worse, and to commit yourself with this woman, whose marriage is but a long scandal."

" But, Rosita, I am not committed to the quarrel, it was she who came in where I was."

" If you had not been at this bad barber's, at the house of this everlasting singer ; if you had not stopped there, with open mouth listening to his paltry songs, you would not have been exposed to being a witness of such a shameful scene."

" But, Rosita, you forget that I must be shaved now and then, under pain of otherwise being mistaken for a pioneer; that this good Ramon Perez shaves me for nothing, as his father did before him ; and that both politeness and gratitude demand of me that I listen with patience when he sings."

" I tell you that it is an abomination to see you among such people, like intimates."

"Rosita, can you speak thus of Ramon, who shaves me for nothing, and of Marisalada, whom ministers and generals have applauded, and who has been so good as to put a cockade on my hat?"

"Yes, a cockade big as a salad! She mocks you. Ah! she is good, this woman, who let her father die in a garret, all alone, in misery and forgetfulness, while she sang herself hoarse on the stage."

"But, Rosita, if she were ignorant of the gravity—"

"She knew he was ill, that should have been sufficient. While a father suffers, a daughter should not sing. Ah! she is good, this woman, in her conduct forcing her husband to fly to the Indies to die there of shame and grief."

"He died of the yellow fever."

"Yes, she is good! And she was the only one who did not come to watch poor old Maria in her last illness; old Maria, who had so much loved her, and who had heaped on her a thousand kind acts. She was the only one absent at the funeral, the only one who did not pray for her either in the church, or at the burial-ground."

"It was immediately after her confinement, and it would have been an imprudence at that time."

"What do you understand about going out soon after confinement?" interrupted Rosita, exasperated by the ardor which Don Modesto exhibited in defending his friends. "Have you ever had any children?"

"No, for—"

"And when brother Gabriel died, soon after old Maria, was it not this Gaviota who dared to laugh, saying, that it was at the theatre only she thought people died of grief and love? This woman is accursed."

"Poor brother Gabriel!" said Don Modesto, agitated by the souvenirs which his hostess revived. "Every Friday he came to pray for a good death from the Lord of Good-help; after the decease of his benefactress he came every day. It was I, who met him one Friday, in the morning, on his knees, near the grating of the chapel, his head resting on the bars. I approached—he was dead! Died as he had lived, without noise, and unconscious. Poor brother Gabriel, thou hast died without having seen the walls of your convent rebuilt—and I, I will die also without seeing my fort rebuilt."

THE END.

LITERAL TRANSLATIONS.

Note 1.

"Banish the importunate complaints :
If you lose me, my handsome godson,
Search where are born the women brown,
Search where the salt alone is found."

Note 2.

" Who was Don Madureira?
The best singer in the world.
God, in his exalted prescience,
Said to him: Die.   He expired;
But reanimated by his zeal,
He wished for a chapel,
And sang things so beautiful
That God himself admired · him.
        'I give you a chapel,'
Said the great Jehovah to him:
' The harmony of my angels
Is not equal to the melody
Of Señor Madureira.'"

NOTE 3.

" Glory to thee, beautiful Andalusian ¡
The sun is in thine eyes ;
Of thee the aurora is jealous ;
Thy love transports me to heaven."

NOTE 4.

" I love better the clash of the glass,
At table with my friends,
Than the lying glow
Of courts and marquises."